LIBRARY

OVERRULED

ISABELLA ALDEN

D0846879

LIVING BOOKS®
Tyndale House Publishers, Inc.
Wheaton, Illinois

Visit Tyndale's exciting Web site at www.tyndale.com

Cover illustration copyright © 1997 by Corbert Gauthier.
All rights reserved.

Living Books is a registered trademark of Tyndale House
Publishers, Inc.

ISBN 0-8423-3195-6

Printed in the United States of America

04	03	02	01	99	98	97
7	6	5	4	3	2	1

CONTENTS

Welcome . . . . *v*

1. A Stormy Evening *1*

2. The Day's Story *11*

3. Poor Hannah *21*

4. Marjorie Edmonds *31*

5. Temptations *40*

6. Poor Jack! *50*

7. A Chance to Choose *60*

8. Pivots *69*

9. "What If I Should—?" *79*

10. An Anniversary *89*

11. A Series of Blunders *98*

12. A Confidential Talk *107*

13. "There Ought to Be—" *116*

14. June Visitors *126*

15. Schemes *135*

16. The Teacher Taught *145*

17. A Crisis *155*

18. Revelations *165*

19. "I Don't Like It" *174*

20. Enter Doctor Maxwell *184*

21. Brothers Indeed *194*
22. A Harvest 203
23. "It Might Have Been" *212*
24. The Unexpected *222*
25. June Again *232*
26. Half the Story *242*
27. Opportunity *252*
28. Another Crisis *261*
29. "For Me—*Heaven*" *270*

WELCOME

by *Grace Livingston Hill*

As long ago as I can remember, there was always a radiant being who was next to my mother and father in my heart and who seemed to me to be a combination of fairy godmother, heroine, and saint. I thought her the most beautiful, wise, and wonderful person in my world, outside of my home. I treasured her smiles, copied her ways, and listened breathlessly to all she had to say, sitting at her feet worshipfully whenever she was near; ready to run any errand for her, no matter how far.

I measured other people by her principles and opinions, and always felt that her word was final. I am afraid I even corrected my beloved parents sometimes when they failed to state some principle or opinion as she had done.

When she came on a visit, the house seemed glorified because of her presence; while she remained, life was one long holiday; when she went away, it seemed as if a blight had fallen.

She was young, gracious, and very good to be with.

This radiant creature was known to me by the name of Auntie Belle, though my mother and my grandmother called her Isabella! Just like that! Even sharply sometimes when they disagreed with her: *"Isabella!"* I wondered that they dared.

Later, I found that others had still other names for her. To the congregation of which her husband was pastor she was known as Mrs. Alden. And there was another world in which she moved and had her being when she went away from us from time to time; or when at certain hours in the day she shut herself within a room that was sacredly known as a Study and wrote for a long time, while we all tried to keep still; and in this other world of hers she was known as Pansy. It was a world that loved and honored her, a world that gave her homage and wrote her letters by the hundreds each week.

As I grew older and learned to read, I devoured her stories chapter by chapter, even sometimes page by page as they came hot from the typewriter; occasionally stealing in for an instant when she left the study to snatch the latest page and see what had happened next; or to accost her as her morning's work was done with: "Oh, have you finished another chapter?"

Often the whole family would crowd around when the word went around that the last chapter of something was finished and going to be read aloud. And now we listened, breathless, as she read and made her characters live before us.

The letters that poured in at every mail were overwhelming. Asking for her autograph and her photograph; begging for pieces of her best dress to sew into patchwork; begging for advice on how to become a great author; begging for advice on every possible subject. And she answered them all!

Sometimes I look back upon her long and busy life, and marvel at what she has accomplished. She was a marvelous housekeeper, knowing every dainty detail of her home to perfection. And a marvelous pastor's wife! The real old-fashioned kind, who made calls with her husband, knew every member intimately, cared for the sick, gathered the young people into her home, and loved them all as if they had been her brothers and sisters. She was beloved, almost adored, by all the members. And she was a tender, vigilant, wonderful mother, such a mother as few are privileged to have, giving without stint of her time, her strength, her love, and her companionship. She was a speaker and teacher, too.

All these things she did, and *yet wrote books!* Stories out of real life that struck home and showed us to ourselves as God saw us; and sent us to our knees to talk with him.

And so, in her name I greet you all, and commend this story to you.

Grace Livingston Hill

(This is a condensed version of the foreword Mrs. Hill wrote for her aunt's final book, *An Interrupted Night.*)

1

A Stormy Evening

ESTELLE Bramlett was in an unenviable frame of mind. The flush on her face was caused by something more than the glow of the firelight in her pretty sitting room, and there was a nervous tremor about her lips when they ceased speaking that betokened keen feeling of some sort and a vain effort at self-control. Life had not shown for her the rose-colored tints that she had meant it should. There had been several months in which she had accustomed herself to looking forward to the time when she should become Mrs. Ralph Bramlett, as the beginning of a future which should be velvet-lined. She had borne that name for more than a year; and the unmistakable lines about her mouth, which had evidently become habitual, showed only too plainly that more or less disappointment had fallen on her.

Mr. Ralph Bramlett was stretched at full length upon a comfortable couch, with down pillows at his head and back and thrust under one elbow. He was listening in gloomy silence to his wife's remarks, making as little response as the claims of decency would allow. His work at the office that day had been nerve trying to a degree that his wife did not and could not understand, and her topics for conversation were not inspiring. She had been tried by his silence and did not improve in her selection.

"Hannah was here this afternoon," she began again, after an irritating silence. "She spent half the afternoon going on about her affairs. I think it is simply disgraceful, the way she is managing. She is the town talk already; and if things continue much longer as they are now, she will not be received into respectable society. I don't believe you have said one word to her about it, notwithstanding all I have told you. She used to condescend to pay a little attention to what you said. Why do you let her go on in this way?"

"Hannah is old enough to take care of herself." These words came at last from behind the hand with which Ralph Bramlett shaded his face, and the tone was exasperatingly indifferent. His wife recognized it by an added irritability in hers.

"Oh, 'old enough!' Wisdom doesn't always come with age, as I should think you might know by this time. I don't deny that she is able to conduct herself with propriety, but the simple fact is that she does not do it. She seems to be entirely indifferent, not only to her own reputation, but to that of other people. You are her brother, and I am your wife; and our social relations must therefore be more or less affected by her actions. I assure you that the matter is becoming very serious. You do not realize what is being said. You are buried all day in that horrid office, and evenings you spend on the couch brooding over something which you keep to yourself; the consequence is you do not know what is going on in the world. If you came in contact with people, as I do, you would understand that it is time something was done. What do you think of having persons like the Greens making your sister's name a subject for gossip in the kitchen? Mrs. Green told Lena that the boys said Miss Hannah went a-walking every night with Jack Taylor, and that he took her to concerts and lectures and everywhere!"

"If I were you, I would not hold conferences with my cook in regard to family affairs or those of the neighborhood."

Mr. Bramlett spoke in his coldest, loftiest tone; and it is perhaps not surprising that he made the color deepen on his wife's cheeks, nor that her eyes glowed angrily.

"That is just like you, Ralph; you are as unreasonable as it is possible for a man to be, and omit no opportunity to blame me. I consider that remark insulting. The idea that I spend my time gossiping with the cook! Lena asked me a civil question. At least she intended it to be civil; as things are going, I do not think she can be blamed for supposing that she had a right to ask when Miss Hannah was to be married. She is a respectable girl and supposed, as a matter of course, that the outcome of such persistent attention was a wedding. But I should think you might be sufficiently well acquainted with your wife to have discovered that I do not gossip with anybody. Since you have decided that your wife cannot be trusted, perhaps it will comfort you to remember that Lena has been in my mother's family for a number of years and has only what she considers the interests of the family at heart. I cross-questioned her carefully, under the impression that I was doing my duty in trying to learn the extent to which gossip had made itself familiar with our name. I made the mistake of supposing that you would not only approve of my efforts but would exert your influence, if you have any, in helping to close the mouths of gossips before it is too late.

"I do not know what you think about all this, you have never condescended to enlighten me; but it does not seem possible that you can approve of the way in which Hannah is conducting herself. It is true, as Mrs. Green says, that she is seen on the street with that odious Jack Taylor nearly every night of her life. Or, if they are not on the street, he is seated on the doorstep, or hanging on the gate, talking with her until a late hour. Yesterday she actually went out riding with him and was gone for hours. Mrs. Green, you may be sure, knows exactly how many hours; and, if she failed to overhear any of their remarks, can draw on her imagination, and make herself and others believe that she did. I hope you enjoy putting your name at the mercy of a woman like her! Now, what I should like to know is whether you approve of Hannah's conduct and mean to uphold her in it, as you seem to be doing."

"I tell you I neither approve nor disapprove," growled her husband. "What I said was that Hannah was old enough to attend to her own affairs, and ought to be allowed to do so. If she chooses to be a fool she has a perfect right to be one, so far as I am concerned, and I do not propose to bother myself about it. I have other matters to think of."

"Oh! It is all very well, Mr. Bramlett, for you to wrap yourself in a mantle of dignity and declare that you have other things to think about. Undoubtedly you have; matters of vast importance, apparently, which absorb all your time. I can tell you one thing about which you rarely think, and that is your wife's comfort. I spend my days alone and might as well spend my evenings in the same manner, for all the pleasure that I have in your society. If I had for a moment imagined what a difference in my life the marriage ceremony would make—" She stopped abruptly, her voice being choked with feeling, whether of grief or anger it might have been difficult to determine. Her husband remained persistently silent under this attack, and after two or three minutes she began again:

"You can neglect your wife, of course; that is nobody's business but your own. I shall not go out on the streets and complain of you, so your dignity is entirely safe there; but I warn you that Hannah is not being so thoughtful. Whether it is your business or not, the public will link your name with it and you will find yourself associated with an unsavory scandal before you are aware. You cannot separate yourself from your entire family. You are by no means so indifferent to what people say as you occasionally like to pretend. I do not know another person who is so sensitive to public opinion as you, and when you open your eyes to the state of things about which I have warned you, do not blame me; that is all I ask."

"Nonsense!" Mr. Bramlett arose to a sitting posture as he gave vent to this explosive word, flinging away the afghan which his wife had thrown over him when he lay down and glaring at her out of angry eyes.

"I wish you would not undertake this sort of scene, Estelle; it was never to my taste—besides, you don't do it well. And I wish, moreover, that you did not consider it your duty to retell to me the gossip of the cook and the washerwoman. I must honor your motives, of course, but I tell you once and for all I consider it entirely unnecessary. My sister Hannah has conducted herself with entire propriety for nearly thirty years, without the breath of suspicion having attached itself to her name, and I have no fear but that she will continue to manage her affairs with wisdom if she is let alone. If you talked to her this afternoon as you have been talking to me, there may be cause for anxiety; there is no telling what a Bramlett might be goaded to do. Why don't you learn, Estelle, that you cannot help people by sticking thorns into them? Were there no letters for me by the late mail?"

It was an unfortunate question in view of all that had passed. Mrs. Bramlett controlled her inclination to burst into a passion of tears and gave vent to her feelings in words instead.

"Oh yes; there are letters of the usual sort. The bill for coal, for instance; I supposed that was settled last month. Your tailor's bill was presented for the third time, and that account from Sewell's. He takes the trouble to state that it will not be convenient for him to wait longer for settlement. Since there is no danger of disgrace to the family through Hannah, it at least looks as though there might be a possibility of it from another source. It is certainly anything but agreeable to me to have the house flooded with tailors' bills and matters of that kind; if it were my dressmaker's bill I should never hear the last of it. I cannot understand why it isn't important to be businesslike about such matters, as well as with the affairs of Snyder, Snyder, and Co. Yet you are always pressing their claims upon me when I need any of your time. May I be allowed to ask why you do not attend to your own business occasionally?"

She could not know how every word she uttered pierced the very soul of her husband like a keen knife cutting into living flesh: it would not have been possible for her to understand what tremendous self-control he was exercising to maintain the outward calm which in itself irritated her. He waited a moment before he replied.

"I am sorry my businesslike habits have proved a cause of offense to you. As to my own affairs, nothing would give me greater pleasure than to be strictly methodical. There is a serious difficulty in the way. I have not yet learned how to pay bills without tangible aid. The simple fact is that my last quarter's salary was entirely spent some weeks before it was due. Some of it, you may remember, went to pay that dressmaker's bill of which you boast. Mr. Sewell will find that he will be compelled to wait until I get ready to pay him; and I shall take care that there shall be no bill hereafter to settle with him. In truth, I am tempted to refuse to pay any of these fellows because they sent the bills to the house instead of to my office. I had no intention of troubling you with matters of this kind." He seemed to realize, before the sentence was completed, that he had put some bitter stings into it, and to feel some sense of regret. He tried to make his voice sound less cold and sarcastic. But matters had gone quite too far for him to thus easily atone. Estelle's eyes were flashing dangerously, and her voice was like steel.

"Pray, do not take the trouble to try to put it courteously; say, rather, the plain truth, that you had no intention of letting me know that you are unable to pay your honest debts. It is certainly a new experience to me. My father is poor, and has always been; but I do not believe he ever owed a person for twenty-four hours beyond the date of payment. It is probably very unbusinesslike for me to wonder what you do with your money, but I confess I am curious. Your salary is larger than my father ever had to depend upon; yet he managed to feed and clothe and care for three daughters, as well as himself and his wife. If I might be allowed to suggest to such a businesslike person, I should say it was quite time you began to keep your own books, instead of those of other people. I supposed it was Hannah who was threatening our respectability, but it seems I was mistaken."

Mr. Bramlett sprang up and began to pace back and forth; it was a way he had when under strong excitement.

"Have a care, Estelle," he said, and his voice was low and constrained; "you may go too far in your sarcasms even with me, who am bound in honor to endure them. It ought to be beneath you to make the insinuations that you have with regard to money when you remember that I furnished this house in accordance with your judgment, not mine; and, indeed, rented it in the first place because your preference for it was so great, although I told you at the time that I felt we could hardly afford it. If you will take the trouble to recall the circumstances, you will remember that there was no other house within our reach which in the least satisfied you."

"That clause, 'within our reach,' is well added, Mr. Bramlett, and most important. Of course I supposed that you knew what you were about; and when you referred the decision as to choice of house to me, naturally I believed that those put at my disposal were within our reach. Why should I not, in such a case, choose the best? As to furniture, when my tastes were consulted, I told the truth, of course; what else would you have had? I suppose I am not to be blamed because my tastes are so unfortunate as to prefer a fifty-dollar couch, for instance, to a twenty-dollar one.

"The truth is," she continued—and, having grown more angry with every word she had spoken, she now laid aside all effort at self-control and faced her hus-

band with a look which said more than her words—
"the truth is, you find yourself in an embarrassing
position. You have chosen to keep your business matters an entire secret from me, and have spent all your
money, in what way you alone know; but now that it
is gone and you awaken to the fact that you have
nothing with which to pay honest debts, you choose
to turn upon me and lay the blame on my good taste
in selecting house furnishings. You have taken pains to
inform me what you consider beneath me; pray, what
do you think of such conduct as that?"

He had taken time to think during that long
sentence; in truth, he had given her words little attention but was engaged in wondering why he had
allowed himself to be betrayed into saying some things
that he had.

"Do let us get done with this distasteful talk," he
said with a wave of his hand, as though he would
throw off all that was disagreeable. "I wonder why it
is that I cannot be allowed to have peace in my own
house? I have business cares and perplexities that you
know nothing about; and when I lock the office door
upon them and come away for the purpose of getting
a little rest, it seems hard that I must be placed in the
witness-box, not only, but must have torture applied
to me. I meant no insinuations in what I said. I merely
referred to the fact that the house had been furnished
in accordance with your tastes and took more money
than we had supposed it would when we began. The
strictest economy is necessary now—has been necessary for some time; and we are neither of us fond of
economizing. If I have been closemouthed about my
affairs, it was simply because I did not consider it
necessary to trouble you with them. But the plain,
unvarnished truth is that I am heavily in debt and have

not a cent of money with which to meet my liabilities. As to where the money has gone thus far, if you are fond of business to that extent, you will find the large drawer of the secretary crammed full of accounts; you are at liberty to study and figure on them to your heart's content. If I have made a mistake in trying to shield you, I will rectify it at once. I fancy you will have no difficulty in discovering where even such an enormous sum as fifteen hundred dollars a year has fled to, and I hope you will find peace and happiness in the occupation."

He had not intended to close his sentence thus; he had meant it to be conciliating. Feeling suddenly how impossible it was for him to control himself further, or endure more that evening, he turned suddenly and left the room, slamming the door after him; not intentionally, but because his nerves had been so wrought upon as to leave him incapable of making gentle movements. He crossed the hall and passed into a small room which had been fitted up in a businesslike manner for his exclusive use. Here he closed and locked the door and even drew the small bolt just below the lock; then threw himself into the leather-covered armchair in front of his desk, with the unpaid bills still in his hand.

2

❊

THE DAY'S STORY

THUS unceremoniously left to herself, Estelle Bramlett bowed her head on the little reading table near her and cried some of the most bitter tears it had ever fallen to her lot to shed.

Do her the justice to understand that nothing about this miserable evening had been in the least as she had planned.

When the tears had had their way, she tried to go over the events of the last few hours and make herself understand how it had all happened. Why had she allowed herself to speak such words as she had to her husband? Sarcasm was one of her besetting sins; she knew it well—she had, indeed, been told it from childhood—and no friend, not even the dearest, escaped her tongue when she was excited; but to Ralph she had never before spoken as she had that evening. How came she to do so? It had been a trying day from first to last. Her husband had been more than usually preoccupied and silent all through the breakfast hour and had finally gone away without even remembering to bid her good-bye. This in itself had tried her more than he could have understood; because, being a woman, she lived on many of the small happenings which men like Ralph Bramlett call trifles. Neither had her domestic machinery moved satisfactorily. Lena, the stout German girl who reigned in her kitchen, had been brought up by Mrs. Bramlett's mother and was considered a treasure that the mother had relinquished to her on her marriage, after the manner of mothers. But even a kitchen treasure may have its faults; and a disposition to have her own way, especially when she knew it to be the best way, was one of Lena's faults. She and her mistress had disagreed about an important matter connected with cookery, and Lena had quoted her mistress's mother in a way which could only be exasperating to the young housekeeper. So Estelle had insisted upon her way, to the detriment of the dinner; and Ralph had found a little fault and assured his wife that his mother could teach her many things. This experience is never soothing, and by dinnertime young Mrs. Bramlett was in need of being soothed. The first to disturb her afternoon peace had been her young sister Glyde. Now, Glyde was a favorite with almost everybody, and as a rule there was no one whom Mrs. Bramlett liked better to see tripping up her side steps. But on this particular afternoon she innocently brought an element of discord.

"I've had such a delicious present!" she began, as soon as she was comfortably seated. Glyde's adjectives could, on occasion, be as startling as those of the average young lady. "I had to rush right over and tell you about it. I wanted to bring it with me, but mother decided that that would be silly."

"A present!" echoed her sister. "Why should you be having presents just now? It isn't your birthday; and it is too near the holidays for extras, and not near enough to count."

"This one will 'count,' I fancy. It is probably intended for my Christmas; only, being the dear, thoughtful creature that he is, Uncle Anthony sent it on after the first frost, so as to be ready for the cold. Can you guess what it is, Estelle?"

"I was never skillful at guessing," Mrs. Bramlett said, a trifle coldly. The truth is, she found it impossible to speak other than coldly when Uncle Anthony was the subject of conversation. She could never forget that there had been a time when his chief interest in their family centered in her, and his special gifts were showered upon her. Although she knew perfectly well that her absence from home two years before had been the sole reason why Glyde was chosen as his companion for a trip to New York, and that Glyde was in no wise to blame for the extravagant fondness which her uncle had shown for her ever since, Estelle could not help feeling aggrieved whenever she thought of it and had sometimes spoken in a way to make a more suspicious person than Glyde feel that she was supposed, in some disreputable way, to have undermined her sister's place. But Glyde's busy, happy nature had no room in it for suspicion. She could not even be made to understand that her sister was not prepared to rejoice with her over the especially appropriate gift that had come to her. Had not Uncle Anthony distinguished himself when Estelle was married? Was there a better piano in town than the one that he sent with his love and good wishes? Had anyone been more delighted with the rich gift than Glyde herself? What more reasonable than to suppose that Estelle would share the pleasure that had now come to her? This, if she had reasoned about it, would have been something like what she would have felt. But Glyde was too entirely above selfishness to have done any reasoning about it, and the voice was only gleeful in which she said:

"If you won't even try, I shall have to tell you. It is a fur cape. Isn't that particularly fortunate just at this time? For you know my winter coat is growing too small, and poor father has had so many expenses lately that I could not endure the thought of hinting about a new one."

"A fur cape! What kind of fur?"

"Seal," said Glyde, a trifle timidly. She had an instinctive feeling that possibly the quality of the gift might not seem sensible to her sister.

"Seal! Do you mean real sealskin?"

"Why, yes, of course, Estelle; Uncle Anthony never approves of imitations of any sort, you know."

"I think you are too young to wear sealskin," said Mrs. Bramlett, her voice as cold and unsympathetic as ice.

But this had tempted Glyde to laugh.

"Why, Estelle!" she said, "you cannot mean that. Don't you remember that they trim even little children's garments with seal; and children wear seal caps and hoods. It must be mink fur of which you are thinking."

"I am thinking of precisely what I said. It is to be presumed that I know quite as well as you what first is worn. What I mean, of course, is that I think rich furs of any sort are not in keeping with the position of a young girl like yourself, who has nothing to match them. However, if Uncle Anthony chooses to load you down with inappropriate finery, it is nothing to me."

She would not have spoken quite so disagreeably if

the rich gift had been anything but a seal cape. It chanced that the words represented her heart's desire for the winter. Only two days before, she had told her husband of some new capes that were displayed at Harter and Beekman's, real marvels of cheapness, considering their quality; and he had assured her in an annoyed tone that even one-third the price she mentioned was entirely beyond his means and that she must not think of new furs for this season at least. It struck her as hard that a young married woman should not have the sort of cape she chose. A husband who had never before been called upon to buy a wrap of any sort for her ought to have been ready to get the first one without a murmur. However, she had struggled with this feeling and conquered it and resolved to tell Ralph in the evening that he was not to worry about her wanting a fur cape; her sack was almost as good as new and quite nice enough for the winter. But it was certainly hard that before she had had time to carry out this good intention, her young sister should come and flaunt an elegant seal cape before her mind's eyes. Of course it was elegant; Uncle Anthony never did halfway things.

Glyde had regarded her sister with a puzzled air and resolved to change the subject. Estelle was evidently not in the mood that afternoon for rejoicing with her over her furs.

"Oh, I forgot; I have something of more importance to tell you: Marjorie has come. You do not seem a bit surprised; I am afraid you have heard of it before, and I wanted to be the first to give the news."

"I have heard nothing about her and thought nothing about her for weeks. What a child you are, Glyde! Do you never mean to grow up?"

"It seems so delightful to have her back," said

Glyde, ignoring the reproof; "I have been happy all the morning over the thought of their house being open again. They came last night; I haven't seen her yet, but I am on my way there this afternoon. Don't you want to get on your wraps and go with me? It is real pleasant out of doors."

"Certainly not. I think I shall have sense enough to call with my husband when the proper time comes. I am not a schoolgirl to pounce down upon people as soon as they get in the house. Has Marjorie brought Mr. Maxwell with her?"

"No," said Glyde wonderingly, "at least I suppose not; I hadn't thought of him. Why no, Estelle; he could not be here at this time of year. He is a college professor, you know, and all the colleges are in session now."

"I do not know what he is," said Mrs. Bramlett; "a gentleman of elegant leisure apparently. I am sure he spent one winter here and then went abroad for I do not know how long; and Marjorie has spent the intervening time with him. I did not know until now that she had decided to come home; she was going to let him accompany her; she seems to have him well under her control."

Glyde's fair face was flushed, and her eyes had a reproachful look; she was sensitive to sarcasm when it was applied to her friends.

"I do not know what you mean, Estelle," she said gravely. "Because Marjorie and her mother chose to spend some of their time in the same town where Mr. Maxwell is teaching, that does not seem to me a reason for speaking almost slightingly of her. They have been traveling all summer, you know, and were absent a large part of the winter; I suppose it was merely an accident that they made the same place their headquarters."

"Some accidents are designed, my dear little innocent. But you need not flush as though I had insulted your idol. Marjorie, having hopelessly lost your respected brother-in-law, has set herself earnestly to the task of securing Mr. Maxwell. Nothing is plainer than that; but I am sure I do not blame her. I suppose he is quite interesting to those who like his style. What surprises me is the length of time that it takes to accomplish her designs. I expected an invitation to her wedding before this. You can give her my regards, and, if you feel disposed, ask if there is anything I can do to help her with her trousseau; that may aid in bringing matters to a focus." She had laughed maliciously as she spoke and realized that she was saying what would bring a still deeper flush to Glyde's face. In the mood she then was, she could not help rather liking to make people feel uncomfortable.

The young sister cut short her call and went away sorrowful. She could not understand why she so often found her married sister in these moods. Perhaps it would have been hard for Mrs. Bramlett herself to explain them. Yet, as has been hinted, life was in many respects a disappointment to her. After Glyde's departure, she sat and brooded for a while over some of her grievances. Prominent among them loomed up the evening before. She had planned that Ralph would come home in time to take her to a certain concert which she was sure they would both enjoy. She had ordered dinner early with this scheme in view, and dressed herself with care; and the husband had returned in time, but would have none of her planning. It was a chilly, disagreeable night, and she ought to know better than to think of exposing herself to it.

Moreover, he was much too tired to dress and go out again; he would not do it if Patti herself were to sing. It had been more of a disappointment to his wife than he realized, but she had done her best to accommodate herself to his moods. Coming in from the dinner table, she had drawn the curtains, and arranged the drop-light, and brought her little reading chair close to the couch on which her husband had thrown himself, and prepared to entertain him. Would he like to be read to? She had a charming new book that Glyde had brought her; she had been saving it to enjoy with him. He replied with utmost coldness. Glyde's taste in books, he said, was not as a rule in accordance with his; besides, it nearly always wearied him to hear other people read. He had been accustomed from his babyhood, almost, to reading aloud himself. Well, then, would he read to her? No, indeed he wouldn't; not tonight: couldn't she see that he was already hoarse? He had been bawling telephone messages all day, all over creation. She might read to herself if she chose, and welcome; he desired simply to be let alone. He had business matters to think about which would require all the brainpower he possessed.

It was not a pleasant prospect, certainly. The wife had been alone all day and was not disposed to continue the loneliness through the long November evening. Still, she had struggled with herself and been silent. She had opened the choice book and read a few pages. Several times she had tried to beguile her husband into a show of interest. "Listen to this, Ralph," she had said; "isn't it a quaint way of expressing the thought?" But Ralph was in a hopeless frame of mind. He saw nothing either quaint or interesting in the quotations. What she called pathetic, he said was silly; and a passage which she pronounced particularly fine, he said was commonplace.

When at last she closed the book and tried to interest him in what she called conversation, she fared no better. He answered her questions only in the briefest phrases, a single monosyllable whenever possible, and finally distinctly intimated that he thought she was going to read her book and leave him in peace.

This had been the drop too much for her; and she had risen in indignation, waiting only to inform him that she might as well have been immured in a convent as to have married, and that if he was so fond of his own company, she would not longer intrude hers upon him. Then she had gone to her own room and cried over the lost evening. He had not followed her, as earlier in their married life he would have done; instead, he was even later than usual in coming to his room. Once there, he moved about on tiptoe, careful not to disturb his wife's supposed rest; and when at last stretched beside her, he gave vent to a sigh so heavy that it smote upon her wakeful ear and made her almost ready to throw her arms about him and ask what troubled him. In truth, she often asked herself this anxious question. Ralph Bramlett had been fitful enough in his unmarried days, but never quite like this. There were times when this wife of a year assured herself that had she imagined he could become the silent, preoccupied, indifferent husband that he was, she would not have married him. But this thought was invariably followed by one of penitence and genuine anxiety for his welfare. Something very serious must be troubling him; matters about which she knew nothing, as he had more than once hinted. Perhaps he was really ill; overworked he certainly was. He complained constantly, sometimes bitterly, of being over-tired. What if he were on the eve of an attack of brain fever or of nervous prostration? Thoughts somewhat after this manner had followed the bitter ones of the evening in question and kept her awake and anxious until a late hour. It seemed almost an insult to find her husband as well as usual next morning; and she had begun the day by indignantly assuring herself that he was well enough and was merely indulging in some of his tempers. Nevertheless, several times through her day of solitude, the anxieties of the night had recurred to her; sometimes with such force that she was tempted to take the next train out and make her way through the great building to his office in order to assure herself that her husband was not seriously ill. It was the thought of the look of unmistakable annoy-ance with which he would greet any such attempt that held her in check, and she would proceed to reason herself back to common sense again.

Following Glyde's departure had come Hannah Bramlett, the woman who since the day of her mar-riage had been one of Estelle's thorns in the flesh.

3

POOR HANNAH

IN ALL the wide range of topics for conversation, there seemed to be no two upon which Mrs. Ralph Bramlett and her sister-in-law Hannah could agree. Poor Hannah had begun by making the mistake which is often made under similar circumstances; that of trying to advise, in some senses even to control, her new sister. Failing utterly in that, she had been unsparing of her censures.

But within the last few weeks the two had in a certain sense changed places, Mrs. Bramlett having turned mentor. There was at first a degree of comfort, or at least a lurking sense of satisfaction, in the thought of something tangible to complain of. A curious state of things existed. Hannah Bramlett had passed her twenty-eighth birthday, and through all the years as far back as her sister-in-law could remember her, had been a pattern of dignity and propriety. She had been a reserved woman always with her own sex and almost, if not quite, prudish in her interaction with gentlemen.

Now, when she had quite passed the age in which

one might naturally look for imprudences, she had become one of the most talked about young women in the neighborhood. And of all persons with whom to associate her name, that of Jack Taylor seemed to her sister-in-law the worst. "Who is Jack Taylor, any-way?" she had asked once or twice of her husband, or of Hannah herself; and her lip had curled in a way which indicated that she, at least, knew who he was, and that her knowledge was not to his advantage.

Poor Jack certainly had an unenviable record be-hind him. "A worthless, drunken fellow," "A ne'er-do-well in any direction," "A man who killed his wife by dissipation and neglect,"—this was the verdict, variously phrased according to the style of the speaker, that one was sure to receive when one questioned concerning him. It is true that Jack had not drunk any liquor for several months and was keeping himself as steadily at work as previous habits of superficiality and his general reputation would admit. But when every good thing which could be said of him was freely admitted, the question was, why should Hannah Bramlett permit his almost daily visits? Not only this, but that estimable young woman walked the streets with him and allowed him to attend her home from the weekly prayer meetings and from other public places. She allowed him to linger at the gate, not merely for a few minutes, but sometimes for a full half hour; indeed, there were watchers who affirmed that on certain occasions it had been an hour and ten minutes by the clock before the vigil closed. Mrs. Bramlett, when in her indignation she had told her husband of his sister's sins, had not exaggerated the stories. The truth is, as they had come to her through the medium of her washerwoman, reported by the aforesaid Lena, they had been sufficiently offensive and she had not been tempted to add even a shade of meaning. The tongues of a certain class of people were undoubtedly busying themselves with Hannah Bramlett's affairs. Mrs. Bramlett was loyal enough to her husband's family to be genuinely alarmed at this. It was one thing to find fault with Hannah herself; it was quite another to have the neighborhood gossips making free with her name. That lurking sense of satisfaction which the matron had felt when she first realized the opportunity for criticism had entirely passed. She realized the importance of urging her husband to the rescue. All things considered, it will be understood, I think, that she came to the evening in question unfitted to be helpful to the nerves of a weary, debt-haunted husband. She had made a braver effort than Ralph Bramlett would perhaps ever understand, to rise above the disturbances of the day. She would have been able, perhaps, to have met him halfway, but, as has been noted, he did not meet her halfway; and when she introduced his sister as a topic for conversation, he did not give her credit for genuine anxiety but believed that she had selected simply another theme for his annoyance. With such a series of discomforts and misunderstandings acting upon two such natures as Ralph Bramlett and his wife, how could the evening have ended other than it did?

While Estelle Bramlett in her pretty sitting room was indulging her disappointed and bitter thoughts, and Ralph Bramlett in his library was staring at unpaid bills and inwardly groaning at the sight, Mrs. Edmonds and her daughter Marjorie sat together in their cheerful back parlor, which, although they had been at home so short a time, had already taken on that mysterious resemblance to themselves which is a peculiarity of certain rooms. Mrs. Edmonds had sew-

ing materials about her; and the latest magazine, with
freshly cut leaves, was waiting for Marjorie to entertain her so soon as the letter she was writing should
be finished. But Marjorie's pen had stopped and was
being balanced on one finger in an absentminded way
while its owner sat lost in thought. Mrs. Edmonds had
watched her silently for several minutes; at last she
spoke:

"Well, Marjorie? Is that letter unusually hard to
write?"

"The letter? Oh no, Mother, that is finished; at least
I have only a sentence or two to add. I had forgotten
it."

"I noticed that your thoughts seemed to be very
closely occupied. If I am to judge from your face, the
reverie is not altogether a pleasant one."

Marjorie smiled. "Did I look cross, Mother? I must
have a very telltale face." Then, after a moment, "To
tell the truth, I have not been able to get away from
some of the things that Glyde told me this afternoon.
She is troubled about Estelle and Ralph."

Mrs. Edmonds sewed steadily for several seconds.
She could not decide whether to question or be silent.
At last she said:

"What about them? Anything new? That is, I mean,
anything different from what you expected?"

"Yes," said Marjorie in a low voice; "I think my
faith had other expectations. We have been praying for
a long time."

There seemed to be no reply to make to this. After
another silence, the mother questioned again.

"What does Glyde say?"

"Oh nothing pronounced, of course; that is, nothing which she meant to have definite. But she is such
a guileless little creature that she tells more than she

imagines. They have both, it seems, quite given up the habit of attending prayer meeting, and they do not even have family worship. In fact, I gather from Glyde's talk that their attendance at church on Sundays is so extremely irregular that it is almost beginning to be marked when they are present, instead of when they are absent. Of course Glyde did not say this; but from her troubled face when she talked about the hindrances in their religious life, I gathered it. Halfway living is not like Ralph; with him it must be all or nothing. What is there, Mother, that we can do to help them?"

It was hard for Mrs. Edmonds to reply. If she had spoken the hope of her inmost soul, it would have been that her Marjorie would let Ralph Bramlett and his wife entirely alone; forget their existence as much as possible, and live her own sweet, strong life without regard to their petty one. But neither policy nor conscience would agree to such speaking, so she hesitated. Presently Marjorie answered her silence:

"I know, Mother, that you sometimes find it difficult to understand my persistent interest in these two; but—we were children together, you remember, and—I realize now that I influenced them both much more than I was aware at the time. I sometimes think that they are living out the life which I fostered in them; and if my influence had been different, why—"

She spoke in half-sentences, with distinct pauses between, as though it was difficult to formulate her thought. But her mother made haste to answer:

"Really, Marjorie, I must say I think that is mere sentimentalism. People must live their own lives. Ralph and Estelle have reached the age of maturity and are responsible for their own doings and their own failures; to foster in them a notion that other people are to blame is merely to help them in a line of self-excuse to which both are only too prone already, if I am not mistaken in them. It was Ralph's besetment from his babyhood."

"I know," said Marjorie quickly; "I remember you used always to say so. Of course I do not mean to say anything of this sort to them; I was merely thinking aloud. But you do not mean that we are not responsible for the influence which we exert?"

"To a degree we are, of course; and I do not deny that if you had been a Christian from your childhood you might have influenced for good not only those two, but your other companions. But all that is past. It is a sorrowful fact that we cannot undo the past. The thought ought certainly to make us more careful of our present; but unavailing regrets, an attempt to accomplish in the present what belongs to the past, weaken our influence over others and savor of sentiment rather than religion."

Marjorie laughed pleasantly. "Mother dear," she said, "it is the first time I ever knew you to accuse me of sentimentality. Have I not generally been almost too matter-of-fact to suit your poetic temperament? I assure you I mean the merest commonplace now. I have shed my tears over past follies and put them away; it is the present that interests me. If I can but do my duty now, I shall leave the past mistakes with him who has promised to hide them. But I frankly admit that I am more interested in Ralph and Estelle than in any other friends of mine; and I daily ask God to show me ways of helping them. It was the predominant thought in our homecoming. I had a feeling that they were in need of help. Aside from this, Mother, you and I can do no less than try. We have covenanted to do so, you remember."

"I promised to pray for them," said Mrs. Edmonds in a low, troubled tone.

"Yes; but what is prayer worth unless we supplement it so far as possible by effort?"

Poor Mrs. Edmonds! She was willing to pray during the period of her natural life for these two friends of her daughter's girlhood; but to come into daily social contact with them, to feel that her daughter was interesting herself in them in a special manner, planning for them, giving herself, as it were, to efforts in their behalf, was an experience from which she shrank with an intensity that she vainly told herself was utter folly. To understand her feeling, one would need to realize what it was for a mother to look forward for a year or two to the probable marriage of her daughter to a young man of whom she did not approve, and then to feel herself suddenly lifted above the danger by the marriage of the young man to another woman; and yet to feel that her daughter's life had been scarred, at least, by the experience. More than that, this mother knew that the scar had been deep. If her daughter had come back to meet Ralph Bramlett with utter indifference, the mother would have been satisfied, would have felt that all was as it should be; but to own to more than common interest in and anxiety for this man who had done what he could to make her life a wreck; not only this, but to proceed on this first quiet evening at home to plan ways of reaching and influencing him, was more than the poor mother's faith was equal to. Once more Marjorie answered the look on her face.

"Mother dear, don't be anxious. I am not going to do anything erratic, nor in the least out of the line of the conventional. I am thinking only of an afternoon call upon Estelle—an informal running in, such as she is not willing to give me, it seems. Glyde said she asked her to come this afternoon, and she declined because it would be more proper to call first with her husband. Think of such formalities between Estelle Douglass and myself!" and Marjorie laughed lightly. "I shall forestall all such proprieties by going tomorrow, I think, to have a little old-time chat with her, and establish her, if possible, upon a friendly footing. Then, in time, I shall hope to be able to influence her in the direction of her highest good, and, through her, to reach Ralph. I am afraid the poor fellow is troubled in more ways than one. Glyde thinks he is unhappy in his business relations. I never believed that his conscience would permit him to continue in peace as bookkeeper in a distiller."

Mrs. Edmonds opened her lips to say that she did not believe he had any conscience, then she closed them again with the words unspoken. Of what use?

"If I could, through Estelle," Marjorie went on, "help him to see that to connect himself with such a business, however remotely, was his first mistake, and persuade him to get right with his conscience in that direction, I should have hope for the rest. Do you not think, Mother, that it may have been the starting point with him?"

"No, dear; I think the starting point, as you call it, was way back in his childhood or early youth. His moral nature was never strong; and his obstinacy, that strong point in a weak nature, was always at the front. The trouble is that you invested Ralph from his childhood with qualities that he did not possess, and because as a man he did not exhibit them, he keeps you in a constant state of disappointment. My opinion is that Ralph Bramlett will have to be entirely made over before he will be other than a disappointment to those of his friends who have his highest interests at heart."

Marjorie made no effort to argue the question. In her heart she believed that her mother was hopelessly prejudiced against this old friend of hers.

"Very well, Mamma," she said quietly. "You and I must remember that the grace of God can do exactly that for people." Then, after a moment's silence, she changed the subject, or rather brought forward another form of what was to her the same subject.

"The gossips of this locality are still alive, Mother; I think it will astonish you to hear whose name they are making free now. Of all women in the world, I should have expected Hannah Bramlett to escape such ordeals."

"Hannah Bramlett!" exclaimed Mrs. Edmonds, surprised out of the instinctive reserve in which she encased herself whenever the Bramlett name was under discussion. "What can they possibly find to gossip about in her?"

"That is the most extraordinary part of it. Do you remember that Jack Taylor whose wife I stayed with while Mr. Maxwell went for a doctor, and who died while I was in the house? Hannah, you know, interested herself in the poor wretch, tried to help him to get work and to keep away from the saloons. She succeeded too; I heard, before we left home, that she was having a really remarkable influence over him. It seems that her efforts have continued and have been crowned with such success that poor Jack has not taken a drop for months, and he works steadily every day. He has earned himself some decent clothes and goes to church quite regularly; but now the gossips, who let him travel toward destruction without a word, are interesting themselves in him and in Hannah, to a degree that is startling."

"But in what way?" asked Mrs. Edmonds, bewildered. "Surely no one disapproves of helping a poor wretch to reform!"

"No; but having reformed he becomes a legitimate subject, it seems, for idle tongues. Glyde thinks poor Hannah has been thoughtless, perhaps. She has allowed him to come often to see her, and has walked with him on the streets quite often, and has stood talking with him at her own gate once or twice, possibly until a later hour than custom approves; and the gossips, who seem to be delighted with the whole subject, have taken hold of it and added what they pleased to make it interesting, until now, Glyde says, the street-corner loungers speak of Hannah as 'Jack Taylor's best girl,' and ask him when he is going to get his house ready for her!"

"Is it possible!" said Mrs. Edmonds. "What an absurdly imprudent condition of things for a woman of her age to be beguiled into! It must be that that Bramlett family are all devoid of common sense."

And then Marjorie resolved that she would talk no more with her mother about the Bramletts.

4

TRUE to her decision, the following afternoon found Marjorie awaiting admittance at Ralph Bramlett's home. A curious half-smile was on her face, and a faraway look in her eyes, as she read the name "Bramlett" on the doorplate. The time had been when this young woman had thought of that name even in connection with such trivialities as doorplates. She remembered a certain June evening when she had waited with Ralph to be admitted to Judge Bartlett's house, and he, calling attention to the name on the door, had said: "It isn't quite Bramlett, but it takes about the same space, doesn't it? However, we shall not have that style of lettering on our door; I detest it. Do you arrange even such matters about our house that is to be, Marjorie? I think no small detail of our establishment escapes me."

She had laughed in response and said gaily, "Our castle is in the air." Yet with the laugh had come a blush, and she had admitted to herself that no smallest detail of that dear castle could be unimportant to her; so entirely a matter of course did it seem to her that, sometime in the lovely future, the name Bramlett would cover her own. Yet here she stood at Ralph Bramlett's door, awaiting admission, and the presiding genius of his home was Estelle Douglass Bramlett!

Was it not well for her that she could smile? Not simply a brave smile, but a quiet, natural one. That time was all in the past, as she had told her mother; and her heart, as well as her conscience, said, *It is well.* She knew now that she had never been intended to become the wife of Ralph Bramlett; that a wise and kind overruling Providence had held her from it, and she could look up thankfully because of the ruling. Yet it was, to say the least, interesting to be standing here at Ralph Bramlett's door. She had speculated a little over their first meeting. How was it possible to do otherwise when she remembered with such vividness their last interview? Probably Ralph, too, remembered it. If they could both forget it, everything would be comparatively easy.

She went swiftly over that last interview while she waited, recalling, almost in spite of herself, some of Ralph Bramlett's wild words.

"Estelle Douglass be hanged!" he had said savagely, when she had haughtily reminded him of his engagement with her. And then he had poured out that alarming appeal to her not to cast him off, to remember how long they had been tacitly pledged to each other, to overlook all the past, and to permit nothing to separate them again. "Let us be married right away!" had been one of his passionate outcries. Oh! she remembered it vividly. The remembrance called the blood to her face even now. But the blush was because she realized that the man who had spoken such words to her was at that moment, of his own will and desire, engaged to be married to another. Long ago she had settled it that some experience of which she knew nothing had caused a temporary insanity, during which he had forgotten his position and gone back into their past. What a humiliation it must have been to him when he came to himself and realized what he had said! It was possible—nay, she had settled it with herself that it was entirely probable—that he had brooded over this interview until it had had much to do with the retrograde life at which Glyde Douglass had mournfully hinted. In the old days she had been well acquainted with him, and none knew better than she what a demoralizing effect a sense of self-abasement had on him. It was entirely within the range of his imagination to believe that she, Marjorie, despised him. If she could but meet him in a friendly way, quite as though they were, and always had been, and always would be, real friends, it might accomplish much. It was this train of thought that had brought her to the decision which she had announced to her mother and brought her finally to Ralph Bramlett's door.

It was Lena who admitted her, and she waited in state in the handsome parlor like any formal caller. When Mrs. Bramlett came, it was evident that she felt formal and dignified. In vain did Marjorie struggle to take her old friendly place.

"What a pretty home you have, Estelle! I have often thought of you in it and fancied myself running in to see you. It is even prettier than I imagined it. Have you grown used to housekeeping? or does it still seem queer to be regarded as mistress, with no mother in the background ready for appeal?"

"Oh yes," the matron said with a cold smile. She was quite used to it. Almost anything became an old story after a few months.

"And have you been well all these months? Aren't you thinner than you used to be? How is Ralph? Does he look just as he did? The truth is, it seems to me years since I went away. I am not used to being so long from home, you know. I may call your husband Ralph, may I not? I cannot seem to bring my tongue into the habit of saying 'Mr. Bramlett'; I think of him very much as I fancy others do of their brothers."

Nothing could be more sincere than this sentence. The time had been when it flushed her cheek and brought a look of indignation to her eyes to have Estelle Douglass talk to her about Ralph Bramlett being the same as her brother. But all that seemed very long ago, like a piece of her childhood that had been foolish and been put away. What she had desired exceedingly was to establish herself on such a footing with this young couple that they would honestly look upon her as a sister; one who was interested in everything that pertained to their life, and ready to be as sympathetic and helpful as possible. If Glyde was not mistaken, Ralph, especially, stood in dire need of a sister's influence. But her heart misgave her as she looked at Estelle's unresponsive face. She had been mistaken, she told herself, in thinking her paler than of old; there was a rich glow on her cheeks. These thoughts floated through her mind as she listened to Mrs. Bramlett's reply.

Ralph was quite well, she believed, though she hardly saw enough of him to be certain. He was like all men, so absorbed in business as to have neither time nor heart for other ideas. As to what name her guest should use toward him, the wife utterly ignored this question. And then, suddenly, it seemed the time for her to ask questions.

"What of yourself, Marjorie? What have you found

to occupy you all this while? I was surprised to learn that you had returned just as you went away. How is Mr. Maxwell?"

"He is quite well, or was when we last heard. He is coming to spend the midwinter vacation with us. I hope you will see a good deal of him then. I feel sure that both you and Ralph would enjoy him."

"And when is the marriage to take place?"

Mrs. Bramlett had not forgotten her old art of asking direct questions when she chose, undeterred by any feeling of delicacy. It may be that she thought Marjorie's frank kindliness justified her in asking so personal a question. But was there ever a stupider guest? For the moment, Marjorie was bewildered. Could she mean Glyde? But that was absurd; she would not question an outsider about her own sister's affairs. Then suddenly the personality of the question dawned upon her, and she laughed.

"You must mean my marriage, I think. My friend, I haven't any idea. Nothing is farther from my thoughts at present. My own opinion is that I shall stay close beside my mother and be a good, useful old-maid sister to all my friends. I have always thought that a more useful life than that could hardly be imagined, and at present it certainly seems a pleasant one."

There was no mistaking the earnestness in Mrs. Bramlett's tone when her next direct question was put.

"Do you mean me to understand that you are not engaged to Mr. Maxwell?"

The rich color flowed into Marjorie's face, but her laugh was free and unembarrassed.

"My dear Estelle," she said, "how could you have imagined such a state of things? I assure you that nothing can be farther from the thoughts of either of us. Mr. Maxwell is a true and valued friend. Speaking of brothers, I am sure no girl could have a better one than he is to me; but that is quite the limit of our relationship. We have never for a moment thought of any other."

"Well!" said Estelle, drawing her breath hard and speaking quickly, as one impelled to speak, whether she would or not—"then all I have to say is, you are even a worse flirt than I took you to be."

"Estelle! Have I ever said or done anything that justifies you in using such language to me?" There was the pathos of wounded feeling in her voice, as well as a strong undertone of indignation. Estelle was instantly ashamed of herself.

"I beg your pardon," she said, trying to laugh, "I should not have said that; it is really none of my business, of course, but you took me so utterly by surprise. Why, Marjorie, everybody thinks you are engaged to Mr. Maxwell; and ever since we heard you were coming home, people have been wondering whether you would be married before your return, or wait to have the wedding at home. I am sure I was never more amazed in my life."

Just what reply Marjorie would have made will not be known. An unexpected interruption occurred. It had been months since Ralph Bramlett had come out from his business by an early train. Indeed, his wife counted herself fortunate if he arrived in time for their late dinner, so all-engrossing had his office business become. Her caller had taken care to assure herself of this fact before she chose the hour for her visit, her plan being to reestablish the most friendly relations with the wife before coming in contact with the husband. Indeed, one must do her judgment the justice to explain that her plan involved influencing her old friend Ralph almost entirely through the medium of his wife. She reasoned that, having so little time outside of business hours, he would naturally want to spend it chiefly with his wife, and of course she would not often see him. In short, she desired and planned to act the guardian angel to this friend of her youth without coming often enough in contact with him to disturb the angelic influence. That is not the way in which she put it to herself, yet it is perhaps a fair explanation of her inward meaning. However, on this particular day the unexpected happened. Mr. Bramlett came home by the early train; and hearing his wife's voice as he entered the hall, and believing one of her sisters to be with her, he pushed open the door without ceremony, and stood framed in the doorway, and ejaculated the one word:

"Marjorie!"

Then Marjorie's self-possession returned to her. Not even positive rudeness on Estelle's part should keep her from trying to be helpful in this home. If Ralph supposed that she cherished indignation against him because, for a single moment, under the power of some excitement, he had lost his head entirely and spoken words which must have been a humiliation to him ever since, it should be her duty at the first opportunity to assure him of his mistake. Accordingly she arose, and advanced to meet him with outstretched hand.

They were to be friends, then. She must have been gratified at the instant look not only of relief but also of unqualified pleasure, which overspread Ralph Bramlett's face. He grasped the offered hand with an eagerness which did not escape his wife's eyes, and drawing a chair beside Marjorie, plunged at once into the most earnest conversation, which was so worded, probably by accident, that Estelle was of necessity left outside. Neither did he appear to notice it when she murmured an excuse and abruptly left the room. Marjorie did, however, and was disturbed; not at being left alone for a few minutes with her old friend—she desired to establish their relations on such a brotherly and sisterly basis as to make this the most ordinary of happenings—but because she felt afraid that Estelle would not realize how hearty and entire was her interest in herself, nor how anxious she was to be her friend.

It is really Estelle that I want, thought this unworldly schemer. *What a pity that Ralph came so soon! I wish he would go to his dressing room, or somewhere else, and give me a chance to visit with his wife.*

Yet although this uncomfortable feeling floated through her mind, she had not, after all, the remotest conception of the state of turmoil into which she had thrown Estelle Bramlett. Be it understood that she had never realized in the past what was patent to some persons; namely, that Estelle was jealous of her influence over Ralph. Why should there be any such feeling? Marjorie would have reasoned, if she had thought about it at all. Did he not choose her and give himself to her? And had he not made her his wife? Of course she was to him above all others. That last interview with him, in which he had spoken words which would imply the contrary, was left out of the matter altogether as soon as it was definitely settled that those words were but the ravings of a temporarily unbalanced brain. Her surprise and consternation would have been great could she have followed the wife and watched her as, having locked her door against all possible intrusion, she walked up and down the room, eyes dry and bright and seeming to flash venom, and hands clasped in so tight a grip that had she not been under the influence of violent excitement it would have hurt her, muttering from time to time such words as these:

"A wicked, *wicked* woman! Worse, a hundred times, than an ordinary flirt! What does she mean? Haven't I trouble enough without having her steal into my house like the serpent that she is? I hate her! I wish I had told her so and gotten rid of her in some way—in any way—before Ralph came. Oh, Ralph! Ralph!"

The name was uttered as a sort of moan, but still there were no tears. Estelle Bramlett was a woman who had no tears with which to relieve her deepest feelings. In her pocket there burned at that moment a bit of paper which she had found on the floor of her husband's study. It was covered all over with a name, written in different styles of his fine hand. That name was Marjorie Edmonds—"Marjorie Edmonds," repeated in German text, in fine flowing hand, in bold business hand, in curves and shades and flourishes, and twice carefully written "Marjorie Edmonds Bramlett!" What did he mean? Why should he employ his idle moments in writing that girl's name in every imaginable style? Why had he actually added to it his own name—her name? Did he wish all the time that it were Marjorie Edmonds Bramlett, instead of Estelle Douglass Bramlett? How was she to bear any of it?

5

TEMPTATIONS

IN THE glow of the moonlight, two figures were distinctly outlined at the gate of the Bramlett homestead. The hour was late, and, especially in that quiet part of the world, most people were sleeping; yet still they lingered, Hannah Bramlett inside the gate, with her anxious face upturned toward Jack Taylor, who lounged against the gatepost and listened with what he meant for an air of respect.

Hannah's voice as well as face was anxious.

"You know, Jack, you own that it is a constant temptation to you and you have half promised me a dozen times that you would give it up. Why don't you?"

"That is the question," said Jack. "Why don't I? It isn't so easy as you womenfolk think."

"I know it isn't easy, Jack; at least, I have heard others besides yourself say the same thing. But you are not a child to yield to a temptation because it is hard to resist it. You have been brave in struggling against a much greater temptation than this."

"There is where you are wrong," said Jack quickly.

"In some ways it is harder to stop smoking than it is to stop drinking. You see, it is like this: if a fellow drinks—drinks hard, you know, as I have to if I do it at all—and staggers through the streets, running against folks and talking to lampposts and things, why, everybody knows about it; and if he is poor, and wears ragged clothes, and all that sort of thing, why, he is a worthless, good-for-nothing fellow at once—nobody trusts him, nobody wants to have anything to do with him. But with smoking it is as different as daylight is from darkness. The nicest men in the world smoke and are respected just the same. Doctor Ford smokes, and you think he is all right. He came into our shop the other day to speak to a fellow and he had a cigar in his hand that minute; it was a good one too. I liked the smell of it; in fact, you may say I hankered after one like it. I went out as soon as I could and bought one. Not like his—I can't indulge expensive tastes, you see, though I have them—but one of my kind. I think maybe I would have got through the afternoon without smoking if it had not been for Doctor Ford; so you see what I mean by being tempted all the time."

Hannah made a movement of impatience.

"Of course I know what you mean, Jack; but cannot you see the difference between you and Doctor Ford? I don't say I am glad that he smokes; I am not. I wish he and everybody else would stop it; but what I want you to think about is, what has his smoking to do with you? Perhaps it isn't a temptation to him; certainly it isn't in the same way that it is to you. Why cannot you live your life and let him live his?—do the best that you can for yourself, without regard to the Doctor Fords or any other people? You know, Jack, you have told me that after smoking two or three cigars you felt sometimes such a hankering for liquor that it seemed to you you must have it; and you know if you once taste it again you are ruined, yet you constantly keep this great temptation before you. How can you hope to become anybody when you refuse to help yourself even by so much?"

Jack Taylor gave a long-drawn sigh and shifted his position from one post to the other.

"I don't hope it much," he said dolefully; "that's the living truth. I'm not worth the trouble you are taking for me, Miss Hannah; I know it as well as the next one. If it hadn't been for you and your kind of hanging on to me and expecting better things of me than I expected of myself, I should have gone to the dogs long ago; and perhaps that would have been the best way, because that is how it will end. There isn't enough of me to have it end in any other way. You see, being a woman, you don't understand anything about it, and you can't understand. It isn't that I don't keep up a constant fight about these things. Take smoking, now, which it seems to you is just as easy to give up as to say I won't go down the street today; why, I've fought enough over that to make a decent fellow of me if there was anything to make it on. I began the smoking when I was a little chap not a dozen years old. I did it to be like my Sunday school teacher, too. I knew he was a big, splendid man, and spent his days in a bank, and went riding in his carriage whenever he liked, and the cigars seemed a part of him somehow. I don't know as I thought that if I got the cigars, the bank and the carriage and fine clothes would come; but anyhow I copied him where I could and took to smoking. I've been at it ever since. Folks talk about second nature; this has got to be first nature with me. I seem to need it too. Why, one time since I have been trying to live up to your notions, I went without cigars for pretty near three days; and a crosser, uglier, more cantankerous beast than I was couldn't be found in the country. I wonder I wasn't discharged any hour in the day; if they hadn't been short of men and uncommonly hurried, I should have been. At last it got so bad I couldn't stand myself. I made up my mind it was no use. I threw down my hammer and went out and got a cigar, and in an hour I was all right."

"'All right,' Jack! When you own to me that after smoking two or three cigars you feel as though you *must* have a drink of beer?"

"That's true, Miss Hannah, and I won't deny it. Everybody may not be so; but with me the two have gone together for a long time, and they seem to belong together. When I get the fumes of a good cigar, it isn't the cigar I think so much about, after all, as the brandy; I seem to see it somehow skulking behind the other smell, and I have to fly out and get the cigar that I know I can have, to keep me from rushing into the thing that I know I mustn't touch. But I shall touch it someday; I feel dead sure of it. Things are getting worse with me instead of better. That is the way it has been all my life; I could keep sober up to a certain point, then I was off, and nothing in this life or the next one could prevent it. You know what I have been through? If anything could have kept me sober, it was that little girl of mine—my wife, you know—and yet I killed her with the drink."

Poor Hannah Bramlett! How utterly helpless she felt before this vision of a tempted soul. It was as if for the first time she had been given a glimpse into darker depths than she had before imagined. Jack Taylor, looking at her, could distinctly see a tear rolling slowly down her cheeks. A tear of sympathy, it may be, but also of disappointment. This shocked and dismayed him, as tears on the face of an habitually self-control-led woman always must dismay those who are not utterly hardened.

It roused him to instant endeavor.

"I'll tell you what, Miss Hannah. I'm not worth all the trouble you are taking for me, and that's a fact. You just let go of me and let me slide. There are fellows in this town who are not so far gone as I, and young chaps who are just beginning, and some who haven't begun yet, but they will. If you will just turn your mind to some of them and save them, you will be doing something worthwhile. But I'm not of any particular account anyway. My wife is dead, and Mother is dead, and there isn't a living soul who cares what becomes of me."

The effect was utterly different from what Hannah would have hoped for, had her tears been planned for effect. They were instantly dried; and Hannah, leaning over the gatepost, laid her hand on Jack's arm. He was watching her intently, a curious, eager look in his eyes. If this girl who had been so kind—kinder than her sort of folks had ever been to him before—would only consent to drop her hold upon him and let him slide, he could then go back to the tastes for which his whole diseased body and brain longed with something like an easy conscience, according to his distorted ideas of conscience. A strange fight was at that moment going on in Jack Taylor's mind. He was making Hannah Bramlett the pivot on which his next action was to turn. If she would only say, "Jack, I am disappointed in you; I have helped you all I can. I must give you up," then would he go as straight as impatient feet could carry him to the nearest saloon and drink until this awful thirst of his was quenched. It was heavier upon him tonight than it had been for weeks before. What she said, with her hand resting on his arm, was:

"Jack, I will never give you up; *never,* as long as I live, so help me God! I have asked him on my knees to make of you a good, true man, and to let me be a help to you in some way. Don't ask me to turn away from that hope and expectation. Jack, you are the first one I ever tried to help in my life, and if you fail me it will spoil my life as well as yours."

It was a strange appeal, and it had a strange effect. Jack continued to look at her steadfastly, but the light died out of his eyes, leaving instead almost a sullen look; and he gave presently that long-drawn sigh and said:

"Well, then I suppose I must try it some more. I thought I wouldn't; but if you *won't* let go of a fellow, what can he do?"

An upper window of the Bramlett homestead opened at that moment—a head appeared, and a voice was heard:

"Hannah, you ought not to stand out there any longer in the cold; I wish you would come in."

It was her mother's voice, and there was more than maternal solicitude for Hannah's health expressed in it. Hannah knew what the admonition meant. So, in a degree, did Jack. He laughed a little bitterly.

"They are watching out for you, Miss Hannah," he said; "you are getting yourself into lots of trouble by trying to help such a worthless fellow as I am. It would be a great deal better for you just to give me up."

"Hush!" said Hannah. "I don't want you ever to say anything of that kind to me again. Remember what I have told you, that I will never give you up. We must not talk any longer now, it is late; but I shall expect to see you at the hall tomorrow as usual. Good night."

By the time she had locked the door and toiled up the long flight of stairs, the door of her mother's room opened and that good lady, in night attire, old-fashioned candlestick in hand, appeared to light her daughter through the hall and speak her mind:

"I wonder at you, Hannah! standing at the gate in the cold at this time of night to talk with that fellow, after what Ralph said to you. I can't think what has got into you; you never used to go on in this way before."

"Oh, Ralph!" said Hannah in a high-pitched, indignant voice; "don't quote him to me, Mother, tonight. If he would help me a little in what I am trying to do, instead of smoking around the streets, setting bad examples for others to follow, I might be more willing to listen to what he has to say. I haven't hurt anybody by standing at the gate for a few minutes with a poor, tempted boy. Our voices couldn't have disturbed you tonight, I am sure; we spoke low enough."

"It isn't the disturbance," said the mother in an injured tone; "you know well enough, Hannah, that I'm not one to be disturbed by folks trying to help others. But there is common sense in all things; and it isn't common sense for you to stand out at the front gate at this time of night, talking with a good-for-nothing boy. It does seem as though you were possessed. What do you suppose people think of you? At your age too!"

"I don't care what they think," said Hannah. She disappeared within her own room without so much as saying good-night to her mother, and slammed the door a little as she did so. By which token it will be seen that an angelic spirit had by no means gotten complete possession of Hannah Bramlett.

As to what people said of her, they were busy saying it that very night. She had been so earnest in her last words to Jack that she had not so much as noticed a passing carriage moving very slowly along the road, while one pair of keen eyes watched with eagerness the scene at the gate. Perhaps Hannah would have been more careful had she noticed the carriage and known that it contained Mr. and Mrs. Jonas Smith; and perhaps not. Hannah had her own share of the Bramlett obstinacy. But Mrs. Smith looked and *looked,* and spoke her mind:

"Just see that Bramlett girl—I s'pose she calls herself a girl, though she is thirty if she is a day—standing at the gate with Jack Taylor, with her hand on his arm and leaning over to gaze into his face! I daresay he is drunk this very minute. What can her folks be thinking about? Haven't they any influence over her, do you suppose? Or don't they know how she is going on with that fellow? I declare, somebody ought to tell them what people are saying. If a woman of her age hasn't learned common sense, it is high time she was looked after, for the sake of the girls, and the boys too, for that matter. To be sure, she can't hurt Jack Taylor! But who would have expected such goings on in a Bramlett!"

Certainly life was bringing to Hannah Bramlett some hard experiences. As she had told Jack Taylor, she had lived her life until very recently without even an effort to help along the work of the world in any way. She had not told him how intense her desire had been to take her place with the great army of those who thought of others instead of themselves; whose days were filled with important work: *service,* instead of with petty routine. But she had been trammelled on every side, chiefly by the feeling which seemed to possess all who knew her, that Hannah Bramlett could not be counted upon in any way.

She was, in a singular sense of the phrase, a girl who had had no place in life. Other girls in their teens had been full of this sweet, fascinating world, charmed with its pursuits, intoxicated, almost, with its pleasures. It had had no opportunity to charm Hannah. She had been a shy, backward girl, living much within herself, always, when at home, busy with the daily burdens of life on an unproductive farm where hired labor was scarce and work heavy.

The long winter evenings that might have been made to do so much for the girl had very largely been spent with her father and mother in the large farmhouse kitchen, gathered around a single kerosene lamp of not modern style, her father carefully reading the daily paper, her mother busy with the interminable mending basket. Hannah had been expected from almost her babyhood to do her full share of the mending and had faithfully attacked this duty which her soul hated. When her brother Ralph was a little boy he had escaped the kitchen by going early to bed. As he grew older, and indeed blossomed suddenly into young manhood, he had gone out into the world and taken his place among the young people as Hannah never had. In fact, he had speedily become a leader among a certain class of young people and had his intimate friends, who included him as a matter of course in all their plans. Oh yes, Hannah had been a schoolgirl, and a faithful, painstaking scholar. She had made fairly good use of such opportunities as had been hers and would have liked nothing better, had the books been at her command, than to fill the long winter evenings with reading and study. But as life on the farm grew harder, she was more and more needed

at home; and as no one recognized for her the importance of her continuing at school—her teachers, as a
rule, being busy with more brilliant pupils—she early
and quietly dropped out of line. She had had but few
acquaintances in school and no intimates.

In short, a greater contrast could hardly be imagined than that which her own young life and her
brother's presented.

6

POOR JACK!

THERE is something very sad about this review of the relation between brother and sister. One cannot help thinking how much they might have been to each other had either or both been different. Had there been less disparity in their ages, matters might not have been so bad. But there was a period in Ralph Bramlett's life during which his sister distinctly ruled over him, not always with a gentle hand. She loved him after a manner which he did not, and perhaps never would, understand; but she made him constantly remember that he was subject to her. Shy and timid with other people, her native energy took the form of aggressiveness with him, and her authority kept that of his gentler mother's in the background. Then suddenly, as it seemed to Hannah, there had come a great change. Ralph escaped her and went out into the schoolboy world, and grew tall and strong, and threw off utterly the yoke of subjection. Had he been the sort of boy he might have been—the sort of which there are a very few in the world—and allowed his dawning manhood to assume a protective form, and clung to his sister, taking her with him on occasion into his new world, telling her about it in a confidential way, he might have done with her almost as he would. Her nature and her love were such that they could have changed relations, and he would have been accepted as the guide and mentor. Hannah herself, when she began to realize the change in him, had for a time a dim sense of this possibility. She began timidly to question him concerning matters in which he had evidently outstripped her. What did people say about thus and so? What was the accepted idea concerning this or that matter? But he had failed to recognize his opportunity; he had laughed at her questions, scoffed at her scruples, sneered into worthlessness all plans of hers, and counted her out of his engagements as a matter of course. Not because he meant to be unbrotherly, but because the four years of difference in their ages seemed to him a great gulf. When he was eleven and Hannah was fifteen, he had looked upon her as a woman; when he became of age and she was twenty-five, she seemed to him to have grown into an old woman, or at least a middle-aged one, who must of necessity be separated from his life outside the home.

Hannah had accepted the repulsion and returned promptly to her character of elder sister and fault-finder. A certain sense of soreness connected with this experience caused her to find fault so sharply and continually that at last he told her in frank, not to say rough, language that she was hereafter to attend to her own business and allow him to attend to his. So they lived their different lives, even when of the same household. Probably Ralph would at any time have been astonished had he known how strong almost to fierceness was the current of love which flowed through his sister's heart for him; but he would have been equally astonished had one told him that his conduct to his sister was at any time unbrotherly.

Meantime, Hannah, having quietly given up certain ambitions which she had had for herself, and of which no one dreamed, had centered all her hopes and expectations on her brother, and in a hundred ways he had disappointed her. He was to have been a scholar, a lawyer, a great man, one to whom hundreds should look for counsel, for help, for guidance. Instead, he had become bookkeeper in a distillery! This in itself was bitter enough. There had been a few months of prospective comfort for her because she had rested her soul on the belief that Ralph would eventually marry Marjorie Edmonds; and once married to her, all that was wrong about him would in some mysterious manner fall away, and he would be all that he could and should be. For Hannah Bramlett, although she had no intimate friends, had one idol. Ever since she could remember, she had looked up to, and felt a sort of reverent admiration for, Marjorie Edmonds. In her secret heart she called her "sister," and revelled in the thought of what it would be to be able to call her that before all the world. "My sister Marjorie says," she would sometimes begin in clear tones, when quite alone, and a happy glow would spread over her face at the thought of the strong, wise words which that sister Marjorie would speak, and of how sure they would be to win respect. Hannah herself, with her curious mixture of timidity and positiveness, which are sometimes found together in suppressed natures, had never been able, outside of her own very small world, to express herself with firmness; yet she gloried in the freedom of speech and gracious leadership which characterized Marjorie and clung to her with a daily increasing intensity of love and a gloating sense of possession in prospect.

And then suddenly had come that crushing disappointment. Instead of Marjorie, the sister was to be Estelle Douglass! As intense in its way as her admiration for Marjorie had been her dislike for Estelle. Perhaps this feeling had deepened instead of decreased since the marriage. Yet, after all, she had borne the disappointment better than at one time she had supposed she could, because she had become absorbed in other interests. Ever since a well-remembered day when she had sought Marjorie and poured out before her some of her ambitions, Hannah might almost have been said to live for Jack Taylor's sake. It was Marjorie who told her of him and actually asked her to try to help him. Following very soon upon her first timid efforts came the discovery which has power to thrill; namely, that she really had influence over a human being, that there was somebody who looked up to her, who was willing, to a degree at least, to be led by her, and who responded gratefully to her efforts to help him. This opened to the hungry-hearted young woman a new world. She put herself between Jack Taylor and the hundred temptations which beset his path. She gave up most of her evenings to work that had to do with him. She begged and pleaded with him to resist the evil spirit that seemed always at his elbow. She went with him, more than once, to places that in themselves had no interest for her; but because they interested him, and because by being with him she could shield him from temptation, she had unhesitatingly sacrificed herself. She had, in fact, done everything for him that a guardian angel in human form could do.

On the evening in question, as the poor girl closed

her door and dropped in weariness and bitterness into the one comfortable chair which the dreary little room contained, and clasped her hands in almost an agony of disappointment, that bitterest of all questions came and stood beside her seeking answer:

"Of what use was all her effort? What had she accomplished?" She had never before so fully realized the force for evil which was pressing upon Jack Taylor—temptations coming daily to him from the very class of people that ought to have been his strength. From men like her brother Ralph, for instance; because this matter of smoking was, without question, a temptation to Jack Taylor, whatever it might be to others. Yet he could not meet even her Christian brother on the street without coming in contact with this temptation! Nay, it was worse than that; her very pastor, *his* pastor as she had tried to have Jack consider him, brought the same power for evil to bear upon him. How could a man like Jack be expected to make anything but a failure, with such fearful odds against him? "Man," indeed! It was folly to call him that; he was a mere boy, with not so much strength of will as had many a boy of seventeen.

But the bitterest drop in Hannah Bramlett's cup was undoubtedly the discovery that she was the subject of gossiping tongues. It was all very well for her to tell her mother that she did not care what people thought; the simple truth was that no one cared more about it than did she. The Bramletts had been poor all their lives, for generations back, indeed, but they had been eminently respectable, none of them more entirely so than Hannah. Unconsciously she had prided herself upon this fact. She was not handsome, she could not lay claim to genius or even talent in any special direction, but she bore with honor and dignity an honored name. No breath from the outside world had ever blown upon her in disapproval, or ever could, so it had seemed to her, entrenched as she was behind generations of propriety. And yet, behold! gossiping tongues had dared to play with her name. To what extent she was not quite sure. If the truth be told, she believed that a very large portion of the tale that had been indignantly told to her had had its birth in the imagination of her brother's wife; but some foundation she must have had, of course, and this thought rankled, struck deep, indeed, in Hannah Bramlett's heart. Was it possible that it was such a mean, wicked world that a woman like herself, who had lived so many years of blameless life, could not show kindness to, and patience with, a misguided boy like Jack Taylor, in order to try to save him, without becoming the victim of cruel tongues? It was characteristic of Hannah Bramlett's character that, although she had cried bitterly in secret over the story when it first came to her through the channel of Estelle's indignation, she had not for a single moment thought of throwing off Jack Taylor, or of changing in any way her efforts to save him. People must talk if they would—it was only the low and coarse who did so—and her brother's wife must lower herself to listen to such talk if she would; but she, Hannah, would move steadily forward in the work that she had undertaken. Jack Taylor was to be saved to the world and to God; and she was to be, in a degree at least, the instrument used to this end. Should any gossiping tongues deprive her of such a joy as that? Not for a second did she hesitate, but the sacrifice was no less bitter. She had told Jack Taylor that night that she would never give him up, and she meant it. Yet as she presently slipped down on her knees to pour out her disappointment and pain to the

One who alone seemed able to understand her, there came at first only a burst of passionate tears. But it is blessed to remember that the Maker of hearts understands the language of tears.

Jack Taylor, left to himself, went with long strides toward the uninviting quarters that he called home. There was in his heart a curious sense of defeat. He actually felt almost indignant at Hannah Bramlett. Why couldn't she let him alone? What was the use in tugging with him any longer? She was injuring herself by it, as he had told her, though the poor fellow had not the least idea to what extent. He only knew that a certain class of people nudged elbows as he passed with her and sometimes indulged in chuckles that were loud enough for his ears to catch. Occasionally they asked him, with sly winks, how his best girl was. It all seemed supremely silly to him; but he had an instinctive feeling that Hannah would dislike it very much, and felt a chivalrous desire to keep her from knowing anything about it. When he heard Mrs. Bramlett's voice that night calling to her daughter, it represented to him a certain other class of people who were saying that Hannah was demeaning herself by having anything to do with him.

"I s'pose she is," said the poor fellow to himself dolefully. "I'm not worth doing anything with, and I told her so. I wish with all my soul that she would let me alone; but she won't, she ain't of that kind. She is going to have me a 'good, true man,' she says. My land! she don't know what kind of a job she has undertaken. Jack Taylor get to be a 'good, true man'!"

Ten minutes' walk brought him to Main Street; as he turned the corner he came upon a former comrade of his, Joe Berry by name.

"Halloo, Jack!" said Joe good-naturedly; "been see-

ing your best girl home? It must be an awful bore to
have to travel so far out with her every night. You will
be glad when you get settled in a livelier place, won't
you?"

"You hold up on that, will you?" said Jack a trifle
fiercely; "I'm not in the notion for anything of the
kind tonight."

"Oh now, old fellow, don't be cross. What if you
have got up in the world, so high that you can claim
the Bramletts as your particular friends? That's no
reason why you should look down to old acquaintances; I thought better of you than that. I didn't mean
any disrespect, you know; why, man, I'm ready to
dance at your wedding whenever you say the word."

Jack Taylor was, as Hannah had called him, nothing
but a boy. The idea of there being supposed to be a
wedding in prospect for him, and of his being allied
with the Bramlett family, struck him as irresistibly
ludicrous, and he laughed outright.

"That's you," said Joe; "treat a fellow halfway,
though you have got up in the world. I'm looking
forward to that wedding, I tell you, with a good deal
of interest. I used to train in the higher circles myself,
and it will seem nice to get counted in once more. You
won't slight an old friend like me, of course. Why, I'm
ready to drink to your prospects any minute; though
I don't know as she will allow that. She keeps you
pretty straight, don't she?"

But Jack's fun had already subsided.

"Look here," he said in his gravest tone, "I don't
want any more such talk as that; you don't mean a
word you say, of course; but some things won't bear
making fun of. Because Miss Bramlett has taken a
notion to try to help a worthless chap like me is no
reason why she should be insulted."

"Never thought of such a thing, I tell you," said Joe, still in utmost good nature. "It is a streak of tip-top luck on your part, and I'm glad it has come to you. The Bramletts are no great things as far as money goes, but they are awful on respectability. There's my Lord Bramlett in the distillery, you know; if you take his notion of it, he is the biggest toad there is in any of the puddles around. Hang me if I'd like him for a brother-in-law, though."

"Shut up!" said Jack fiercely. "I told you I didn't want any more chaffing of that kind. If there wasn't anything else in the way, you might remember that you are talking about a woman who is almost old enough to be my mother. But the thing is ridiculous in every way; and there never was any such notion about it, of course."

"Honor bright? Well, now, really. I didn't know. Old girls like that are queer sometimes. They've lost most of their chances, you know, and there's never any telling. What does she hang around you so for, if there isn't anything in it?"

"She wants to make a man of me," said Jack, "a 'good, true man'!" Then he laughed. There was bitterness in the laugh; he had no heart for laughter. In truth, no human being knew how near Jack Taylor was to the verge, that night.

Joe Berry laughed uproariously. "That's the dodge, is it?" he said. "Next thing she'll be getting you converted; that's the way they do it. The very next thing I expect to hear of you, Jack, is that you have been down on your knees somewhere, making all kinds of promises. I hope you'll keep 'em! I've made a good many myself in my day, and kept some of 'em—for a week or two. I say, Jack! Let's go into Old Tawney's here and take a drink to treat what may be."

"No," said Jack; "I won't go into Old Tawney's. What is the use of making it harder for me by asking?"

"The old girl won't let you, eh? Well, that *is* hard. Suppose we go in and have a smoke, then? That isn't wicked, you know. My Lord Bramlett puffs cigars all the time."

He was only good-natured and rollicking. He had no conception of the harm that he might do. He had not even an idea of the awful burning thirst which seemed to be consuming Jack that night; much less did he know of the drawing power for evil that the mere smell of tobacco had over the poor fellow. Jack, listening to the evil spirit that had been at his elbow all day, said within himself, "What's the use? I told her it would come some time. I gave her fair warning. If I go into Old Tawney's tonight, I shall drink; I know I shall. Why not tonight as well as any time?"

Poor tempted Jack!

7

A Chance to Choose

HE STOOD irresolute, almost within the jaws of the tempter. The door of Old Tawney's saloon kept opening and letting out odors that were as ambrosia to the poor diseased appetite. Voices that sounded cheery to him, and laughter, floated out with the odors; it was bright in there, and warm, and the night was cold; and Jack in his insufficient clothing shivered and longed for the comfort and companionship to be found just inside. He argued the question with himself. He was tired; he had worked harder than usual that day and been held to it later; perhaps the smell of the liquor would not tempt him as much as he thought, and a pleasant smoke in there would rest him. What if it did tempt him? He had been tempted before and had resisted; why shouldn't he do it again? He placed his foot on the lower step.

"That's right," said Joe Berry encouragingly. "Come on, it will be nice and warm inside; it is uncommonly cold tonight for this time of year."

"Oh, Jack Taylor! I'm so glad it is you. Won't you take me home? I've been down on Carnell Street at the mission to help them with the singing. My brother-in-law was to come for me at nine o'clock; but there must have been some misunderstanding, for he hasn't come. I've been waiting at the rooms for more than an hour. I'm afraid to be on the street alone at this time of night."

It was a pretty girl, in the neatest of street costumes, who thus addressed Jack. He, as well as his friend Joe, knew Glyde Douglass by sight. Jack, indeed, could boast of more knowledge than that—he had met her several times at the mission. She had spoken to him in a friendly way, and he had bowed afterward when he met her on the street. By so much was he ahead of Joe Berry in respectability. Joe would not have thought of such a thing as bowing to Glyde Douglass, although he had known her by sight from childhood.

"Of course I'll take you home," Jack said with cheerful alacrity; and he took his foot down from the lower step of Old Tawney's saloon and walked away briskly with the young lady by his side. Joe looked after them interestedly, giving a low chuckle the while.

"I wonder if they'll git him?" he asked himself. "They are trying for him for all they're worth; if that little Douglass critter is going in too, maybe it will amount to something. She is pretty enough for 'most any fellow to do as she says. Well, it would be funny if Jack Taylor would out and out reform, that's a fact. I'd 'most think *I* could, after that. And he ain't got no mother, either."

Joe, poor fellow, had a mother who would have cried tears of joy if somebody had only "made something" out of him.

As they walked down the moonlighted street, Glyde explained more fully the perplexity in which she had been because of her brother-in-law's non-appearance, then suddenly returned to a matter that had troubled her before the question of getting home came up.

"Jack, do you know a young man by the name of Seber? William Seber?"

"I reckon I do," said Jack promptly, "and I don't know any good of him either."

"I was afraid so," spoken sorrowfully. "Is he very bad, Jack?"

"Well," said Jack reflectively, "I don't know as he is any worse than dozens of others; but he's a bad lot now, that's a fact. He's good-natured, though, when he hasn't too much whiskey aboard; a real jolly kind of a fellow, but he does some pretty mean things—things that some of the fellows won't do, bad as they are in some other ways."

"And do you know a girl named Susie Miller?"

"Oh yes, after a fashion I do; her brother and me used to be chums when we were little chaps; and I've drawed Susie to school on a sled many a time. I ain't known her much of late years; her brother died, you know; seems as if all the decent folks I used to know died; but I see her at the mission when I go there, of course. I've seen her with Bill Seber a good many times lately."

"I suppose so. Jack, what do you think of it? If Susie were your sister, would you be willing to have her on friendly terms with Bill, taking walks with him, and letting him see her home from places, and all that sort of thing?"

"No," said Jack, scowling fiercely. "She shouldn't do it if I could help it, you may be sure of that. It isn't the thing, perhaps, for one like me to be finding fault; but there's a difference in fellows, just as sure as you live, even when they don't any of them amount to much.

If Bill Seber tried to make up to a sister of mine, I'd knock him down for it."

"I think I understand your feeling, Jack, and I am very much worried about Susie. She is in my class, and of course I am especially interested in her. I have talked with her about this matter, but so far it hasn't done any good. She is with him tonight, and I think he had been drinking. I did not like the way he looked or acted. It is not that Susie is especially attached to him; but she thinks she can help him by going with him, and ought to do so. I have tried to explain to her that the way to help him would be to show him that he cannot have the society of a respectable girl unless he is willing to be a respectable young man; but she has her heart set on reforming him. I am sure I wish she might; but I cannot think that that is the wise way to attempt it."

Jack gave a series of low, amused chuckles before he attempted any reply.

"Reform Bill Seber?" he said at last. "That is a job, I tell you!—a bigger one than ever Susie Miller will accomplish, or my name isn't Jack Taylor. I should as soon think of setting a little gray mouse to reforming a great green-eyed cat, and a tiger cat at that. I tell you, Miss Douglass, reforming ain't such easy work as some womenfolk that never had any temptations think it is."

The tone had changed from its half-amused note to an almost despairing gravity. Something in it suggested to Glyde a personal question. "How is it with you, Jack? Are you getting along well?"

"No, I can't say that I am. Fact is, I guess I am getting along about as bad as I can."

"Oh, I am sorry to hear that! Why, the last time I heard Miss Hannah speak of it, she was very much encouraged about your prospects. She is a good friend to you, Jack; you ought to try to please her."

"That's so," said Jack; "a fellow never had a better friend. But it is hard work pleasing her. She wants folks to be angels, you know; and that isn't in my line." He laughed a little and tried to speak in an utterly careless tone, but Glyde detected the heartache underneath it.

"What do you find so hard?" she asked encouragingly.

"Everything," said Jack in gloom; "a fellow can't turn a corner without coming across something that he used to do, and would like to do, and mustn't do. It's just pull and haul yourself all the time, and nothing much to keep you back from it either. I haven't any folks, you know, to care; if I had, it might make a big difference. There's Joe Berry, now—that fellow I was talking with tonight when you came along—he's got a mother, as nice an old lady as ever was; she would give her two eyes to see him a 'good, true man.' If I had a mother, it kind of appears to me as though I could do it; though maybe not. When I had folks of my own, it didn't make a mite of difference; but I'm a little different now from what I was then. Still, when there isn't anybody to care, what's the use?"

It occurred to Glyde to remind him of what he owed to his citizenship, and the respect that he might win from his fellowmen, and the love that might be his in the future, if he made himself worthy of it; this seemed the natural thing to say to him. He had heard it often. Hannah Bramlett had earnestly tried to rouse his manhood along all these lines. But something made the young girl feel like passing them and going at once to the fountainhead.

"Jack," she said, "do you remember the Lord Jesus Christ, and what he did in order that you might become a 'good, true man'? Do you remember that he is more interested in you than father or mother or any earthly friend could be? How is it that you are willing to disappoint him?"

For a moment Jack Taylor was dumbfounded; he knew the Lord Jesus Christ by name certainly. In his childhood he had had some teaching concerning the central truths of the Christian religion, and in later years in the Chapel he had, of course, heard the sacred name in hymn and prayer; but certainly he had never heard anyone speak of Jesus Christ quite as Glyde Douglass did. He looked around him, half in superstition. He was conscious of a curious sensation, as if a third person had come quietly up in the moonlight, and it was he whom Glyde was introducing.

"I don't know as I understand," he said after a moment, in a tone that had a touch of awe. "He doesn't expect anything of me, of course, nor care. Why should he?"

"Oh, Jack! Why shouldn't he? Isn't he interested in manhood to a degree that no one else can be? Doesn't he understand as none of us, if we do our utmost, can understand, the possibilities of real manhood? Doesn't he know what we could accomplish in the world if we would? It is all out before him as a map might be to us; he sees the roads that may be taken, as well as those that have been. Moreover, he sees beyond this world and knows the possibilities that there are for us in that other world where none of the obstacles now in the way of what men call success come in to interrupt. Don't you believe that he is deeply, *awfully* interested in what you will decide to do?"

"That's a queer way to put it!" said Jack. "I never heard anything like it before in my life. But now, Miss Douglass, I just want to ask you one question. If he is so awfully interested, why doesn't he do things for a fellow? I don't mean anything disrespectful; I s'pose I don't understand how to talk about such things, but I couldn't help getting that off. Of course I understand that God can do anything he has a mind to; and if he cared for a fellow like me in the way you say, why, I should think he'd make things easy for me. Kind of *make* me get into the right road, you know, and stay there whether I wanted to or not. I'd do it in a minute for any chap that I was interested in, if I could."

"No," said Glyde positively; "he will never do that for you. When he made you, he put a man's soul within you and arranged that you should have a man's possibilities. He has given you a chance to choose for yourself."

"Now, see here," interrupted Jack, speaking almost fiercely, "folks talk about God being a father to them. Down there at the hall the other night that man talked about the verse: 'Like as a father pitieth his children'; and he said God was the best and wisest father, and all that. Now, I'm not very wise nor very good, the land knows! But suppose I had a little boy—I had a little chap once, Miss Douglass; he didn't live but three weeks. I have sometimes thought if he had, everything might have been different; but he didn't. Suppose he had. If I had the power to take that little fellow, and put him on the right road, and keep him there, don't you suppose I would do it quicker than a wink?"

"No," said Glyde firmly; "I don't. Look here, Jack, suppose you had a very pleasant house into which you could put your little boy, and keep him there with locked doors and windows grated, so that it would not be possible for him to escape. You could keep him from a good many wrong roads by that means, couldn't you? He would not be tempted by gambling saloons nor drinking saloons; he would not stand around on street corners, nor mingle with men who used evil words—oh, there are a hundred wrong roads from which you could surely shield him! Would you do it? Keep him there all his life, surrounded with pleasant things, books and flowers and birds, and everything that love could furnish, but still a prisoner? Would you do this, instead of letting him go out in the world to choose his own way?"

Jack laughed. "I reckon I wouldn't, Miss Douglass."

"Indeed you wouldn't. You would be too wise. You would be sure that your boy, in order to amount to anything as a man, must go out and see the different roads and choose for himself, or his goodness would be mere weakness. I think it is a little bit of an illustration of the way in which our heavenly Father treats us. Not a good one, Jack, because there are so many things about our future that we do not understand. There are so many possibilities that are not known to us. I suppose that God, knowing all about us, took the best way, did the very best that he could in order that we might get ready for that highest good. You can easily see that love for your little boy would lead you to give him a certain degree of freedom. You would show him as well as you could the right way, and teach him what he ought to do; you would guard him while he was a little fellow, but as he grew older, you would know that he must choose for himself. Isn't that, in a sense, the way that God has treated us? Oh, he has done infinitely more than that, of course! It is only a very faint illustration. But after you had done your best for your boy, if he should persist in choosing the wrong road, you wouldn't feel as though he had treated you very well, would you?"

"No more I wouldn't," said Jack frankly. "But, after

all, Miss Douglass, it ain't possible for folks to think—for me at least—to think of God caring for me like that. If I could once feel as though he did, why—it seems to me—"

He stopped abruptly; his voice had begun to tremble, and he did not choose to show his heart even to this simple-hearted girl.

"If you could believe that God loved you as a father, you think you would try to please him; is that it, Jack? I will tell you what I wish you would do. You have never read the Bible much, I suppose—you have a Bible of your own, haven't you? I wish you would read in it the story of Jesus Christ on earth. Read what a lonely, friendless life he lived here, and how his followers treated him—the very best of them. In the hour of his greatest human need they all forsook him and fled. Worse than that, one disowned him, declared with oaths that he never knew him! Read how his enemies mocked and struck him, and spit on him, and pierced him with thorns, and how in agony unimaginable he died at last on that awful cross; then ask yourself why he bore it all, why God permitted it. If the reason he has himself given should prove to be the true one, because he 'so loved' Glyde Douglass and Jack Taylor that he 'gave his only Son' that they might have eternal life, ought you and I to need any other proof of love? Oh, Jack! I don't want you to be one of the men who are going to disappoint such a Savior as that. One verse in the Bible comes often to me. Do you know it says, 'He shall see of the travail of his soul and be satisfied'? I cannot tell you what a joy it is to me to think that I am actually going to help satisfy the Lord Jesus Christ! I want you to remember that you must either satisfy or disappoint him, and that you have it in your power to choose which you will do."

8

PIVOTS

JACK drew one of those heavy sighs that seemed to come from the depths of his soul as he said:

"Well, Miss Douglass, maybe you are right. It looks more reasonable to me than it ever did before; but I'll tell you what it is, I'm afraid I've got to disappoint him. You see, the trouble is I've got onto the wrong road somehow, and I've been on it so long that I can't seem to help it. Miss Hannah, she's done her best for me, and I've tried the best I knew how. For months now I've been at it, trying to satisfy her, but I can't do it. I feel tonight as though it is all up with me and there is no use in trying any longer. I've felt so for two or three days. Perhaps a fellow does have a chance to choose. I guess it's so, as you say; but I had my chance and chose the wrong road, and there I am. I know folks say that you can get back if you want to, but it isn't true. I want to, bad enough, and there needn't anybody say I haven't tried; but I've just about made up my mind tonight that there's no use in it."

Nothing more utterly cast down and discouraged

than Jack's tone can be imagined. It put energy into Glyde's.

"Jack, I know what you need; you have *got* to have the help of the Lord Jesus Christ, or the fight will be too much for you. I know something of how you have felt all these months, just as though you were on slippery ground and might fall any minute. Don't you see that you need to get on solid ground? Why don't you try that way, if you are in earnest? And I believe you are. Give yourself up to the Lord Jesus Christ and follow his lead. There is entire manliness in that course. Do you understand what I mean? That boy of yours about whom we have been talking, suppose he were a young man and you were his good, wise father. You would not order him what to do and where to go; you would recognize his manhood and his rights. But suppose he came to you saying, 'Father, I want you to direct me; I realize that you are wiser than I, and I desire above all things to be guided by you.' Wouldn't you do the best you could for him? The illustration isn't a good one; it is too weak. But don't you know, Jack, that Jesus has undertaken to meet us more than halfway? He offers to make a contract with us; our part is to give ourselves to him."

Jack listened in silence. When the earnest voice ceased, he still kept silent, feeling that he had no words for such a subject. After a minute Glyde began again anxiously, "Don't you understand, Jack? I am afraid I haven't made it clear. I don't know how to talk about these things very well. I wish you knew Marjorie Edmonds; she could tell you just how it is; or Mr. Maxwell, if he were only here." It struck the young Christian worker suddenly as a strange thing that in all her circle of acquaintances, many of whom were members of the church, she could think of only these two who would be likely to be able to direct Jack clearly. Oh, there was Doctor Ford, of course; but young men like Jack were afraid of clergymen. She had tried to persuade some of the boys at the mission to talk with Doctor Ford, but had not succeeded.

"I don't know enough to understand such things," Jack said humbly.

"But, Jack, it is all very simple. Listen: suppose you had a friend—a strong, wise friend, one who never had done, so far as you could see, other than just right; and suppose it were possible for him to go with you wherever you went, and stay with you day and night, directing you just what to do, and what not to do; suppose he would promise to do this for you, provided you would put yourself under his care; would you do it?"

"I reckon I'd try it," said Jack promptly, "if I could find any such fellow on this created earth; but I couldn't, Miss Douglass."

"Never mind that. You would know just how to do such a thing, wouldn't you? You would say—I wonder what you would say?"

"Why," said Jack, growing interested in the supposition, "maybe I should say something like this: 'If you are willing and able to do all that for me, I'm your chap; lead on.'"

"Very well. Don't you see what I mean? Jesus Christ is both able and willing to do all that for you; he has promised to do it. You can say, 'I'm your chap,' to him as well as to a man walking by your side. The question is, will you do it?

"I have given you only the human side of the story. There is a divine side. That good, wise friend whom we have been imagining might do a great deal for you, but he could not change a thought of your heart, no matter how much you might wish him to do so; but the Lord Jesus can take from you all desire after the wrong road. More than that, he can blot out all your past sins—*blot them out,* Jack; it is his own word—and give you peace and victory all along the road."

By this time they had reached her father's door and there was no opportunity for Jack to reply, even had he felt inclined. In awkward silence, he received her hearty thanks for his protection, then, turning, walked swiftly homeward with eyes bent toward the ground. He passed several saloons without so much as noticing that he did so. Strange, new words had been spoken to him that night.

Hannah Bramlett was a Christian woman, and her daily life was a constant struggle not to dishonor the religion she professed. She prayed daily for Jack Taylor, sometimes with strong crying and tears; and she believed that if he were ever to be a saved man, the power of God must save him. Yet she had not known how to talk with him about these things. An almost overpowering timidity had taken possession of her whenever she attempted to speak to him of the way of salvation. She had struggled with the timidity and had tried more than once to point him to Christ. That is, she had told him that his heart was "unregenerate," and that he needed to be "converted," and that nothing but a "real downright conversion" would ever make him sure of himself, even for this life. Poor Jack had been willing to believe that he needed everything; he had even reached the point where he was willing to "get religion" and "stand" the mockery of the "fellows." To this end he had gone several times to the weeknight services at the mission and listened patiently to talk that was as Sanskrit to him, because the speakers either did not realize his depths of ignorance on such topics or did not understand how to reach his level. For the most part they used the accepted terms, the "shibboleths" if one may so speak, of religion—more wisely, it is true, than Hannah Bramlett in her inexperience and timidity had been able to, and they reached and helped many. But Jack in his early life had learned only words and names, and in later years had not come in contact even with these; he did not understand. It had been given to Glyde Douglass to reveal to his astonished ears the simplicity on the human side of that wondrous plan of salvation. And then was Jack Taylor, if he had but understood it, at the most perilous point in his life's history. There had been made plain to him the fact of two distinct and ever separating roads, either of which he could choose if he would. Nay, having admitted that, and hidden behind the apparently humble statement that he had chosen wrong and must abide by his decision, suddenly had been revealed a Friend so infinite that He could not only guide and guard for the future, but could blot out the past. In short, Jack Taylor understood that he might begin again. He had helped to make plain the revelation by his own admissions. Had he not distinctly said that if such a human friend could be found he reckoned he would follow him? He knew, as well as the best-taught regular attendant at church and Sabbath school could know it, that here was a chance for him, an offer, as it were, for his soul. What would Jack Taylor say in reply?

Meantime, what had become of that brother-in-law whose absence had occasioned Glyde Douglass so much anxiety and embarrassment? He had given a somewhat reluctant consent to her petition to be called for on his way home from the meeting of the Library Association. It is true, it would be but two blocks out of his way, or at least would have been had he gone to the Association meeting. He had not chosen to explain to Glyde that he did not intend to be present at the meeting, having dropped his connection with it, as he had with most things of like character. To do him justice, it was not the walk or the trouble to which he objected, but the fear of meeting some of the mission workers, who had urged him earnestly and frequently to help them in their efforts to save men. The harassed man had pleaded all the excuses he could think of except the true one, and felt that he wanted to hear no more about it. Still, Glyde had been very urgent; and being not willing to give the real reasons for refusing, he could think of no others and had yielded.

But at the appointed time he had been so engrossed with thought and care that all memory of his young sister-in-law waiting alone in a part of the town that ladies did not like to frequent unattended, escaped him. What was the occupation that so engrossed him? It did not appear on the surface. He was locked and bolted into his own home study, but not so much as a scrap of paper was before him. He sat at his desk, elbows leaning on it, his face held between his two hands, his eyes fixed on space, and so sat for hours. If anyone could have told him that he was reviewing his life, he would probably have contradicted the statement. Yet in a certain sense this was true. At least a limited panorama of what he fancied he had been moved solemnly before him, strangely intermixed with pictures of what he might have been, and would have been, if only.

Perhaps it is true to the experience of human nature that not many sadder pictures confront the lives of men than the one suggested by the hackneyed quotation, "It might have been." Yet whether or not such a retrospection shall be profitable is often determined by the clause connected with that potent word, "if." "If I had taken that turn to the right instead of to the left," says the dreamer, "all might have been well." Perhaps he is correct in his statement, and perhaps it is the weakest sentimentality to allow himself to brood over it; or it may be the truest wisdom to hold his mind steadily to that view. How shall he determine which? But that is a very easy question. Think, my friend. Is that turn to the right possible now, after the lapse of years? Putting aside the failures, the heartaches, the blotches that can never be erased because of the mistake made then, will the future be improved by your making the turn now, though it may be hard and involve much sacrifice? Then, hold your heart and your conscience steadily to that point until your manhood rises to the height of the sacrifice involved and says, "I will do it *now.*" If, on the contrary, the turn once made, however foolish it may have been, is one that ought to remain settled, if the decision cannot be reversed without sin, close the eyes of your soul to the alluring "might have been," ask God to forgive you, and move steadily forward in the path that is.

What, think you, was Ralph Bramlett's most serious "if" in the review that he was taking?—"If I had been true to the voice of my conscience away back there in my childhood when I decided for what I *wanted* to do, instead of what I knew I ought?" "If I had been true to the vows that I took upon me publicly in the church of God?" There were so many such "ifs" that might have been wisely considered, and that would have suggested the wisdom of making haste to cover the mistakes as much as might be by the decision of the present. None of them presented themselves. Pity the miserable weakness, even while you despise the wickedness of the man who could hold his haggard face in his hands and say, "The mistake of my life was in marrying that girl! If I had married Marjorie all would have been well with me." And the woman whom, unurged by anything but his pride and his passing fancy, he had asked to be his wife, was locked outside and sat brushing away the dreary tears over the thought that she was locked out and alone!

By this is not meant that Ralph Bramlett spent the hours in staring at that one regret; there were questions having to do with the immediate present that might well hold his thoughts. Those unpaid bills were haunting him day and night, were accumulating with every passing day. Some of them he did not know how to ward off longer; and they were bills that he did not keep in the secretary to which he had proudly pointed his wife. He owed many hundreds of dollars; but none of the debts gave him that sense of overpowering shame that he felt when he looked at a page of his private memoranda and read there certain figures and initials and dates that only he could understand. The first one was dated nearly a year before. How vividly he remembered the day. He had stood in the hall waiting for his chief, and, being in excellent humor, had chatted pleasantly with the bellboy, who had just been paid his month's wages, and who confided to the handsome bookkeeper, who seemed to him like a great man, that he did not know how to keep his money safely. He wanted to save it until he had enough to buy his mother a house so she need not pay rent anymore. His mother did not need it now, and she wanted him to put it in the bank, and keep it until he got enough to buy a suit of clothes; but he meant to do without clothes and surprise her some-day; only he did not know how to invest his money in a way to make it earn a lot more. Ralph had been amused with the boy's mixture of ignorance and brightness and pleased with his deference to himself, and had offered in good faith to become his banker, since there was not a savings bank within convenient reach, and to pay him eight percent interest until such time as he could do better.

The boy had been delighted with the offer and felt himself in some way immediately connected with the great firm of Snyder, Snyder, and Co. He had regularly brought his savings each month to his new friend, until there had accumulated something over fifty dollars. And now a dark day had come in the boy's life. His mother had fallen sick, and the money that was to have bought her a home was needed to pay the doctor's bill and furnish nourishing food. Five times had the bellboy waylaid his banker with anxious face and great troubled eyes, only to be put off with very small sums and promises. In a fit of indignation with his wife, Ralph had, at her complaining, emptied his pocketbook on her dressing table, and had actually but a two-dollar bill to depend upon until his next quarter's salary fell due. It was horrible to remember that when it came, not a penny of it was honestly his. The bellboy's need, and his inability to meet it, accentuated Ralph's misery to a surprising degree. Curiously enough, he, who was not as a rule attracted to young people, had taken an unaccountable fancy to the boy and had given him from time to time much whole-some advice, as well as shown him many kindnesses. The result was that the manly little fellow had given his whole heart to the bookkeeper and believed that all goodness, as well as all wisdom, was embodied in him. It was maddening to Ralph Bramlett's pride to have to be lowered in the esteem of this wise-eyed boy; yet he had not a friend of whom he was willing to try to borrow fifty dollars.

9

"What If I Should—?"

BUT it was more than the past with its "might have been" that was torturing Ralph Bramlett: the immediate future must be met. Out of the chaos of embarrassment and bewilderment that the future showed, stared one definite proposition; but it was of so strange a character that, if it required any studying at all, it is no wonder it required long studying.

There had been a time when Ralph Bramlett would have turned scornfully from such a proposition and felt that it needed no consideration. It had come to him from one of the junior members of the firm of Snyder, Snyder, & Co. It appeared that that gentleman owned a valuable corner lot in the town where Ralph lived. The building had been occupied for years as a drugstore; but the prosperous druggist had lately died, and his business had been closed up by his heirs. The building had now been unoccupied for several months. It had been the opinion of the owner, even before the drugstore closed its doors, that that corner afforded special advantages for the setting up of a first-class retail liquor store. He did not use the word *saloon;* the phrase *retail liquor store* had a better sound to him.

He proceeded to explain that there was a decided need for a business of the sort in that end of the town. Several estimable families, some of his own acquaintances indeed lived in that vicinity, and doubtless often found it inconvenient to go so far as they were now compelled to for supplies. He had been spoken to more than once concerning the excellent site that corner would be for a retail store. "In short," the philanthropic gentleman had said, "I am really growing anxious about that part of the town; my early home was there, Mr. Bramlett, and of course I feel a special interest in the place. I have been approached several times by persons who, to speak frankly, I am not willing to see established in such a business in that vicinity. I have been offered very fine rentals for the building; but thus far I have held off, making all sorts of excuses. Of course, I cannot continue such a policy very long. You know, without my mentioning it, that it makes all the difference in the world what sort of men take hold of this business. The men who have come to me are well enough in their way, and would undoubtedly have paid the rent—though I mentioned a very large figure to them to help me in getting rid of them—but they were not the class of persons to establish on that corner: persons who lacked judgment, you understand, and forethought; men who would be in danger of consulting their pocketbooks instead of principle. I'm afraid they would have been as willing to sell to minors, for instance, or to habitual drunkards, as to responsible persons. I felt that they would be almost sure to get themselves and me into trouble. There are people living all about that region, who, if the business were conducted in accordance with not only the letter but the spirit of the law, would be glad to countenance it, even though they do not themselves use the goods; whereas, if another sort of person should take hold of it, those very men would make trouble.

"I am sure you understand the peculiarities of the situation; and to come to the point at once, Mr. Bramlett, as we are both busy men, it has occurred to me to definitely propose that you occupy the said corner yourself. Not in person, of course, in a way to take any considerable amount of your time—we consider your services here much too valuable to be willing to give them up. What we thought was that we could supply you with a man here to do a good deal of the office drudgery that now occupies you, and let you have leisure enough to look after this other business. You could secure good, reliable men to do your bidding, you being merely the brains of the establishment. Men of that kind can easily be found, who are capable and entirely willing to do as they are told, who are yet not exactly the ones to shoulder responsibility and do as they please, you understand. I have been talking it over with the other members of the firm, and they are willing to make the arrangement that I have suggested. I may say that they are more than willing. The fact is, Mr. Bramlett, we are all interested in you as a rising young man and would like to do you a good turn—put you in a way to make more money than you can on a mere salary. You know, of course, what terms we could offer you for goods— at least, you know the usual wholesale rates. I do not hesitate to say that, if it should come to an actual business transaction, we should be ready to make even better terms, on the score of personal friendship.

"I suppose I hardly need say that I know of at least

a score of fine young men who stand ready to accept such an offer as I am making, but I haven't felt inclined to make it to them. I don't know but I am something of a crank—my friends tell me that I am—but I am really very particular indeed as to whom I put in my buildings. I want not only reliable men in the ordinary acceptation of those words, but men of thoroughly conscientious views. Men, in short, who will not only understand the law, but abide by it in every particular. I am a law-abiding citizen myself and want no underhanded proceedings. There is a sense in which you might look upon it—and I confess I have thought of it more in that light perhaps than any other—as your opportunity for doing a good thing for the community in which you live. A good citizen is always glad of such opportunities of course. I am sure you can see what danger might result from putting an immoral man, for instance, in such a place—a man who would sell to anybody who would bring him the money, without regard to whether or not he ought to be trusted with the goods. I think myself that you could not serve that part of the town better, perhaps, than by controlling the business carefully.

"Such a business as ours is, of course, capable of doing great harm; in the hands of unprincipled men, whose only object in life is to make money, it does do harm. I have never shut my eyes to that fact and trust I never shall. It is because I judge you to be entirely capable of managing the business, not only in a way to be entirely satisfactory to yourself, but to your townspeople, that I have made the proposition I have. I do not want an answer today; take time, by all means, to consider it, Mr. Bramlett. There, by the way, is our private price list; the second line of figures represents the ruling prices at retail. If you need to refresh your memory and wish to make any estimates of probable income, that will save you time perhaps. I ought to say before this interview is closed that, as the building in question is not fitted up for the purpose proposed, I had thought, if you took hold of it, to suggest that I advance you, say a thousand dollars; you to spend as much or as little of it as seemed to you well, and fit up the place to suit your own ideas. I want the whole thing to be attractive, and entirely in keeping with the surroundings. The whole sum might or might not be required, you could hardly tell for several months perhaps; but, of course, whatever was placed in the building as a fixture would belong to me, to be paid for out of the fund. The balance, if there were any, could be handed back to me at any time, or included in the rent. You see how entirely I trust you; that sort of proposition would not be made to many men, I assure you."

Then the philanthropist had sat back in his chair and beamed a benevolent smile upon the young man whom he was willing, even anxious, to set up in business.

Ralph Bramlett had by no means listened in silence to this long-drawn-out proposition, but had from time to time interjected words expressive of surprise or bewilderment, of which the junior partner had taken no notice, except to repeat and try to make clearer some of his points. While he talked, Ralph had had, as in a vision, a view of himself standing there, say three years before, listening to such a proposition. A faint smile hovered over his face as he thought of the indignant way in which he would have declined an offer that connected him in any way with the business of rum selling. But the smile was one of contempt for the fanatical notions of a boy; he was a *man* now, and such narrow-minded, wholesale condemnations as those in which he used to indulge did not become him.

He sat down to his work, after being courteously dismissed by his chief—at least, he sat before his desk, but his thoughts were on what he had just heard; especially were they concerned with what he admitted was a new idea; namely, that a man could serve his townspeople by conducting a liquor store. However, why not? Of course a thoroughly well-managed liquor store, that not only never infringed upon the law but was, in a sense, a law unto itself, having a care how it dispensed dangerous beverages even to those whom the law recognized as fitted to buy them, would be infinitely better for the neighborhood than one of the ordinary kind. The idea was not only new, but interesting.

All day long, though occupied with even an unusual amount of business, he had kept going this second train of thought. For the first two or three hours he had assured himself that, although there certainly was good sense in some of the arguments advanced by the junior partner, still he, Ralph Bramlett, could never have anything to do with the retail liquor business. The Bramletts for generations back had been too pronounced on the temperance question, and his father had suffered too keenly because of his present position for him to entertain any idea of going farther.

Moreover, he admitted that he himself shrank from it; that is, he told himself that he was not equal to the sacrifice, although good could undoubtedly be done by preventing evil. But he, a member of the church, a member of a well-known family, could not place himself in such a questionable position.

He might talk until he was gray, and yet not make clear to certain people the arguments that had been brought to bear upon him that morning. There, for instance, was his sister Hannah, who had no head for argument and was as set in her way as self-opinionated old maids generally were; she would be sure to give him no peace of his life if she imagined he thought of such a business. Yet he had immediately curled his lip over that objection and reminded himself that Hannah had enough to do at present to take care of her own reputation without concerning herself about other people's. But there were others. What would Doctor Ford, for instance, think of the junior partner's arguments? he wondered.

And what, above all others—oh! it wouldn't do, of course; he wasn't considering it for a moment. Then he took pencil and paper and fell to calculating what the profits would really be, and exclaimed over their enormity. He had been conversant with wholesale prices for several years, but had never before given his attention to the retail trade. Then there was that hint about special reductions on the score of friendship. It certainly was a way to make money; and money would undoubtedly be made on that corner. Why not by him? Did it make such a tremendous difference, after all—except to the person who received it—into whose pocket the money went? Yes, of course it made a difference—here was a chance for that new and most alluring argument to present itself again—if the money went into the pockets of an honorable man, one who would under no circumstances allow his goods to be sold to persons incapable of judging for themselves what was good for them, it certainly ought to make a great difference in the morality of the community. The argument looked clearer than it had before. Why did not those fanatical people who were always prating about the evils of the saloon study up this phase of the subject, and, until they could do something better, try to get respectable, moral men put in charge of saloons? Yes, he was actually so befogged that he used the phrase "respectable, moral men" in such connection, and failed to see its absurdity! Yet why not? Had not the junior partner, who represented millions and understood business and respectability, used the same?

When Ralph Bramlett walked toward his train that evening, he was saying to himself, "There would be no occasion for my name to appear. All he wants of me is to be responsible for the rent and look after the men whom I put in charge. It is no more, in a sense, than I am doing now."

He had by no means told himself that he would undertake the work; but he took his seat in the car still studying the profits that might be made and the feasibility of entirely suppressing his name, thus silencing foolish tongues.

There came and sat beside him one of the workers at the Carnell Street Mission, who began to tell of the wonders that were taking place there. Did he remember Harvey Barnes who used to be a schoolmate of his? He knew of course how low the poor fellow had gone? A regular gutter drunkard. But he was making an honest effort to reform. He signed the pledge nearly two weeks ago; and last night stayed to the after-meeting and not only talked with one of the workers, but actually went down on his knees and prayed. "Think of Harvey Barnes *praying*, Bramlett! The age of miracles is not past, you see."

The Christian worker had a more definite aim than merely to tell good news. He proceeded to say that they had been planning how best to help tide the young man over the dangerous weeks which were now before him; and somebody had remembered that he was an old schoolmate of Ralph Bramlett's and used to be much under his influence. And somebody else had wondered if Ralph would not be willing to take hold with them and try to help his old friend.

Ralph was interested and touched. He remembered Harvey Barnes when he was the best scholar in their class. He had gone down rapidly, an inherited taint, people said. Ralph had lost sight of him for years; hadn't he been out of town? Yes, he used to have a good deal of influence over him. He recollected that he once told Harvey he was too easily influenced and would never amount to anything because he had no mind of his own; and he had replied with his genial laugh, "I'll let you be mind for me, Ralph; you may go ahead, and I'll follow in your footsteps. You are such a proper fellow that the road will be sure to end right."

Certainly he would like to help Harvey Barnes. It must be interesting to help people; it was what he had meant to do when he united with the church. He parted with the mission worker thoughtfully, having promised that he would do what he could for Harvey and added a sort of half promise to come to the mission some evening. He was silent about his engagement to meet his sister-in-law there that evening and take her home, because, as a matter of fact, he did not mean to be there until the meeting was safely over. His half promise to attend the meeting had not meant so much that he cared to emphasize it by appearing at once. Yet as he walked from the station with his mind full of the tender thoughts that the news of his old schoolmate had awakened, he wondered how it would seem to start afresh and carry out some of the plans that had once been his. Estelle, he reminded himself, had not been interested in that sort of thing, or it would have made a difference. But perhaps she would be willing to go even to the mission now, if he were with her. And then he admitted that he had not spent much of his time with her and that he had been out of sorts that morning and spoken somewhat roughly; but she had certainly been very aggravating.

As he let himself in at his own door, he said, still to that interesting person, himself, "What if I should surprise everybody with an entirely new departure?"

10

An Anniversary

ON THE hall table had lain three letters for him. Every one of them contained bills—two for much larger amounts than he had expected; one was presented for the third time with a peremptory demand for immediate attention. He threw them down with a sense of having been injured. Why should bills be allowed to force their ugly faces upon him just as he was meditating radical changes for the better? He went on to the dining room. He was later than usual; those private calculations had consumed time. Mrs. Bramlett sat alone at the head of her table. She looked up at his entrance with an injured air.

"Here I am eating my solitary dinner; it is the third time this week. It is very pleasant to be married and have a house of one's own where one can enjoy solitude! Your friend Marjorie wanted to know if I had become used to it. I told her I was becoming used to most things, and so I am. Although I will confess that, since this is my birthday, I did think perhaps you would make an effort to reach home at least at your usual early hour!"

Such had been his greeting. He had given a slight start at the mention of the birthday; he had forgotten it. But he told himself drearily that it was just as well, since he had no money for birthday offerings.

He looked at his wife critically as he took his seat opposite her and wondered if it would be worthwhile to tell her some of the thoughts awakened in him by the news from the mission. She had changed a good deal since their marriage; she was by no means so pretty as she used to be. He was not sure but there had come to be a look of habitual gloom on her face. No, that was not quite fair; only a few evenings before she had met him with smiles and winning words and had tried to rest and comfort him when he complained of weariness. His conscience reminded him that he would have none of her comfort. But that, he hastened to tell himself, was because he had been so tried by business cares. Any woman of sense ought to expect such times. If she were in a like gentle mood this evening, she would find he could meet her halfway. But nothing was more evident than that no such mood possessed her. What if he should himself take the initiative? Suppose he should remark that he was sorry to have been late, especially on her birthday. One wonders that it did not occur to him to be amazed over the fact that such a commonplace courtesy as that would have been unusual. Furthermore, what if he should ask her to walk down with him by and by to the mission to meet Glyde? He might tell her about Harvey Barnes; she used to know Harvey, and would no doubt be interested in hearing of his new departure. These thoughts passed rapidly through his mind; and he opened his lips to put some of them into words just as his wife broke forth:

"If you have nothing whatever to say, Mr. Bramlett,

now that you have come, I may as well begin at once upon the interesting items that have been dinged into my ears this afternoon. Your immaculate sister Hannah has been here again, giving me a benefit. I do not know why she does not choose an hour when you are present; she talks about you continually. She is terribly exercised, let me tell you, about your reputation. She has heard, from I don't know how many sources, that you are hopelessly in debt. According to her ideas the businessmen meet on the street corners and discuss the alarming nature of your affairs. If you have any reason to give why you do not pay that odious Dunlap, for instance, I wish you would rush right down there and tell Hannah; she will proclaim it from the housetop before tomorrow night. At least, she will mention it to that confidential friend of hers, Jack Taylor, and he will see that it is spread abroad."

Was it wonderful that Ralph Bramlett, being the man he was, lost every vestige of a desire to speak kind and conciliating words to his wife? His reply was icy in its dignity:

"I wonder, Mrs. Bramlett, if you could explain why you consider it necessary whenever you mention my sister to insult her?"

"Insult your sister? That is an exquisite suggestion. It is not I, let me tell you, who have helped to place your sister's name in the mouth of every street loafer. Instead, I have done my utmost not only to warn her but to rouse her brother in time to save her reputation. Is not this true? Don't talk to me about insults. It is your wife who has been insulted, I can assure you. If you had heard Hannah's words to me this afternoon, even you might have been roused to at least a show of interest."

But why soil these pages by recounting the words

that followed from both husband and wife? They were not many. Almost immediately following the last sentence recorded, Mrs. Bramlett remembered the possibility of the girl, Lena, being within hearing. Therefore, while she said a number of stinging things, she lowered her voice so that had Lena's ear been even at the keyhole, she would not have been much enlightened.

As for the husband, he was never loud-voiced; strong excitement had the effect, with him, of quieting any outward manifestation, so that his tones were even lower than ordinary when he had anything particularly trying to say.

He arose from the table before the second course had been completed and, without a word of excuse or apology, retired to his private room, leaving his wife to control face and voice as well as she could and explain to Lena that they did not care for any dessert that night. Mr. Bramlett had been too tired to wait for it; and as for herself, having been in the house all day, she had not much appetite for anything. Then she, too, made a precipitate retreat to the darkness of her own room. It was after this home scene had been concluded that Ralph Bramlett allowed himself to bow his head on his hands and groan out to his heart that miserable "It might have been!" Not in any sense did he consider himself to blame. Had he not come home with the intention of turning over an entirely new leaf? He called it now a deliberate intention, though the reader will remember how far from decision he had been. No, he corrected that last phrase and put it that he had come home intending to carry out the plans which he had long ago formed and would undoubtedly have followed out had it not been for the millstone hung about his neck. In his bitter anger and pain he allowed himself to designate in his thoughts the wife of his choice.

But, as has been said, he had not given himself long to that train of thought. Truth to tell, like experiences were becoming too common in his home to hold his attention long. He did not change his attitude, but his thoughts turned quickly to the proposition which had been made him that day. With the unpaid bills lying beside him on the table, he thought again, as he had a hundred times before, of the thousand dollars that would be given him in advance with which to furnish that store; and remembered that it would be left to his judgment as to whether much or little of it should be so spent—and the remainder could be paid back at "any time" during the winter. It is wonderful what a delightful sound that indefinite "any time" had to the debt-burdened man.

Long he sat, going over all the arguments in favor of his acceptance of the business offer, all the phases of relief that would come to him in such a case, as well as the network of perplexities and embarrassments that would continue to entangle him should he decline. Was public opinion worth such a sacrifice as would be involved? For that matter, what reputation had he now? Suppose a tithe of what Hannah's narrow mind and his wife's ill humor had flung at him was being said? Could there be a greater humiliation for a Bramlett than that? Would it not be infinitely better for a man to pay his honest debts than to squirm over a question of taste? Moreover, his name need not appear. That thought seemed to have charms for him; he repeated it in various forms. The Bramlett name was undoubtedly being sullied now, or at least would be as soon as the true state of affairs should become known. He had it in his power to prevent the stain, and no one need know by what means he prevented it. So far as that was concerned—and he drew himself up slightly, preserving his dignity by the thought— suppose everyone knew? There was nothing to be ashamed of; it was a legitimate business, sanctioned by the government under which he lived, and capable of being carried on in a way to protect the community from evil. Why should he hesitate longer? Then, for a few minutes, he allowed himself to stand face to face with a question that had all day been pushing to the front and been resolutely held in abeyance. It was not, What will the Lord Jesus Christ, whose name I bear and whose honor I am bound to consider, think of this business? but what would Marjorie Edmonds say if she knew that I was planning such a way out of trouble as this? He arose at last, and kicking away angrily the slippers that had been his wife's latest Christmas gift, made ready for the street again. All thought of the mission and his engagement with his sister-in-law had passed from his mind; but an over-powering desire to talk with Marjorie had taken possession of him. Not that he by any means meant to tell her definitely what he was considering, not that he had the slightest doubt of what her opinion would be should he do so, but simply because he could not rid himself of the desire to ask her certain questions and hear her replies. He did not own, even to himself, that he knew a way to put questions which she would not understand, and to draw from her such sympa-thetic replies as he could shape to his own needs, even to his defense if need be.

Mrs. Bramlett, still sitting in her darkened room, saw through the closed blinds the tall form of her husband as he strode down the street. What could have taken him away again? He was not fond of going out in the evening after a hard day's work; it required a special effort to get him to do so. Never before, since their marriage, had he stalked away without word or sign to her. Was he too angry ever to forgive her?

The poor wife's heart ached after him so that she was tempted to push up the window and call. What if she should shout out into the night and the darkness, "Ralph! Oh, Ralph! forgive me. I did not mean to hurt you. I did not mean any of the cruel things I said. I love you, and am miserable day and night because we cannot be happy together as I thought we should be. Come back, dear, and let me put my head on your shoulder, and my arms about your neck, and tell you how sorry I am." What wild words those would be to fling out after him! If she should try it, would he come back? She pushed open the window a few inches; not with the slightest idea of speaking any of those eager words, but wondering if she should call him. Suppose she should say, "Ralph, wait a moment; I want to speak to you." That would sound well enough for any passerby to hear; and Lena, if she were listening, could make nothing of it; then, when he was once beside her, with the door closed after him, she could— She pushed the window down; she *couldn't* do it. She had a vision of his cold eyes and could hear his icy voice as he came back promptly enough at her bidding—he was always in these outward forms a gentleman—and stood before her asking, "What is it you wish?"

She couldn't do it. All she wished was to put her head on his shoulder and cry and ask him to forgive her. No, the trouble was she wanted more than that; she wanted him to ask her to forgive him; she knew that he would not; and she knew that he was to blame, as well as herself, for the cruel state of things that now existed between them. Oh, more than herself! What had she done but speak irritably to him a few times under strong provocation, and what had he not done to repel her, especially of late? No, it would be not only humiliating but a species of falsehood to ask his forgiveness as though she alone had been to blame. It was well that she had not called him back. Let him go his way, wherever it was. He should see that he had married a woman who had self-respect, at least.

She had struggled hard with her anniversary—this poor, unhappy wife. Evidently her husband had not so much as noticed it, but she had prepared certain dishes that she knew he enjoyed; she had arrayed herself in the dress that he used to like, and before his plate had placed a tiny bouquet of the flowers that were his favorites. And there was the birthday cake, over which she had hovered even while it was baking, to see that it was done to just the right shade of perfection, that he had not even waited to see. Oh, why had everything gone as it had, when she had worked so hard and tired herself out just to please him! Why had Hannah Bramlett come that afternoon of all others, to thrust those wretched pinpoints of criticism into her very flesh?

The idea of Hannah daring to hint that she was afraid his wife's expensive tastes had brought trouble upon Ralph! and pointing, in proof of her charge, to certain expensive articles with which she had had nothing whatever to do—articles that had been Ralph's gifts to her in those early days of their married life that now sometimes seemed centuries away!

The idea of Hannah Bramlett finding fault with *her* because they paid such an enormous rent and lived in so large a house—an "absurdly large house for two people!" What business was it of hers how many rooms they had? And why should she suppose that

Ralph had had nothing to do with the choice? Why should Ralph allow his sister, who was disgracing herself, whose name was tossed about carelessly by the street gossips as "Jack Taylor's girl," to come and force her criticisms on her? To come, too, in the name of affection for Ralph! To look distressed while she repeated the vile slander—brought to her, probably, by Jack Taylor—that he not only did not pay his debts but did not mean to pay them and was borrowing money of poor people who trusted him, and deceiving them with the story that he had invested it for them! She, the wife, would have thrown anything she could reach at the head of any person who had dared to come to her with such tales; but Hannah had only wiped her eyes and looked the picture of misery and begged her, Estelle, to change her manner of living, and reduce their expenses, and help poor Ralph out of this terrible embarrassment.

Mrs. Bramlett, as she thought it all over, hardened her heart, not only against Hannah, but against her husband.

11

A Series of Blunders

MEANTIME Ralph Bramlett, unmindful of the distressed watcher at the window, strode off down the street, bent on the desire of his heart. When was Ralph Bramlett bent on anything else save his own desires?

It was now some months since Mrs. Edmonds and her daughter had reached home; and Marjorie, if she had not made much headway in the work that she wanted to accomplish, had at least seen more or less of Ralph. This, however, had been the result apparently of accident, certainly without design on her part. To all appearance, Ralph was a more regular churchgoer than his sister-in-law had led her to suppose; and invariably he and his wife joined her mother and herself for the homeward walk, keeping directly behind them, Ralph, at least, eager to enlist them in conversation. Several times it had occurred that in crossing the streets the couples would of necessity become separated; and again, without apparent design, it would be found that when they came together Ralph was beside Marjorie, leaving his wife to walk with her mother. This arrangement tried Mrs. Edmonds more than she would have cared to express, but it was apparently so purely an accident that nothing could be said.

Then, too, the number of times in which Marjorie had met Ralph Bramlett on the train, and traveled homeward in his company, were surprising when she recalled them. She had carefully avoided what was supposed to be his regular train, lest he should get the idea that she was trying to stand guard over him in any way; but take whatever train from town she would, he was nearly certain to have chosen the same one. In her innocence, it did not occur to her that he had skillful ways of possessing himself of her intentions. A like experience had been hers a number of times when she had arranged to spend an hour or two with his wife. It was sure to be the day in which he surprised his wife by coming home early. In these, and various other ways, she had certainly seen much of Ralph Bramlett; yet she could not feel that any good results had followed. Unquestionably Ralph was glad to talk with her, and upon any subject that she chose to bring forward. Moreover, he took high ground on all these subjects; either his sister-in-law had been deceived in regard to him, or else he talked in this strain from force of habit. Marjorie sadly feared that the latter was the case, because from her standpoint a man could not be growing spiritually and maintain a position in a distillery. The original plan that she had formed of reaching and helping him through his wife seemed a failure. Although she had made extraordinary efforts to establish herself on the familiar footing with Mrs. Bramlett that the intimacy of their girlhood warranted, she found herself constantly held at a distance.

She puzzled over the reasons for this. With the single exception of a few months before her marriage, during which time Marjorie had decided that she was so absorbed in her new relations and future prospects as to be indifferent to all former interests, Estelle Douglass had always shown not only a willingness but an eagerness to be on intimate terms with Marjorie. Why had she changed so utterly? Studying the question with utmost care, Marjorie's only conclusion was that Mrs. Bramlett so felt her dignity as matron and mistress of a home of her own that she was prepared to resent anything which foreshadowed possible advice or suggestion of any sort. So, although there were some points on which she would have liked to advise her, Marjorie carefully held herself from all such temptations. She realized, from hints that Estelle had dropped, that the young wife had to endure more or less advice from her sister-in-law; perhaps this made her suspicious of others. At least, it was the only solution that this young woman, who could be very stupid on occasion, could furnish.

On the evening in question, Marjorie chanced to be seated quite alone in their cheery parlor, her mother being closeted in the dining room with a poor woman who had a tale of woe to pour out intended for no ears but hers. When, therefore, the little maid whose duty it was announced "Mr. Bramlett," it was Marjorie who advanced to meet him.

"Alone?" she said inquiringly. "Where is Estelle? I recognized your voice in the hall and hoped you had both come to spend the evening."

"I am alone," he said.

"How is Estelle? Not ill I hope? But of course she is not, else you would not be here. Why did not this pleasant winter evening coax her out?"

"I did not bring her," was his brief reply. Then, "Is it a pleasant evening? I did not know. I am too weary in body and soul to take note of weather, though it is pleasant here. What a charming home you have, Marjorie! I remember it, of course. I remember every detail of the rooms; sometimes I think of it as 'Paradise Lost.'"

Marjorie gave him a swift, anxious glance. Certain rumors had come to her from time to time as to his being much embarrassed about money matters, but she had given slight heed to them—there was always gossip afloat that had little or no foundation; but on this evening, as she saw his troubled face and listened to his dreary words, she wondered whether it could be that he was in such trouble financially as to make the carefree days of his younger life seem almost like a paradise lost.

"I want to talk with you," he said, drawing forward a chair for her and sinking into one near it. "I am glad to find you alone; it seemed to me that I must talk to somebody or go wild."

"Oh, Ralph!" she said in tones of earnest sympathy; "what is the matter?" Here was evidently some trouble from which he meant to shield his wife, and from sheer force of habit he had come to his old friend. She would not fail him. He hesitated. Just what was the matter? Or rather, what did he mean to say to her? It was not exactly sympathy of which he had come in search, but the moment he stepped into that sympathetic atmosphere, the desire for it overpowered him.

"Everything is the matter," he said tragically; "nothing is as it should be in this world. Did you know it?" Then he laughed cynically and added, "You live a safe, sheltered life, do you not, Marjorie? Shut away from the disagreeable of every sort. Well, I am glad; that is as it should be."

The sentence closed with a heavy sigh and in a tone which hinted that a great deal more might be said were he at liberty to say it.

Of course he was referring to business embarrassments. Marjorie had not supposed that, to a salaried man, these could be very serious. After a moment's silence, during which she reflected what it was best to say, she resolved upon a bold stroke.

"Ralph, at the risk of seeming to be unsympathetic, I will confess that I do not feel so sorry for your business troubles as perhaps you think one ought. If I were to speak quite the truth, I would confess that my strongest wish for you is that they should become so great as to cause you to break at once and forever from all association, however remote, with the liquor traffic. I am sure it is a business that must be distasteful to you in every way. I know you will forgive my plain speaking. I have never been able to look with any degree of endurance upon the position which you now occupy. The only thought I have had in connection with it has been one of pain and disappointment. It is not because you did not study for a profession," she added hurriedly; "I do not mean in the least that I consider a clerkship beneath you, or that it was other than the honorable course if it seemed necessary to you at the time to earn money immediately; but some other clerkship than the one you hold is surely possible. There are so many honorable places waiting for men like you. I shall have to confess that if your present position were so distasteful to you as to cause you to leave it tomorrow, I could only be glad."

She stopped abruptly. The young man's face looked so hopelessly dark as to oppress her with the fear that this was, after all, no time to broach this subject.

"You ought to be satisfied with it," he said gloomily; "you are to blame for my occupying it."

She gave a little inward start. This was the first attempt that he had made to refer to the peculiar relations which they used to sustain toward each other. In their reference to the past, both had gone away back to the time when they were schoolmates. The sentence pained her more deeply than he could imagine. Must she add yet this to the number of ways in which she had influenced others to their injury? Perhaps if she had not allowed her girlish sense of dignity to take such full possession of her and had remained his friend during those early beginnings of their misunderstanding, she might have saved him from this mistake. But of what use to mention it now? It would be better for him not to talk about it. She was silent and distressed. He also realized that he had struck a wrong note.

"You surely understand," he said at last, determined to ignore his blunder, "how a man who has made a false step in life and who yet has a family of his own to care for, to say nothing of his father and mother, finds it difficult, in fact, finds it impossible, to retrace his steps. I may not approve of my work; I may hate it, indeed; yet it is all I have to depend upon, and I must abide by the position in which my folly has placed me."

His listener's face brightened visibly. He did hate it then. His conscience was not at rest, and this accounted for much of the gloom his face was wearing. She spoke with intense earnestness:

"No, Ralph, no! What would become of any of us if we could never take back false steps? I can understand how hard it was for you at the time, feeling perhaps that your father needed help; and I can imagine some of the specious reasons that may have been brought to bear upon you. I have heard them advanced since, but I am sure that your conscience has long ago told you how false they were. Throw up the position, Ralph. Do it at once. Your friends will rally around you. Why, no one will be more rejoiced over it than your father. I heard him but a few weeks ago expressing the strength of his feeling on the liquor question. And Estelle, I am sure, will rejoice in it. She will feel that your truest manhood has reasserted itself. As for any temporary embarrassment that there may be while you are getting established in a new business, we, your friends, will be—" She stopped abruptly, distressed over his rapidly darkening face. Ralph Bramlett was a proud man; it was a bitter trial to have Marjorie Edmonds offer him pecuniary assistance.

"Excuse me," he said coldly, "there are some things that even I cannot bear. And while we are upon the subject, I may as well say to you that you are utterly mistaken in some of your premises. My wife is the last person who would counsel me to give up a certainty, meager as she considers it, for a fanatical idea, as she would be sure to call it. She is the last person who would help me in any way. I tell you, Marjorie, that you do not know what I have to endure. I have made an awful, an irreparable, blunder in my life, and I am miserable."

There was no sympathy now in Marjorie's face, only cold indignation. Her voice expressed it promptly, "You are making a very serious blunder now; you are criticizing your wife and allowing yourself to speak words concerning her that the vows you have taken ought to make you ashamed to utter."

He saw his mistake and made haste to try to cover it.

"I beg your pardon, Marjorie; of course I ought not

to have spoken. It is the last thing I meant to say; but, indeed, I am so nearly beside myself at times that I wonder I do not go wild. I want you to forget it. Believe me, I did not come here to say anything of this kind. I mean to live my life as best I can and keep my misery to myself. I came to talk with you about other matters, and I do not know how I could so far forget myself."

It was almost the first word of self-rebuke that Ralph Bramlett had ever been known to utter. Miserable as was the occasion, was there not a shadow of encouragement in it?

Marjorie was silent from very doubt of what ought to be said. The next moment the sliding doors were rolled back, and Mrs. Edmonds entered the room.

"Good evening," she said, "Mrs. Bramlett is well, I hope?" Was her voice colder than usual? How much of that last outburst had she heard?

Ralph Bramlett arose on the instant. He could not talk platitudes with Marjorie's mother. He stammered some incoherent reply as to his wife's health and got himself out, he hardly knew how, into the night.

Perhaps a wilder storm of pain and disappointment and rage never burned in human heart than that to which he gave free rein for a few minutes. The only redeeming feature in it was that for once in his life he criticized his own actions. He asked himself why he had been such a consummate idiot as to go to that house at all if he could not exercise common sense? What insane spirit had possessed him to drag in his wife and say spiteful things about her to Marjorie? He might have known, if he knew anything, that no better way could be devised for making her withdraw her sympathy. What had been his object in going to her in the first place? In the confusion of brain which then possessed him, he could not satisfactorily answer even that question. He had felt impelled to seek her; therefore, he had done so. It was a ridiculous idea, and deserved to fail as ignominiously as it had. Marjorie Edmonds was a fanatic of the fanatics on that entire question, and he had always known it. What was he about? Why should he, Ralph Bramlett, moon along after this sentimental fashion? Why allow himself to be persuaded and cajoled by any woman living!

He would do exactly as he pleased, of course, as any man of sense would. What was Marjorie Edmonds to him? She had chosen to toss him aside as of no consequence. What right had she to try to tutor him now? The fact was, she had insulted him. Offering to take care of him until he could get a situation that suited her! His face burned at the thought. Where would Marjorie Edmonds get her money with which to be so generous, save of that insufferable Maxwell who had spoiled his life? Didn't she know that he would go to state prison rather than accept help of him?

By this time his mood of self-criticism had passed, and it was once more other people who were to blame for all his misfortunes. He tramped long that night, passing once his sister-in-law whom he was to have taken home; but he was on the opposite side of the street, and she was in such earnest conversation with Jack Taylor that she did not notice him.

When at last he reached his private room once more, the first thing he did was to sit down at his desk and write a formal acceptance of the junior partner's business proposition.

12

A CONFIDENTIAL TALK

THERE was silence in Mrs. Edmond's parlor for some minutes after their caller's departure. Marjorie had dropped back into her seat near the open grate, and, with hands clasped in her lap, was staring at the coals. Mrs. Edmonds had taken up a book and was supposed to be reading. In reality she was occupied in thinking of her daughter and trying to decide whether it would be wiser for her to speak what was in her heart or to keep silence.

At last she decided that longer silence was neither being honest to herself nor just to her daughter; and, after the manner of people who have planned for some time just how to commence a conversation, she said the very words that she would have chosen not to, springing, as it were, to the center of her subject instead of approaching it by degrees.

"Marjorie, do you think you are doing just right?"

Marjorie started like one roused from a painful revery, raised troubled eyes to her mother's face, and asked:

"What do you mean, Mother?"

"I mean, dear, is it just right to receive and hold a long and apparently confidential conversation with a married man who has left his wife at home alone while he comes to visit with you?"

Certainly this was not what Mrs. Edmonds had planned would better be said. Her sentence had gathered force as she talked; force born of an indignation that she had meant to suppress.

"Mamma, I do not understand you in the least. Why should I not receive and converse with any gentleman of our acquaintance? You speak almost as if it were a premeditated arrangement. Certainly I did not plan that you should be engaged elsewhere this evening, nor that Ralph should come. I do not know what to think of such strange words from you."

Mrs. Edmonds struggled for self-control and spoke gently:

"I know, Daughter; of course I did not mean what my words may have suggested. I am entirely sure that there was no premeditation, on your part at least. But, dear, think what you are doing. I have felt for some time that I ought to speak; tonight I feel that I must wait no longer. Only today you were telling me a painful story of gossiping tongues that are making free with the acts of people who you know are above suspicion. Why do you not think of yourself in such connection? You cannot have forgotten that Ralph Bramlett used to be very intimate in this house, and that people who had no right to know anything about your affairs freely reported you as engaged to him. Can you imagine that he can single you out for attention in the way that he has been doing ever since we came home, and, above all, call upon you without his wife, and not furnish food for gaping eyes and censorious tongues?"

"Mother," said Marjorie, distressed almost beyond speech, "how can you think—how is it possible for you to think—that there are any people so low as to talk about *me* in connection with a married man!"

"My daughter, you talk as though you did not live in the world. Probably you have never realized how easy it is for a certain class of people to talk, nor out of what small material they can build their theories. But I want to ask you frankly if, as a looker-on, you are sure you would call this small material. Is it customary for a young married man to call frequently without his wife at houses where there are no gentlemen? I am sure you do not realize the number of times that Ralph Bramlett has rung our doorbell in the last few weeks. I remember that he has nearly always had an ostensible errand—you must forgive me for saying ostensible, for some of them were flimsy enough—and I knew that he has made short calls, at least until this evening; but I must frankly own that I have no confidence in him. At the same time, I will try to be just and admit that I do not suspect him of any other motive than a selfish desire to enjoy his own pleasure for the time being, without regard to appearances or the comfort of others. I have never known that young man to consult anyone's comfort but his own; and I think it is only too apparent that he is trying to draw you into a very confidential friendship with himself—a friendship that shall exclude his wife. This does not surprise me in him; but I confess that to see my daughter permitting such a state of things has given me more pain than I ever expected her to cause me."

Marjorie sat in dumb distress. Only an hour before, she could have made indignant answer; but that hour had brought her revelations. She was not benefiting

Ralph Bramlett. A man who felt toward her in such a manner that he could arraign his own wife before her, and expect her sympathy, was not one whom she could benefit by friendship. Perhaps her mother was right, and she had been making a mistake. But not surely in the way her mother feared. It could not be possible that any of those gossiping tongues would dare to touch her name! No, she was sure such an idea was but the creature of an over-anxious imagination. Mothers were always overcareful; and such wretched stories had come to her lately, it was no wonder they had preyed upon her nerves. She spoke at last, gently, soothingly.

"Mamma, you remember I told you not long ago that I believed you were always right and I wrong when we differed? I will say it again. I have perhaps been—not wise, in my anxiety to help poor Ralph. He is in great trouble and needs help almost more than anyone I know; but he is a boy still, not a man at all; and I—" a moment's hesitation, then a disappointed sigh—"am not the one to help him. I did not mean to try directly; I meant to reach him through Estelle; but she holds aloof and will not see what I could do for her."

"And her very holding aloof, Marjorie, ought to show you how impossible it is for you to help her. Do you not see, is it possible you have not understood all this time, that the poor creature is jealous of you?"

Marjorie's face was aflame. "Mother!" she said, controlling her voice and choosing her words with care, "if that sentence were spoken by anyone but you would it not be almost insulting? How is it possible for any woman to think of *me* in such a connection as that? Do you mean that I have given her cause?"

Mrs. Edmonds made a movement of impatience.

"I used to think, Marjorie, that you had splendid common sense. Indeed, I have leaned upon you for years; but I confess that your knowledge of the world and of human nature seems to me to be not much more than a baby might have. Given such a character as you know Estelle Douglass to possess, married to such a man as Ralph Bramlett is, what is she to be but jealous of the woman for whose society her husband leaves hers on every pretext? And then, too, child, you seem to ignore his past intimacy with you—a thing which you may be sure his wife never does. Unwittingly you have given her cause for discomfort. You could hardly help it, unless you were willing to tell her husband frankly that you did not want to see or talk with him. I do not say you are to blame, dear, because you are strangely blind in some directions; but I have no doubt that he sees her pain and is indifferent to it."

Here was food for thought for the already perturbed girl. If she accepted her mother's theory, much that had been mysterious in Estelle's behavior was explained; but what a humiliating theory! Jealous of *her*—when Ralph had deliberately deserted her and chosen his wife before her eyes! She studied over it so long that Mrs. Edmonds had time to determine upon another question that she had long desired to ask.

"Marjorie, has it not occurred to you that Mr. Maxwell might think this renewal of friendship with Ralph Bramlett rather strange?" She studied the girl's face carefully, but could see in it only perplexity.

"I don't think I get your idea. I think Mr. Maxwell would be among the first to understand that I would like to help poor Ralph if I could. But whether he approved it or not would, in a sense, make no difference to me. I mean, I should have to do what I thought was wise and right, not what he thought."

"But such a friend as he ought surely to have influence."

"Influence, yes; I should like to please him; but not more, of course, than I want to please you, Mother; and I have not understood that you did not want me to try to influence Ralph and Estelle in right directions if I could. Why should you introduce Mr. Maxwell's name?"

Poor mother! To most mothers it is a pleasure to be put first; to her it was a positive pain. Was, then, her precious air castle, on which she had been at work for so many months, to come tumbling about her ears? It was dreadful to think that she was precipitating its fall! But she must go on now. She would go on; it was folly to be moving aimlessly around in the dark. She made a bold plunge.

"I don't want to force your confidence, Marjorie; I have been willing to wait until you were ready to give it, but you ask me a direct question. I will confess that I thought Mr. Maxwell's name ought to have greater weight with you than any other—than mine even. There are some for whom even mothers are willing to yield their place." But Marjorie only gazed at her in open-eyed anxiety.

"Do you mean, Mother—I wonder if you can possibly mean—that you think Mr. Maxwell and I will, sometime, marry? If you do, I cannot imagine what has given you that idea. Nothing was ever farther from our thoughts. From the first hour of our intimate acquaintance he has seemed to me like the dear older brother that I always longed for and never expected to find. I am sure he has been like a brother to me all through the months—years they are getting to be now; and I have rested in his friendship and trusted him as I could no one else, save you; but I have never thought, and could never for a moment think, of him in any other relation."

For a little, Mrs. Edmonds was dumb with disappointment and pain. That which she had hoped, at first with trembling, and during these later months with something like assurance, had fallen to the ground. She was growing older every day, and some dreary morning Marjorie would waken to find herself alone. She, the mother, who would at any time have laid down her life for her, must leave her alone. Oh, it was a bitter world! Should she hazard one more question? It was foolish, but she could not help it.

"While you have been rejoicing in the thought of having a brother, has it never occurred to you that you might be doing infinite harm to one who could not look upon you simply as a sister?"

"No, Mamma, it hasn't in this connection. With some persons I might, of course; and, indeed, as a rule, I should not approve of brotherly and sisterly friendships among young men and women: but there are exceptions to all rules; and Mr. Maxwell has, from the first of our acquaintance, shown such patient and persistent brotherliness that I should have been simply foolish to think of him in any other way."

"Yet there is a bare possibility that you have been mistaken. Suppose you were?"

"Then, I should be very sorry indeed—distressed beyond measure; for I should feel that the result could be only pain. But there is no such mistake, Mamma; I am glad to be sure of it. If Mr. Maxwell were indeed your son he could not be more truly my brother than he sometimes seems to me, and I am sure there is nothing that a brother could do that he has not been ready to do for me. I have done a good deal of harm in the world, Mother; but it is a comfort to me to feel sure that in this case I need not blame myself: I can enjoy Leonard Maxwell with a free conscience."

It would be difficult to describe the tumult of pain in Mrs. Edmond's heart as she listened to these assured words. It was not alone her own disappointment, which was bitter, that she felt she had to bear. Mingled with the pain was an undertone not only of resentment, but self-accusation. This state of things she believed to be the direct outcome of her daughter's early intimacy with Ralph Bramlett; and who had been to blame for permitting that intimacy? She could not resist the temptation to test her belief.

"Since we are on this topic, may your mother ask why you suppose it is that a man, so worthy of winning a true woman's heart, has not reached yours? I think I have not been a mother anxious to dispose of her child; but mothers who remember that they have only one to leave cannot help looking forward anxiously sometimes. Do you never mean to marry, dear? And if not, why not?"

Marjorie's nerves were highly wrought that night. She resisted the temptation to laugh and regarded her mother tenderly. "Do not let us borrow trouble, Mother dear; surely that would not be a grave calamity. You and I have each other; is not that all that either of us wants?"

But the shade of disappointment, almost of reproach, did not lift from her mother's face. After a moment, Marjorie added gravely:

"I mean to be very frank with you, Mother. I think you sometimes have a feeling that I do not show you my whole heart; but, indeed, I wish to. I do not think I can be quite like other girls. Most of them seem to think of marriage as a matter of course, but I feel quite the contrary. I do not expect ever to marry. When I was young and foolish, I thought to marry Ralph Bramlett and built my girlish air castles with that idea for a center. Now, I bless the Providence which held me from that; don't you remember, I told you so when we first came home? At the same time I realize how entirely my ideas, as well as feelings, have changed. I have neither intention nor desire ever to leave you. Let us be everything in the world to each other, Mother, and admit no one else."

That night, after Marjorie had been kissed with even more than usual tenderness, and gone away assured that her mother did not intend to blame her, Mrs. Edmonds wrote this letter:

My dear Friend: *I fear I have a bitter disappointment for you. I have just had a plain and exceedingly confidential talk with my daughter, and I find that you are quite mistaken in your thought of her. It is a trial to have to write it, for you know how dear you have become to me, and how much I should like to leave my darling in your care; but honor demands that I should tell you that Marjorie regards you only as a brother, and I believe will never have any other feeling. She is also so sure that you think of her simply as a sister that she has not a qualm of conscience concerning you—of course I have not enlightened her. Dear friend, there is no one else, and I fear me there will never be. It is that old mistake of mine bearing its fruit. I must leave my darling alone in the world, because I did not early shield her from the mistakes that the world constantly makes.*

13

"THERE OUGHT TO BE—"

GLYDE Douglass stood at the door of the tenement house which was Susie Miller's home, awaiting admission. She had called before, several times, but had failed to meet any of the family. During the day Susie was at the factory, so indeed was her mother much of the time; and as Glyde's calls had to be made in the daytime, she knew nothing as yet of Susie's home life. But on this day she expected to gain admittance. A guest was in the home that even the factory respected. Mrs. Miller had not been at work for several days; and on this morning Susie's loom was silent, and word went quietly among the workers near it that "Susie Miller's little sister was dying."

"It will be an awful blow to Susie," the homely red-haired girl who worked next her said, her usually harsh voice soft with sympathy. "It is that little curly-haired young one that she is so proud of. A cute little thing. I'm awful sorry for her."

"It's hard on Susie," volunteered an older girl; "but after all, it's the best thing that could happen to the young one probably. That house is just running over full of children, and the Millers are as poor as poverty. What chance is there for any of 'em? Why isn't it better for them to die and be out of it all before they understand what a mean place this world is?"

This phase of the subject was freely discussed; the weight of testimony being on the side of "sticking it out," and seeing what would "come of it." Something might "happen."

Meantime, Glyde heard by accident of the child's illness and was waiting at the door. Somewhat frightened it is true; serious illness in any form was new to her, and of death she knew nothing; but of course she ought to call.

Susie opened the door to her; the girl's eyes were red with weeping, and she burst into tears again at sight of her teacher.

She said it was true, she supposed. Nannie was going to die. The doctor hadn't been there since yesterday; but he said then he couldn't do anything, and "Ma" said she knew that the baby was worse.

A strange revelation was that home to Glyde Douglass. The way to the little bedroom where the child lay, led through the main living room of the family. Sometime during the morning there had been an attempt at breakfast; the odor of fried pork was distinctly in the air, and the soiled dishes and pork rinds still lay about on the bare table that had been pushed into one corner. The coal in the cookstove had burned itself to a red glow, and the room was stifling. Huddled into corners, in various stages of dishevelment, curiosity, and terror, were gathered the little Millers of all ages. There was very little furniture in the room, and the carpet that covered part of the floor was so worn that unwary feet must constantly have been tripped by it. Within the bedroom, which to

Glyde's horror was absolutely dark save for the light that filtered in from the large room, tokens of poverty were still more marked. The bed on which the child lay gasping for breath seemed to the eyes of the horror-stricken girl but a bundle of rags; but the mother had as intense a look of agony on her haggard face as ever a mother wore; and her voice, as she bent over her dying baby, was tenderness itself. Clearly here was love, struggling with ignorance and poverty.

"Mother," said Susie, "here is Miss Douglass come to see if there is anything she can do. My teacher, you know, at the mission."

Mrs. Miller gave her one quick glance and nod, then turned her eyes back to the child as she said, "It's too late, Susie, to do anything. Oh, my baby, my baby! What *shall I do?*" The old cry wrung from a mother's heart in the midst of the awfully incongruous surroundings. Poor Glyde had never in her life felt so utterly powerless. She made an effort in search of what seemed to her the first necessity.

"Ought she not to have air?" she said. "She breathes so hard; it is dreadfully warm and close here."

The mother turned heavy eyes on her inquiringly. "Where would I get it?" she asked. "I couldn't have the outside open; the young ones would get their deaths, and it would be bad for her. The doctor said we mustn't let no wind blow on her. And we can't get the windows up; they are nailed in and pasted up. We had to, to keep from freezing."

The child died, of course. How could it do otherwise? Then began another phase of Glyde's education, in watching the preparations for the funeral. They chose, at much inconvenience to themselves, and against the judgment of the physician, to wait until Sunday for the service.

"Seems as if I must!" the mother said; "Sunday is the only day that poor folks have time even to cry."

Her neighbors from the other tenement houses gathered after factory hours, and cleaned, and made that living room habitable. Then they spared each a chair or two from their meager stores, until there were seats for all. Meanwhile the wardrobe, not only of the mother and Susie, but of all the little ones, was a source of no small anxiety.

"'Tain't decent not to have a bit of black about 'em somewheres," so the mother argued, "poor little wretches; they all loved her dearly, and they as quiet as mice that day she was so bad. Get a black ribbon for 'em, do! I'll make it up somehow, and a few bits of black ribbon can't cost much."

It was then Glyde learned that while the very wealthy and aristocratic will sometimes ignore altogether the custom of wearing black, and the moderately poor and respectable can often be easily persuaded to follow such example, those in abject poverty, who have not yet discovered the latest fashions, cling to their black dresses and ribbons and veils as tokens of love for their dead. The same thought appeared in other ways. Glyde was indefatigable during those two intervening days. She secured warm flannels for the living children, and, in several cases, the much-needed shoes; she discovered in somebody's storeroom a half-worn overcoat for the little boy; she brought a warm flannel sack for the mother; she furnished, from Mrs. Edmonds's kitchen, nourishing food for the half-starved family; but it was when, on the morning of the funeral, she had brought a wreath of choice flowers tied with white satin ribbon that the young ladies of the church Bible class had sent to lay on the little coffin, that the poor mother broke into tears and exclamations of gratitude. Flowers in March on her baby's coffin, and tied with soft white satin ribbon in unstinted quantities, seemed to mean more to her than clothing and food. She cried again when Mrs. McPherson, in whose attic the little overcoat had been found, sent her carriage for the mother, and the half-drunken father, and all the little Millers to crowd into and ride to the grave. Here, too, was what she seemed to consider a love token to the waxen-faced baby who was riding in state in front of them.

Other discoveries Glyde made. During those three days, when the Millers by reason of their bereavement came into prominence among their neighbors, it was Bill Seber, the worse than worthless fellow against whom she had exhausted her ingenuity in warning Susie, who was on the alert day and night to serve them all. It was he who looked after certain homely details for the heavy-eyed mother; it was he who watched over the irresponsible father to see that he did not drink enough to disgrace his dead child; it was he who superintended the arrangement of the chairs on the day of the funeral and who moved the heavier pieces of furniture out of the way, and received and seated the neighbors as they filed in, and placed Susie beside her mother in the carriage, and tucked all the little Millers swiftly and quietly into place. Alert, thoughtful, eager to serve, certainly a mine of strength was Bill Seber during those trying days. Glyde could see how, in a sense, Susie was not only grateful to him, but proud of him. Perhaps his virtues showed in stronger light because of the utter absence of young men of a higher grade. In vain did Glyde, when she awakened to the importance of such influences, try to secure some of the young men from the mission to attend the Miller baby's funeral. A few of them were engaged in Christian work elsewhere at that hour; but the majority needed it for rest, for dinner, for whatever they chose to do, and could not be made to see the importance of sacrificing their own ease and inclination for even a single Sunday. So impressed did Glyde become with the power of these minor matters, that, failing in others, she hinted her desire to her brother-in-law and was sorry afterward that she did so; for he came and walked decorously beside Marjorie Edmonds to and from the little "factory cemetery" where these people buried their dead. Glyde was beginning to feel, rather than see, reasons why this should not have been.

All things considered, the trouble that came to the Miller family was an education in several ways to this young Christian worker. An education that troubled her. She told over some of her thoughts to Marjorie as they sat together in the latter's parlor one afternoon.

"There are so many puzzling things about it all, Marjorie. One doesn't know what to try to do. Take those Millers, for instance; they are representative of quite a large class. Poor—much poorer than they need be, on account of whiskey; it is dreadful to think how many of those factory people drink up their earnings—yet see how they have managed. They had no bread in the house yesterday, and no credit with which to get it; but they *had* to have black dresses and a bit of crape on their bonnets, and all that sort of thing. Isn't it sad, Marjorie, to think of their poor, hard-earned money being spent in that way? If they could have taken it beforehand, and bought flannels for the baby, and good milk for her to drink, and a decent bed for her to sleep on, it would have saved her life perhaps. But saved it to what? I am so distressed when I think of it all, that it seems as though it would break my heart. See how they go on for generations—no improvement. I presume Mrs. Miller's mother was such another as she, and I am afraid Susie will be much the same. Why, Mrs. Miller simply does not know how to make her room clean! While as for bread, she would have to buy the miserable stuff they get at the bakery in any case, because she has not the least idea how to make it. She doesn't know what to do with the meat she buys in order to get any nourishment from it; why, she doesn't even know how to manage her coal fire! And as for making a home for those children—*oh, dear!* What chance is there that she will ever know any of these things? How is she to learn? No homes worthy of the name are open to her. She represents at least a dozen other families right around her who are not one whit better off than she."

"Yet they manage to dress themselves in a way to look very bright and stylish," interrupted Marjorie; "the younger ones, I mean. Your Susie, for instance, I could not but notice her when she came out in her new winter hat; it was quite in the style as to shape, and had fully as many flowers as the fashionable people wear."

"I know it, and that illustrates what I am talking about; they have no sense of the relative value of things, or rather, values have changed places. They *must* have new bonnets and dresses made in the prevailing style, even though the children go shoeless and all of them without proper underwear. Susie spends her wages largely on herself and thinks that she must do so; and her mother sympathizes with her. There's another thing about Susie that perplexes me. You remember I told you how distressed I was at her being so much on the street evenings? But there is excuse even for that. Think of their one room, Marjorie, with not a decent chair in it, with the father forever puffing away at an old pipe when he is at home, with children of all ages forever not only underfoot but quarreling and crying and shouting, with one stuffy little lamp that smokes as constantly as the master of the house does. Add to all this the perpetual smell of the last pork and onions that were fried, mingling with bad whiskey, and what sort of a place is it for a girl like Susie to invite a friend into? She cannot ask even Bill Seber to come in and take a seat; for the chances are that there will not be a whole chair to give him. What is she to do? How shall she be taught that she must not put on her pretty bonnet and her stylish-looking coat and parade up and down the nice gaily lighted streets where the well-dressed people walk? I confess to you, Marjorie, that the whole problem is such a hopeless tangle to me that I am lost in it. There ought to be a room, a home, where girls like Susie could come with their work and their books and their friends and have comfortable sittings and pleasant surroundings, and learn how people live. I do not mean Young Women's Christian Associations, nor clubs, nor guilds, nor anything of that sort; those are blessed, of course, but they are on a large scale. Who is it that says they are Homes spelled with a capital *H?* That expresses it. There ought to be little homes scattered about where those young people could drop in and feel that they belonged and could make cups of tea or plain little stews occasionally for their friends. They ought to be shown how to do all these things; not by classes, not in large numbers, but by the half-dozen, or sometimes by only two.

"I can invite them to my mother's parlor, you think, and so I can, and do; and you invite them here. I have by no means forgotten all the delightful things you and your mother have done and are doing for my girls;

but I am talking about something else now. I don't
want them always to have to come ever so far away
from their homes and the streets where they live for
their happy times; the home ought to go down to
them and make a center for them to gather in and get
ideas."

"A college settlement, for instance," suggested
Marjorie.

"Yes; or no, not quite that, either. That is too large;
it has a secretary, and a board, and is *managed*. Don't
you know what I mean? If I had a home of my very
own—" here a soft flush suffused itself over her
earnest face—"and could put it where I liked, I should
like to go right down among them and have a large,
cheery, homely sitting room that, on certain evenings,
for instance, should belong to Susie Miller, to manage
as she would. And between times I should like to show
her how to manage." She laughed a little over this and
added, "You think me an idiot, and perhaps I am; but
there are certain experiments that I should like to try."

"Whether or not Susie Miller is being educated,
Glyde Douglass certainly is." This was Mrs. Edmonds's
remark after Glyde had left them. She had sat apart, a
silent, amused listener to the girl's eager outburst.

Marjorie gave a detailed account of the conversation in her letter to Mr. Maxwell, and closed with the
following:

> In short, when a certain Paul Burwell gets ready to
> set up his home, may I be near enough to observe
> its workings; for little Mrs. Paul—that is to be—
> is certainly getting ready to undertake some
> astonishing experiments. Oh, but she is delicious!
> Such a rest from all the other girls! And it is such a
> comfort to me to think that the young man is evi-

dently ready to meet her more than halfway. She does not suspect that I know it; but the mouse gets some of her most startling ideas from him, just as I have no doubt that he gets some of his sweetest ones from her. Indeed, Leonard, I believe they will be a couple after my own heart.

14

JUNE VISITORS

JUNE came early that year, or at least it seemed so to the busy ones. And with June, history prepared, apparently, to "repeat itself." That is, Mr. Leonard Maxwell was coming, as he had one June before, to take possession of Mrs. Edmonds's second floor front room and spend the summer. He had been disappointed in his plan for enjoying the holidays with them, imperative duty having called him elsewhere; but now he was arranging for a quiet vacation to be spent in preparing his writings for the press; and where could a better abiding place be found than Mrs. Edmonds's home?

Mother and daughter seemed to be looking forward to the close of the college year with equal satisfaction. The mother, it is true, would not have liked to confess what hope she had hidden in that coming summer. She was not, as she had said, a scheming mother, nor had she, in the vulgar sense of the phrase, the slightest desire to "marry off" her daughter Marjorie. Yet perhaps the strongest wish of her heart for this beloved daughter was to see her, before her mother died, the happy wife of Mr. Maxwell.

On the surface, all the people connected with this history were moving on in the even tenor of their ways; yet there had been changes. Notably in Jack Taylor, for instance. No class of people who had ever thought of him before had difficulty in discovering this change. Jack slouched and shambled along the streets no more. Instead of the uncertain, vacillating gait that had been his for years, his step was alert, and his whole manner suggested energy. He whistled in these days as he passed saloons, and rejoiced in every fiber of his being because he had not the slightest inclination to enter one of them. He had steady employment now, at good wages, and worked hard every day, and was piling up quite a little sum at the savings bank. He attended the evening school that had been started in connection with the Carnell Street Mission and was making fair progress in the art of reading, writing, and kindred elementary studies. He wore respectable clothing and clean linen and conducted himself everywhere in a manly way. These were the observable changes. Great as they were, Jack knew of another far more astonishing to him. Locked into his room at night after the day's work was done, and every morning before the day's work commenced, Jack bent his knees and held communion with God. Is there anything more wonderful than that in human history? Not only men of giant intellect, but men with such minds and opportunities and wasted energies as Jack Taylor represents, may at will hold audience with the infinite God, commune with him as long as they will, and live in the daily increasing strength which such communion bestows!

Yet Jack knew of something more wonderful still! Not alone when locked into his room did he hold communion with the infinite One; but that One actually walked beside him, shielding, guiding, foreseeing, and planning for him! Jack had a simply unanswerable argument with which to prove the truth of this. That argument was his life—what he had been without God, what he was, having permitted him to take control. Jack felt that only those who wished and intended to doubt could get away from this argument. From the night when Glyde Douglass had made her earnest appeal to him not to disappoint the Lord Jesus Christ, a new life had begun in him. Not only new ambitions and hopes, but new strength with which to reach after them. Jack did not understand it fully—who pretends to?—but he understood at least the human side, and the infinite Lord attended to the rest. "If any man will do his will, he shall know of the doctrine." Jack Taylor was doing his will as well and as fast as he understood it; and no talkative infidel, however ingenious, could have moved his feet from the firm foundation whereon he knew they had been placed.

Jack took part nowadays in the mission prayer meeting, being always in his seat even before the hour for opening. No, not in his seat either, but at the door, watching out, darting down, on occasion, to the sidewalk or around the corner to the alley hard by, to put an eager hand on some poor fellow's shoulder and speak his word of invitation. Oh, the best of them could not work down in that vicinity equal to Jack.

"Jack Taylor has been converted," said his old-time friend Joe Berry; but though, not long before, he had chuckled at the idea, he spoke the words now with an entirely grave face and respectful manner. "It is a dead sure thing," he said; "'tain't like mine. It's queer, too, what a difference it makes! Mother ought to have had Jack for her son instead of me." The curious regret closed with a grave sigh. But be sure Jack Taylor had not forgotten his old friend; he was watching out for him.

Following that long, confidential talk between Mrs. Edmonds and her daughter had been some anxious days, during which Marjorie went over and over again the details of that interview, her face burning afresh every time she thought of the possibility of her name having been on the tongues of the gossips. It will be remembered, however, that she had felt sure at the moment that her mother's words were born of motherly anxiety and oversolicitude. This idea gained in strength. It seemed quite natural when she remembered her mother's recently acquired knowledge of the world's wickedness, through putting forth her strength to help some of its victims; but despite its naturalness in the mother's thoughts, of course it was preposterous. They had no enemies, and it would require an enemy to couple her name even with an impropriety. As for Ralph Bramlett's own words that had started her so much, due consideration must be made for them also. They were utterly unpremeditated, and he had failed, in his excitement and pain, to realize how they would sound to her; evidently for the moment he had forgotten her presence, and simply thought aloud. It was only too apparent that he did not love the wife of his choice as he ought. This was terrible, certainly; yet by so much more did he need help. The hasty conclusion she had reached that she was not the one to help him was next taken up and studied carefully. She was by no means sure that this was true. Had not Ralph sought her almost by instinct, one might say, when he was in bitter trouble? What her mother felt concerning him must really be taken with allowance, because poor Mamma had never been able to think of Ralph in an entirely unprejudiced way and had never understood him. Still, of course, she must be careful not to worry her in any way.

The final conclusion she reached was that she would be entirely frank with Ralph. She would say to him at the first opportunity that they should always be glad to see him at their home, but that for the sake of idle, gossiping tongues he must not come to them without his wife. Also, she would so order her trips to and from the city as to leave no possible chance for him to join her, and she would make her visits to Estelle in the mornings.

All these resolutions she had carefully acted upon. Ralph, being duly warned, had taken offense, as might have been foreseen, and for a time did not come at all. But that mood had not lasted. Perhaps he could have told better than anyone else what influence he brought to bear upon his wife, but certain it is that they together spent many evenings with Mrs. Edmonds and Marjorie. No reasonable fault could be found with this; although Mrs. Edmonds realized what Marjorie did not, that it required much diplomacy on her part to keep the conversation general. Neither had the morning visits been entirely as were intended. To the equal surprise of the guest and the wife, Ralph adopted the fashion of appearing suddenly at any hour of the morning. It was always "business connected with the firm" that had either detained him in town or brought him back unexpectedly; but evidently Mrs. Bramlett knew no better than Marjorie what the distillery could have to do with their end of the town. On the whole, imperceptibly upon Marjorie's part, June found Ralph Bramlett and herself upon nearly the same footing that had been interrupted by that confidential talk. Not quite, for Ralph attempted no more private interviews in which to talk wildly of his troubles and draw out her sympathy; on the contrary, he carefully avoided any personal references and was entirely silent as to his business.

Marjorie, much as she hated it, could not but hope that some arrangement had been made which was more satisfactory in a money point of view. Certainly the Bramletts seemed to have tided over their anxieties in that line. Estelle exhibited proudly some costly gift from Ralph at almost every visit of Marjorie's. The time for the seal furs upon which she had set her heart early in the winter had of course gone by, but a costly lace-trimmed garment had taken their place; and the anniversary of their engagement was remembered by a handsome pin with a diamond center.

Marjorie was genuinely glad over these. They not only implied prosperity, but, she believed, something better—that Ralph was ashamed and amazed because he had allowed himself to grow cold toward his wife, to blame her too severely perhaps for trifling faults; he was trying to atone for the injustice that his thoughts had done her, and took this graceful and expressive way. She could not but hope, as she studied the signs, that Ralph was gaining ground in many ways; his silence to her, even when he had occasional opportunity to speak a word in private, augured well. She even, as the days passed, conceived the idea that he was planning a happy surprise for his friends. He had spoken gloomily once of some business ventures which had not proved a success; perhaps he had been happily disappointed in them and now saw and was arranging a way to escape from the position that he had admitted he hated. If only that escape could be brought about, she felt that her hopes for his assured future would be great. It seemed to her a perfectly evident thing that his association with the liquor trade was what was holding him back from church work and from Christian usefulness generally.

The hopeful calm into which she had fallen while she waited was broken in upon in an unexpected manner. The surprise began with a call from Mrs. Bramlett; not Estelle, but Ralph's mother. Marjorie, as she sat opposite the little old woman with her worn face and anxious eyes, found herself wondering, while she kept up the commonplaces of conversation, what could possibly be the object of the call. Years before, in the days when she was so young and ignorant that to run in to see Ralph about some matter was as natural to her as to call upon a girlfriend, she had known his mother fairly well; but after she attained to young ladyhood and propriety and dropped entirely her visits to Ralph, her acquaintance with his mother had also dropped. Mrs. Bramlett was a woman who went to church as often as she could and who went almost nowhere else. To make a formal, or even an informal, call was an act entirely outside of her life.

"Old Mrs. Bramlett, did you say, Jennie?" Marjorie had questioned the little maid. "Do you mean Mr. Ralph Bramlett's mother? Then she cannot want to see me. Are you sure she did not say 'Mrs. Edmonds'?" Jennie was very sure she did not. She hadn't said either "Mrs." or "Miss," she said she wanted Marjorie Edmonds. So Marjorie commented on the lovely spring they had had, and the warm summer that was prophesied, and waited for some errand to develop itself.

Suddenly, without responding to a suggestion as to the beauty of the day, Mrs. Bramlett began, "I suppose you are rather surprised to see me, Marjorie; perhaps I ought to say Miss Marjorie, but I knew you so well when you were a young thing that it doesn't come natural. I may as well tell you right away what I've come for; I'm not good at going around a thing. I've sat at home and thought about it just as long as I could, and it came over me this afternoon that I would come up here and see if you wouldn't be willing to help me. I want you to talk to our Hannah. I know she is a good bit older than you, but that doesn't make any difference. If there is a living mortal who has any influence over Hannah, it is you; she has always set more store by you than she has by anybody else, and I don't know another person to go to. Ralph is so out with her that he won't speak to her at all, and I don't know as I blame him altogether, either. A brother, you know, always wants to see his sister do just right; and if she doesn't, why—"

Here Marjorie interrupted in amazed anxiety. "But, dear Mrs. Bramlett, what is the matter? I thought Hannah always did just right."

"Oh, dear, no! Hannah is human like the rest of us. Not but that she is a good girl; she has been as faithful to her father and me as any girl could be, and a good sister to Ralph, too. She has helped him lots of times in his younger days, in ways that he doesn't know anything about, besides a good many that he does know. But you know how the talk is going, Marjorie; you must have heard—about Hannah and Jack Taylor? They say he has been converted and is behaving first-rate; and sometimes I can't help wishing he had died after that and gone to heaven, instead of staying here to make all this trouble. Why, they've been telling around that she was going to *marry* him; and that wasn't bad enough, but they have been saying real downright low things, Marjorie, about my Hannah! Think of it! A Bramlett getting mixed up with such talk as that! Not that there's a word of truth in what they say, of course. All that honest people can say of Hannah is that she has been dreadful silly in letting him tag after her as she has. She had good motives, and I always knew she had; still, it isn't the way to do in this wicked world, and I told her so; but Hannah is that set in her way, sometimes, for all she seems so quiet, that it didn't do any good. Now she is the victim of sinful tongues. I didn't know we had an enemy in the world; but it does seem as though some enemy must have got up these last stories anyhow. Haven't you heard anything, Marjorie?"

No, Marjorie had not. At least nothing that she had heeded. A long time ago, when she first came home, she had heard of some silly rumors that were afloat; but she had not given them a second thought, beyond a feeling of indignation that a Christian girl could not try to help one in need without being the victim of idle tongues. But she had heard nothing of late and had forgotten all about it. "Does Hannah know what is being said of her?" she asked.

"Oh yes," the mother said with a sigh; "she knows well enough. I've talked to her by the hour; but it didn't do any good. It made her kind of mad; and when a Bramlett gets his spunk up there is no end to the things he will do, just to show his independence. Hannah won't give up teaching Jack Taylor—she's got him in her arithmetic class down at the mission; and she won't stop his walking home with her and stand-ing at the gate a while to talk. He tells her all about his affairs; acts as though she was his grandmother, and she seems to have some such notion herself.

"Ralph's wife hears all the stories; it does beat all what that woman hears! Seems as if folks must run to her with the news as quick as they happen, or some-times before they happen. But it doesn't seem as though people would tell her about her husband's own sister, does it?"

15

SCHEMES

AT THIS point Marjorie was called from the room for a moment, giving Mrs. Bramlett time to reflect on what she had been saying. She looked up at Marjorie on her return with a timid, half-questioning glance as she said:

"It seems kind of queer to you, I suppose, to hear me going on as I have about my own flesh and blood; but I've sat there alone and thought about it so long that it seemed to me I should go crazy unless I talked it over with somebody. And I haven't anybody to go to. Mr. Bramlett is so poorly now that I can't say a word to him. I wouldn't have him know for anything that Hannah is being talked about; it would break his heart. She is the only daughter, you know, and he has always set such store by her. That is one of my troubles—for fear someone will think it his duty to get off a long story to him. Hannah doesn't have any kind of a notion what it would be to her father to go through such a thing about her. It's queer that children never seem to know what they are to their parents. To hear her talk sometimes, you would think she believed there was no one in the world who cared for her, and there's her father just bound up in her. She's having a real hard time. Ralph is so out with her that he won't speak to her at all. I tell him that is a dreadful way for brothers and sisters to be—but there, he's a Bramlett too. You see, Estelle has said so much, and in such a way, that Hannah got all wrought up, and I suppose she said some pretty sharp things back; and Estelle ran right to Ralph with them, and he says Hannah has insulted his wife. You can't blame a man for standing up for his wife, can you? I wouldn't give much for one who didn't stick to her through thick and thin; though of course Hannah didn't mean anything like an insult."

Poor Mrs. Bramlett, in her earnest desire to be true to all the members of her family, was being continually switched off on sidetracks. "And so, Marjorie, I just made up my mind this afternoon that I would come up and tell you the whole story and ask you if you wouldn't send for Hannah, or come over and see her and have a talk with her. I am sure you can influence her if anybody can. If she would just give up going with Jack Taylor, or letting him run after her—if she wouldn't have anything to do with him at all for a spell, why the stories would die out, and nobody would be hurt. They haven't got anything to grow on, you know—nothing but made-up stories; but she keeps them afloat all the time by the way she does. She's got a notion, you see, that people feel above Jack Taylor and won't have anything to do with him, and that if she drops him, he will be discouraged and go back into bad ways. I tell her even if he does, she isn't bound to ruin herself, and him too, in order to try to help him! But you can't convince her; at least I can't. She thinks that Estelle has turned Ralph and everybody else against her and that she must do her duty in spite of them. It's all *duty*, Marjorie; anyway, she thinks it is. She believes she is a kind of martyr, you know. It's my belief that some folks like to be martyrs, if it isn't too hard work: it gives dignity and importance to what they are doing to feel that they are suffering because of it in some way or other; still, Hannah was never one to turn back. I don't believe she would if the old days were back again and she was on her way to the stake; and I believe in her and have no kind of doubt but that she helps the fellow in a hundred ways. But you *don't* think it is right for her to go on like this; now, do you?"

"No," said Marjorie, distressed into an emphatic answer. "It isn't right for a girl to peril her own name, of course, and bring trouble upon others by her good works; but this is all so new and strange to me, Mrs. Bramlett. I cannot imagine the gossips saying anything but the merest twaddle about Hannah."

"That's about what she thinks," said Mrs. Bramlett, nodding her head sagely. "She says Estelle imagines two-thirds of it, but I told her that Ralph had spoken plainly enough for her to know better than that; still, she believes that Estelle has prejudiced Ralph. Will you come over and talk with her, Marjorie, and tell her what she ought to do, and get her to promise to do it? It does seem as though I couldn't stand much more of this—Ralph and his wife not speaking to her, and staying away from our house for fear they will meet her, and saying she has disgraced them, and all that kind of thing; and Hannah feeling like death a good deal of the time, but going straight on doing her 'duty'; and her father breaking down right before our eyes. We have trouble enough coming to us without making any of it ourselves."

Here the poor mother hid her face in her handkerchief and let the tears that had been forcing themselves upon her have free course for a minute or two; while Marjorie, with all her heart on the alert, hastened to assure her that she would certainly have a talk with Hannah at the first opportunity, and that she would meantime take pains to inform herself as to the exact nature of the reports. Then she made haste to prepare for her guest a cup of tea, talking cheerily the while about commonplace matters and making every effort to draw her thoughts for a time from her burdens. Just as her last drop of tea was drained, Mrs. Edmonds appeared at the gate in the little pony phaeton that she used on her errands of mercy; and Marjorie, mindful of the long, warm walk to the farm, proposed driving her guest home. But she would have none of it.

"Oh no!" she said, shaking her gray head and rising. "I mustn't do that; it would never do for me to go back in state. Hannah would know right away where I had been, and then she would suspect something. I wouldn't have her know for the farm that I had been here talking with you about her. It would just upset the whole thing. She is so wrought up that she can't listen to anything I say anymore, and she would be sure to think I had prejudiced you. I want you to talk to her just as though you had heard the story from the gossips themselves, and don't mention Estelle nor Ralph if you can help it. Oh, I can walk home. I had an errand at the store that I had to see to myself; they didn't know I was coming any farther, and I don't mean they shall know I did. I feel quite chirked up; it does beat all how you manage to comfort a body! I always knew you were to be depended upon, Marjorie, and I used to think in the old times—Oh, well, dear me! Never mind."

There was a heightened color on Marjorie's face as she turned back from the gate with her mother, having said good-bye to their guest. They both knew what Mrs. Bramlett used to think.

Perhaps Marjorie had never had a duty to perform more disagreeable to her than this which had been thrust upon her. She had always an instinctive aversion to interfering with other people's affairs, especially the affairs of one whom she knew so little as she felt that she did Hannah Bramlett.

"But it was I who set her to work, Mother," she said with a little self-conscious laugh; "I suppose there is a sort of poetic justice in my having to interfere with it now. Poor Hannah! it seems such a pity that she need be disturbed when her protégé is doing so well, and when, I presume, she can help him in many ways as no other person can."

"It is a pity that she isn't sixty years old, or else that she hasn't common sense," said Mrs. Edmonds dryly. For Mrs. Edmonds, estimable and sweet-spirited woman as she generally was, could not be depended upon for a perfectly unbiased judgment where any of the Bramlett name were concerned.

Nevertheless, she discussed with Marjorie ways of managing the proposed interview. The first suggestion was that Hannah should be called upon informally, and that, as opportunity offered, the delicate subject should be broached and frankly discussed. But Marjorie was opposed to this. She wanted Hannah to come to her.

"I can manage the details so much better, Mother," she said, "without fear of interruption at the most inopportune moment; besides, if I should become really unendurable, Hannah could leave me at any moment and go home, whereas if I were her guest I should have to be endured to the end."

Half a dozen ways of securing a visit from Hannah Bramlett that would look sufficiently unpremeditated and friendly were discussed and abandoned. It was wonderful to see what a difficult thing even so simple a matter as that became, when one had a special end in view. One proposition from Marjorie was to give the boys of Hannah's mission class, including Jack Taylor himself, a treat; have ice cream and cake in the evening, accompanied with music and games, and ask Hannah to come in the afternoon and help to prepare for them.

"Would she be so distressed by our talk, do you think, as to spoil the evening for her? It is not as if it were something new. Her mother says she understands it fully, that she has talked to her by the hour. Poor creature! I do not wonder that she is obstinate, after being talked to by the hour about anything. What I am to do is simply to use my influence to help her to see things in the right light."

"And by way of doing so," interrupted Marjorie's mother, "invite her to spend the evening at your house with Jack Taylor and walk home with him two miles afterward! I am afraid, Daughter, that Mrs. Bramlett would not commend your judgment. How would it do to ask Hannah to come and help prepare the work for the sewing classes? There is an enormous quantity of it to be made ready before Thursday, and she is probably an expert in that kind of work."

"The very thing!" said Marjorie gleefully. "Why did you not mention that sewing basket before? I'll have her stay to tea, and we'll get up the nicest little supper and smooth over all the trying things I shall have to say to her with it. I believe we can make it a pleasant afternoon for the poor girl. She must be desperately lonely. I have been thinking of her all the morning, and I do not know of any persons of her age who would be in the least congenial to her. Perhaps she has been willing to give Jack Taylor so much of her time because she did not know what to do with herself. Oh, Mother! there are so many things to be done in this world. Somebody ought to be interested for the people who haven't resources within themselves. I wonder if it is I?"

The scheme of the sewing basket worked well. Hannah Bramlett, who would perhaps have felt suspicious of almost any other form of invitation, was more gratified than she cared to own over being the one chosen to assist Marjorie. And Mrs. Bramlett not only made no objection to the plan but assisted her daughter to make ready for the afternoon's outing with an alacrity which in itself would have been suspicious had Hannah not been too busy to notice it. Mrs. Edmonds, having assisted in assorting the various kinds of work and offered what advice was needed, when everything was arranged, left the two young women to themselves. Marjorie saw her depart with a great shrinking of heart; she dreaded the ordeal before her more even than she had at first. True to her promise to Mrs. Bramlett, she had instituted careful inquiries to learn the extent of the gossip, with the result that she stood appalled before its magnitude.

It was not that any respectable person seemed to credit the stories, unless one excepts those vicious creatures who lay claim to respectability, yet who shake their ugly heads and affirm that they "do not know; there must be some fire where there is so much smoke"; and one added that those "old girls who had lived such circumspect lives up to a certain date were often queer." Marjorie blazed with indignation over it all and spoke keen, cutting words in Hannah's vindication; but she came home sore-hearted, with the conviction upon her that even good work, such work as angels might rejoice over, must be done carefully in this sinful world. She shrank from beginning the conversation with Hannah and talked commonplaces until she was ashamed of herself. At last she made the effort.

"I want to ask you about your protégé, Jack Taylor. Is the progress that he is making in every way satisfactory?"

"You need not call him my protégé," said Hannah with a good-natured laugh. "It would be more appropriate to say that he is Glyde Douglass's; she accomplished more for him in a half hour's talk than I succeeded in doing all winter. I don't know how to talk religion to people, Marjorie; I wish I did. There ought to be a school for teaching folks what to say about such things; though I don't know but Glyde would have to be appointed a teacher—the youngest one among us." This last with an amused little laugh.

But to get into a discussion upon methods of teaching theology was not what Marjorie desired. She repeated in another form her question about Jack.

"Yes," said Hannah unsuspiciously; "Jack is doing very well. He is dull in arithmetic, poor fellow; but who would expect him to be anything else? I was dull enough, I remember. Perhaps that is why I seem to succeed pretty well in teaching him. I remember perfectly how out of patience my teachers used to get with me, and so I try to have patience at least. There has been a great change in Jack. I often wish that some boasting infidel could have been well acquainted with his life up to a few months ago and watched the change. Among Ralph's books there is one called *Evidences of Christianity;* Jack would make a good volume of that kind, I think."

"Yes," said Marjorie with ready sympathy; "no one can doubt the change in Jack. I like to hear him pray in the prayer meeting; he is so simple and quaint in his language and so manifestly asks for what he wants and nothing else. But, Hannah, will you forgive me if I say something now that may hurt your feelings? Do you not think that he is far enough advanced for you to safely drop him, in a sense? I do not of course mean that you would lose your interest in him, but could he not do without so much of your time and attention?"

She felt that she was bungling wretchedly. There was an instantaneous change in Hannah's manner, and her face suggested the Bramlett obstinacy of which Marjorie had heard all her life.

"Why should not I give my time as well as to leave the work for others?" was the cold response, "He needs a great deal of somebody's time in order to make up for the years that he has lost."

Clearly circumlocution was not going to serve here. There must be plain speaking.

"I know," Marjorie said gently; "and you naturally feel that you can be more helpful to him than others could. But, Hannah, there are reasons why it should be some other's time than yours. Don't you know there are, dear friend? I suppose you have heard some of the foolish gossip that is afloat. It is utterly without foundation, of course, as all your friends know. Still, isn't it wise to silence wicked tongues when we can as well as not? Wouldn't it be better for you, and for Jack himself—to say nothing of all your family—if you should transfer him to some other class and give up any special attention to him, for a time at least?"

"No," said Hannah passionately, "it wouldn't be any such thing; not as I look at it. It would be simply a confession that I had been doing something of which I was ashamed, and it is the only work I ever did in my life that I am proud of. I have neither said nor done anything for Jack Taylor that might not have been said and done before all the world, if that was the commonsense way of trying to help people. I know about the stories, you may be sure. My precious sister-in-law takes care that I shall miss nothing from them. I know more, I think, than has been said. Estelle has a way of hearing more than was said, when she feels like it. But the stories haven't influenced me one bit, Marjorie; and I am disappointed to find that you considered it necessary to send for me to come up here in order to tell me that I ought to give up the only bit of real work that I ever did in my life. I've got used to hearing other people talk like fools, but I must say I didn't expect it of you."

16

THE TEACHER TAUGHT

"NOW, Hannah," said Marjorie in a kind, quiet voice, "that isn't the way to talk, dear friend; you shouldn't receive a word of friendly warning from a Christian sister in any such spirit. Do you think you should?"

Hannah stitched fiercely for a few minutes without speaking; then she laid down her work and looked her mentor squarely in the face.

"Marjorie Edmonds," she said with a kind of suppressed fierceness, "do you mean to tell me that you, *you* of all persons in the world, counsel me to give up my work for Jack Taylor because of the lies that some malicious tongues have chosen to tell?"

"Yes," said Marjorie firmly, "I do. Not because I do not believe with all my heart both in you and in Jack Taylor, but because I know it to be a very wicked world, more wicked I have discovered of late than I had imagined it could be, and because you and I must take care of our influence. In our working orders we find no plainer directions than that. Think how many girls in the mission you lose your influence over if you allow acts of yours that could be avoided to furnish food for gossiping tongues."

"Then, why don't you follow your own advice?" The words seemed to force themselves from Hannah's lips almost without her consent.

Marjorie regarded her with grave surprise. "I do not understand you," she said, a tinge of coldness in her tone; "in what way does it seem to you that I am not doing so?"

"Why, of course you know—I wonder if it is possible that you don't know—what the gossips are saying about you?"

The blood mounted in rich waves to Marjorie's temples, but she kept her voice quiet.

"What do you mean, Hannah? Speak plainly, please."

"I wish I hadn't spoken at all," said Hannah, conscience smitten over the look on the girl's face. "Perhaps you don't know a thing about it, and I thought you did and gloried in the way you were taking it—going straight on doing what was right, and letting folks talk."

"Hannah, I shall have to ask you, if you are my friend, to tell me just what you mean. This is all new to me."

"I wish I had been dumb before I began to say anything about it," said poor Hannah. "Why, it is just this—it is pretty near as hard for me as it is for you—it is about Ralph, you know; they say, the gossips do, that you and he are too intimate. Part of what they say has some truth in it—that he used to think the world of you before he was married, and never got over it; but they say you never did either, and that you two are keeping company as well as you can, since there is a wife in the way. And because the woman always gets the most blamed when people gossip, they say that the way you treat Estelle is shameful, and they wonder she doesn't go insane; and, well—a lot of tales that it is a disgrace to repeat, and that I don't think deserve a second thought."

She had turned her face away from Marjorie, and was stitching rapidly. Had she been watching her, she would have seen the blood recede, and the girl's face grow very pale. With a great effort, Marjorie held her voice to something like naturalness while she questioned further.

"Hannah, nothing but the story in its completeness can satisfy me now. Who says these things? Where have you heard them? To what extent are they talked?"

"That I am sure I don't know," said Hannah, nervously stitching a sleeve to its lining upside down. "The first I heard of it, to pay any attention to it, was one evening when Jack Taylor came to me feeling dreadfully because he had got into a quarrel with a worthless fellow on the wharf and knocked him down. That was after he was converted and had given up such doings. I insisted upon knowing what was the cause of the quarrel so that I could decide how much provocation Jack had had, and I discovered that the fellow had insulted you and Ralph; and because you were my friend, and Ralph my brother, Jack thought he ought to take up a cudgel in your defense. At least, he was roused to such a pitch of anger by what was said, that he went to fighting before he knew what he was about. I questioned Jack so closely that it began to open my eyes to the kind of talk that was going on, and I followed it up a little. I made Susie Miller tell me what some of the factory girls were saying, and I found out that Bill Seber had had a pitched battle with another loafer for the same reason. That was to please

Susie, because she did not like Glyde Douglass's brother-in-law to be insulted. They are faithful to their friends, those factory people, in the ways that they understand best. That is about all there is of it, Marjorie. I've heard enough since to let me understand that it was general talk among the class of people who depend on such talk for their daily food; and I supposed that of course you and Ralph knew what was being said and treated it with the disdain which it deserved. Ralph generally knows what is going on. As I said when I began, I just gloried in the way you took it. It seemed to me the only sensible way, but of course I was a good deal hurt to think that he should pitch into me as he did. The only thing I could think of was that it was Estelle's influence, because she didn't like anything about me, and never did; but when you began to criticize too, that seemed almost too much to bear. I wonder if it can be possible that Ralph doesn't know either what is being said?"

"You may be sure," said Marjorie, "that your brother has not a thought of such a thing. Regard for his wife, to say nothing of justice to me, would have compelled him to take notice of it if he had. I confess that I am overwhelmed. I knew it was a wicked world, but I certainly did not know that there was anyone who would dare to couple my name and that of a married man."

From that point on the two young women seemed to change places. From being on the defensive, Hannah turned exhorter and would-be comforter, reiterating her earnest belief that dignified silence and a steady continuance of the same line of conduct was the best way to meet such attacks. She affirmed that any other way was equivalent to a confession of wrongdoing. She declared more than once that she wished she had been deaf and dumb for a year rather than to have brought such a look of misery to the face of her friend. Certainly she exerted herself to her utmost to make Marjorie's pain less bitter; but viewed from that young woman's standpoint, the afternoon was a wretched failure. It seemed to stretch its length along interminably. She put away with dignity, after a little, all personal questions and essayed to hold the interest to the aprons and dresses and sacks that were being prepared for the sewing class; but she felt all the time an almost overpowering desire to get away to her own room, and look this intolerable humiliation in the face, and decide what she should do with it. Jack Taylor, and even Bill Seber, resorting to hand-to-hand fights in her defense!

Mrs. Edmonds performed her part of the afternoon's program to perfection. Nothing could have been daintier or more homelike in appearance than that tea table, and more toothsome viands had probably never been spread before Hannah Bramlett—who was a stranger to the finer details of the culinary art; yet even this was a failure. Hannah, who was grieved for Marjorie and angry with herself, tried in vain to talk commonplaces with Mrs. Edmonds. She was at all times tempted to be silent before a third person and inclined to be half afraid of Mrs. Edmonds. As for Marjorie, she seemed to have to struggle with herself in order to utter even the few sentences that she did; and her mother, much bewildered, tugged at her end of the burden as best she could and found herself wishing once more, as she had a hundred times before, that Marjorie had never met a person who bore the name of Bramlett. The family seemed destined to bring trouble of some sort upon her.

"What is it, dear?" she asked, as soon as the door

had closed upon Hannah's departing footsteps; "was it all so much of a failure that you cannot rally from the disappointment? It is too much to expect of a Bramlett, I suppose, that she should have sense enough to accept adverse criticism kindly."

"Do not be hard on poor Hannah," Marjorie said, trying to smile; "she bore the criticism quite as well as could have been expected under the circumstances. I do not think any good results will follow, however. Hannah has what I suppose is a false idea of the way in which gossip that has no foundation in truth should be treated; but one can respect her for being willing to move bravely forward in the line of what she thinks is duty, despite wicked tongues."

And then, to Marjorie's intense relief, a woman belonging to her mother's Bible class came to claim her confidential attention; and the girl was able to escape to her own room, where she locked and bolted herself in and began to walk up and down her room like a caged creature, doing what Marjorie Edmonds had not done three times in her life—wringing her hands in a kind of passion of despairing indignation. I am sure there are pure-hearted girls by the score who can understand just how terrible it was to her to think of her name being bandied about the streets, not only by the thoughtless and careless, but by the coarse and low. Perhaps the deepest sting in this experience came to her through the thought that she was, in part at least, to blame. Had not her mother warned her? And had she not found again and again that her mother's intuitions were to be trusted? that her mother's estimate of the world was truer than her own? Yet she had been so wise in her own conceit, so sure that in this particular case it was not wisdom but anxiety which had dictated the warning, that she had allowed it to slip from her almost unheeded and gone on in much the same way as before. Now, how was she to live through the humiliation of it all? Hannah's straight-forward course, mistaken though it might be consid-ered, was worthy of all praise as compared with hers. Hannah had had an object in view and had accom-plished it. Jack had steadily improved under her tute-lage, and she was able to see each day some definite result of her efforts.

But—so Marjorie sternly told herself—her own plans from the first had been ill-formed and vague. She wanted to influence Ralph and Estelle for good, true; but could anything be more vague than that word "good"? What had she hoped to do, after all? What had she aimed at? And even in the most general sense, what had she accomplished? Worse than noth-ing. Estelle barely tolerated her; perhaps because she was compelled to—here this self-accusing spirit felt her cheeks burn with shame, there came to her such a feeling of certainty that Ralph had known all along of the infamous talk, and instead of making an effort to shield her had gone loftily on doing as he pleased. It was like him, indeed—this imagining himself "su-perior to public opinion" whenever it suited his passing fancy not to notice it. For the first time since his marriage, she let a feeling of burning indignation against this selfish man take possession of her heart. Before that it had been so full of pity for him, in view of the mistakes he was making, that there had been room for no other feeling. Now she let it have full sway.

Indignation and a sense of self-injury may, under some circumstances, be a good teacher. At this time it enabled Marjorie to get her mother's view of Ralph Bramlett and to realize, as she certainly had never done before, what an embodiment of selfishness he was. It enabled her also to realize what is perhaps one of the most important lessons that the young people of today have to learn; namely, that the views of good mothers are at all times worthy of careful consideration, and perhaps nine times out of ten are correct.

Among other questions claiming consideration was that trying one as to whether her mother must be told of the extent to which gossip was now meddling with them. If not, how was her anxiety to be satisfied as to the outcome of the afternoon's effort?

Fortunately other interests came in to help her in this. The late train brought Mr. Maxwell three days earlier than he could reasonably have been expected. He was with them at breakfast the next morning; and Mrs. Edmonds, in the relief at seeing him, forgot Hannah Bramlett.

It will be remembered that this good woman was indulging in certain strong hopes as to the outcome of this summer's companionship. It is true she had felt it her duty to write a very discouraging letter about them, but she, too, had done some reconsidering. The reply to that very letter had helped her.

"Do not be troubled as to myself," Mr. Maxwell wrote. "I am entering into this effort with eyes very wide open, and if I fail, I have certainly been duly warned. Above all, do not disturb Marjorie's peace by any confession of my feeling toward her. If I may have no other place, I certainly want to be to her as a brother, and I would not by any means have her startled into fear of me. Let the summer take care of itself. I confess I look toward it with eagerness."

A reasonable person might have been satisfied with the greeting that Marjorie gave their guest. She was openly and heartily glad to see him, and within twenty-four hours of his arrival their companionship was established on the old basis. Perhaps it might be said that the intimacy was greater than ever before. Marjorie, who had found it impossible to put away from her mind Hannah and Hannah's information, found herself on that first evening making a confidant of Mr. Maxwell, so far at least as to let him see how sorely she was being tried. He entered with even more heartiness into her feeling than she had expected; indeed, she will probably never know how he longed to visit some swift and condign punishment on the creatures who had dared to toss her name carelessly among them. For her sake he controlled himself and tried, after the first outburst of indignation, to treat the matter lightly.

"People must talk, you know," he said; "I remember I used to think that they were especially given to talk in this part of the world, and they naturally like to choose the choicest possible victims. Suppose we turn their thoughts into a new channel? Compel them, as it were, to talk about our two selves? I propose, with your permission, to be so constantly your companion for the summer that it will not be possible for even their ingenious tongues to separate our names."

Marjorie laughed, though her eyes shone suspiciously; she thought she recognized the delicate chivalry that was ready to sacrifice its own convenience to her welfare.

"But that would be only exchanging one of the victims," she said, mindful for a single instant of another warning of her mother's. "It would relieve poor Ralph, it is true, but what of the substitute?"

"The substitute enters into the snare with wide open eyes," he said cheerily. "In fact, that is a wrong figure; it is we who are preparing the snare for the unwary tongues of gossips, don't you see? I think I shall rather enjoy the situation."

It was such a hearty and apparently heart-free response that Marjorie was immediately relieved and reflected gleefully that in this one thing her mother was undoubtedly mistaken. Leonard Maxwell, who had loved a sister once, and lost her, had adopted her in the vacant place, and jubilantly did she receive him. No brother, she believed, could have been more appreciated. Certainly none could be more unselfish.

17

A Crisis

MRS. Estelle Bramlett was moving with an air of uncontrollable restlessness about her pretty parlor.

Although it was not the time of day for such employment, and she had no duster in hand, yet there was an apparent attempt to put things in order. She took up and laid down again various books and papers on the reading table, brushed away with her hand an imaginary fleck of dust, then suddenly turning, began to walk up and down the room, with those restless hands tightly grasped as if in an effort to control them.

Occasionally, although quite alone, she broke into snatches of talk, as though arguing with someone, and being responded to in such manner as to increase her indignation. Then she would recollect herself and, breaking off in the middle of a word, move swiftly over to her mantel and rearrange the elegant trifles thereon, as though all her thought was centered upon them, only to replace them in a very few seconds as they were before. Clearly the poor lady had been terribly moved.

Perhaps in reviewing all the days of her not very

happy existence she could not have found a harder one than this. It was all the harder to endure because, in some respects at least, her life had been pleasanter of late. For several months her husband had seemed less moody and disturbed; certainly his monetary troubles, whatever had caused them, appeared to be over. He had proved this in numberless extremely pleasant ways. Elegant and expensive trifles that she had admired but never expected to possess had been lavished upon her to such an extent that—and this constituted a large share of her enjoyment in them— she had had something new to show Marjorie Edmonds nearly every time she called.

That young woman continued to be the wife's special "thorn," although there had been improvement here also. Her husband did not now spend hours alone with Marjorie, as she had been sure that he did on two or three occasions, and as her intense jealousy had caused her to imagine that he did many times when such was not the case. He was punctilious now in his determination to have his wife with him whenever he called at the Edmonds's home; but he was willing, nay, anxious, to call there whenever the slightest pretext for doing so could be invented, and he was not ready to call anywhere else. It was rarely indeed that she could prevail upon him to spend an evening with her at her old home; he frankly admitted that he considered such evenings hopelessly stupid. Her sister Fannie was always entertaining some special guest in the front parlor, and Glyde could talk of nothing but her Mission scholars, or some such invigorating topic. When in a fit of indignation she had one day accused him of caring to see nobody but Marjorie Edmonds, he had been equally frank, assuring her that Marjorie was the only lady of his acquaintance worth talking to. So these were all old grievances and could not account for Estelle's miserable day.

It had begun, as she angrily told herself that most of her misery did begin, with either Hannah Bramlett or Marjorie Edmonds—this time it was Hannah. Mrs. Swansen, her Swedish washerwoman, had called upon her that morning on what she believed to be an errand of justice. Mrs. Swansen was no gossip, as she took pains to explain. She heard a great deal as she went from house to house, which as a rule "went in at one ear and out at the other." But on the day previous she had heard so cruel a story connecting itself with the name of Hannah Bramlett, and had heard it from so many different tongues, that she had made up her mind to come with it to Mrs. Bramlett to see if "the master," as she called the husband, could not do something with the talkers.

The story had been cruel indeed, worse than Estelle had before imagined. Being compelled to wait until her husband should return at night before she could do anything definite, directly as the door had closed upon Mrs. Swansen she had relieved her nerves by seizing her hat and walking with much more rapid steps than usual out to the Bramlett farm; arriving there, warm and almost breathless, to find the elder Mrs. Bramlett sitting drearily in a kitchen chair, with one corner of her apron doing duty every few minutes to wipe away a tear that would steal down her cheek, and Hannah dashing about among the dishes in a way that betokened strong excitement.

"What is the matter?" asked Mrs. Estelle, arrested by the tears—her mother-in-law rarely made such exhibition. "Where is Father Bramlett? He isn't worse, is he?"

"He is in bed," said his wife, shaking her head

drearily. "He is clear tuckered out this morning, and no wonder; he has had a stroke that I just expect he will never get up from."

"A stroke!" said Mrs. Estelle, startled. "You don't mean of paralysis?"

"No," said Hannah, "of tongues! That is worse."

"I wish I had a stroke of something," murmured the mother, "before I let that meddling, gossiping Mr. Sharp up to see him; I might have known something would come of it."

"Oh!" said Mrs. Estelle; she thought she comprehended. "I don't think I would worry about that. For my part, I believe it is just as well. Somebody would have told him sooner or later; you can't keep a father in ignorance of his daughter's doings, even if it were wise to do so."

"It doesn't happen to be his daughter that is troubling him," said Hannah, with a sort of grim triumph; "it is something of vastly more importance. But I suppose you know all about it, and have this long time. It is only his father and mother and sister who must be kept in ignorance until they hear things from strangers."

Estelle's face was paling under the possibilities that this language suggested.

"What are you talking about?" she asked sharply. "Can't you speak plain English when you have anything to say?"

"Hannah," said her mother, putting down her apron and speaking in a tone of grave rebuke, "why do you talk as though you believed it? There isn't a word of truth in it, not a word. I never thought so for a moment. What I am worried over is that your father, being weak and feeble, cannot rise above it, and had a

sleepless night over it; and sleepless nights are dangerous things for a man in his condition."

Estelle in her excitement, and in her fear of she
knew not what, fairly stamped her foot as she said:

"What *are* you talking about! It seems strange that
you must wait to have an argument before you tell me
what has happened."

"Nothing has happened except some more talk,"
said the mother with dignity; under her daughter-in-
law's disrespect she was overcoming her tears. "I let
Mr. Sharp in last night to see Father. He was so
anxious to have a talk with him, and Father had been
so kind of quiet and lonesome all day, I thought it
would do him good. Ralph hasn't been to see him for
three days, and I knew he was grieving over it and
needed heartening up; but I made a dreadful mistake.
What did he do but go to work and tell him a lot of
stuff that I suppose you have heard—though not a
breath of it has come to us, but you seem to hear all
the stories that are going—about Ralph running the
liquor store at Marsdon Place that all that fuss has
been made about. People have got it around, it seems,
that Ralph is at the head of the business, and Clark
and the other man who run it are only hired by him.
They say he is there every day, and two or three times
a day, and that the lease for the building is signed by
him, and that the men have to report to him every
month and get their wages, and he pockets the earnings. All stuff, the whole of it! Between eight o'clock
last night and this morning I suppose I told Father a
hundred times that I wondered at him for having the
patience to listen to such out and out folly. But you
see he is feeble, a great deal feebler than anybody,
except me, senses, and he couldn't get away from it. I
don't believe he slept an hour all night. He would just

lie there and think; and every once in a while he would give a groan, softly like, as though he was afraid of disturbing me, and say, 'My son, a rumseller! My one boy, that I thought I brought up to hate it, and fight against it, and vote against it! O God! forgive me; I must have failed in my duty awfully, or such a curse would not have fallen upon me. How can I go and meet my Maker and tell him that the boy he gave me to take care of for him is getting his living by ruining lives?' It would have made a stone cry just to hear him."

Mrs. Bramlett's apron was needed again before her sentence was completed. With the last word she retired entirely behind it and cried softly; the poor little woman never did anything in a loud, fierce way. But Mrs. Estelle was angry.

"I should not have cried," she burst forth fiercely. "I should have been indignant. I should have ordered a man from the house who talked about my son in that way. I never heard anything like it—coming into his own home and slandering him vilely before his father and mother, and they merely crying over it! The man shall be arrested for slander and tried and punished. I don't care if he is seventy years old; if he were seven hundred, it should not save him. Hannah, I should think you at least might have had spirit enough to stand up for your brother and tell that creature what you thought of him."

It was Hannah's opportunity. Could she be expected to do other than use it?

"Oh no," she said; "I believed every word he uttered, of course! And just as soon as I get the work done, I'm going to rush down to Ralph's office and tell him he is a disgrace to the family and he ought to be ashamed of himself. That is the way to manage gossip, don't you know it?"

"I understand your insinuations," said Mrs. Estelle with great dignity, "and consider them beneath my notice. Of course this is a very different matter. In your case, you provoke the stories by your daily doings, while as regards your brother there is not the shadow of a foundation for them to work upon. Well, Mother, I might as well go home if there is nothing I can do. I am sorry Father Bramlett allowed himself to be disturbed by a false and foolish story; one would suppose him to be too old a man to be so easily deceived"; and not deigning to take further notice of Hannah, she turned and swept from the room.

She deceived them both by her sudden calmness; she did not deceive herself. Never in her life had her passionate nature been in such a whirl of excitement. Was it anger, or pain, or fear? or a mixture of all three? Was she angry with the repeaters of the story, or with the foundation on which it rested? What did she fear in regard to her husband? Not certainly that he was, in so many words, a rumseller; but—she did not allow her swiftly flying thoughts to formulate themselves in distinct phrases, yet despite her trying to push them aside there came to her reminders of facts which she had not understood. Her husband's sudden apparent prosperity where before he had been on the eve of disgrace. He had brought her one evening, with a triumphant smile, receipts for every one of those bills about which she had haunted him, saying that he presumed she would like to keep them among her treasures. He had responded promptly and freely to her calls for money for household or personal expenses. He had been lavish of his gifts to a degree that she had never noticed before. She had believed him to

have speculated with some of his salary and to have apparently failed, and then to have met with sudden success; but—was this the explanation?

More strange than this experience had been the lately acquired habit of coming home to luncheon, or of darting in perhaps at ten or eleven o'clock for something forgotten, and explaining that business had detained him in town until that hour. What business? When she had questioned, it had always been "matters connected with the firm, in which she could have no interest." Was it certain that she had no interest in them? Oh, she had no fear, of course, of anything like what those Bramletts had allowed that odious old man to pour into their ears; but was it possible that he might have permitted himself, for a large increase of salary, to take the general supervision of the retail liquor-store which was so hated in that part of the town? Perhaps some member of the firm was conducting the business and paying her husband to oversee it for him? Could this be possible?

She did not, as has been said, put the thought into definite form before her; she simply pushed its shadow from her and hated it, and grew more angry every moment over its bare possibility. Was Estelle Bramlett, then, such a fierce and consistent temperance advocate that she shrank thus from the smell of its contact? One must move carefully here and try to do her justice. She hated the liquor traffic certainly— all respectable people belonging to her world did. Like her husband, she had been brought up among the "temperance fanatics." Then did she hate the distiller? Well, that was different; it was *wholesale;* and anyway, Ralph was but its bookkeeper—books had to be kept. She would have preferred, certainly she would much have preferred, that he should be a lawyer, for instance.

But would she have preferred him to keep books at the shoe factory for eight hundred dollars a year, rather than for the distillery for fifteen hundred a year? No, distinctly she would not. They could not live on eight hundred a year. What was the use of considering it? But a retail liquor store set down in their midst! a store that her friend Mrs. Hemmingway hated with all her righteous soul—a store that Mrs. Gordon Potter unhesitatingly called a rum saloon! Mrs. Edson declined to call upon the wife of the man employed there, because she would not have the wife of a rumseller on her calling list. Ah! all this was distinctly another matter. Mrs. Ralph Bramlett knew that in the circle in which she chiefly moved, to be the wife of a rumseller meant social ostracism. To be connected, however remotely, with the retail liquor trade meant a distinct drop from unquestioned respectability to the ranks of those who were *talked about*. Mrs. Bramlett could not endure it. Hannah Bramlett had been a sufficiently bitter cup for her to drain. If Ralph had been inveigled into a closer connection with this business, had dared to enter into it without consulting her, without even allowing her to know it, she simply would not tolerate it. Nothing should tempt her to do so. Ralph Bramlett should see that even a wife would not endure everything.

In this mood she went home, and in the mood she remained during the long hours of that trying day. Nay, her indignation increased as Glyde came, in the course of the afternoon, frightened and anxious. Glyde had heard the story, heard other forms of it, some of them more trying than the first. What did Estelle think would have started such reports? Did she think Ralph could have said anything to lead people to suppose such an absurdity? Did she not think he ought at once to be told, in order to take measures to have the people understand that there was absolutely no foundation for the stories?

Estelle did not choose to say what she thought, beyond the fact that she "evidently had occasion to be ashamed of all her relatives, since they were so ready to listen to lies." She hurried Glyde away more disturbed than when she came in, told her to rush over to her dear friend Marjorie and publish all the gossip she had heard against her brother-in-law, and be sure to let that immaculate Mr. Maxwell hear every word.

In this mood, growing stronger with its nursing, she met her husband when he came home late, tired and harassed by a burden that he was carrying quite alone.

18

REVELATIONS

DOES anyone need to be told how Ralph Bramlett was received? There had been stormy periods in his married life before; certainly none stormier than this. Estelle waited not even for her husband to make ready for dinner. She followed him to his dressing room, and while he tried to wash from his hands the soil which had accumulated that day—some of it soil that no soap could cleanse away—she burst out upon him; not with questions, not even with a hint that she had no faith in the stories, but with as complete a tirade against his acts as though every syllable of the gossip had been proved. Had she not been too much occupied with herself, she would have noted that he grew deathly pale; but he did not in any other way make known that he heard her. He went on washing those hands that were well shaped and had always been a comfort to him, with punctilious care. That, and his silence, exasperated his wife still more.

"It is like you," she said, "to insult me by this silence and unconcern. Do not pretend that you have no regard for what people say about you; I know better.

You would give all you are worth to stand well in the eyes of Marjorie Edmonds, even if you care for no one else." Then he spoke:

"It is not necessary to drag her name into this remarkable scene, I should think."

Perhaps he could not have said anything that would have added greater fuel to the flame.

"Oh no," his wife said, "of course not; her *name* even must be shielded from everything disagreeable, while I, your wife, must endure everything. You would better think of your own name, since you care nothing for mine. Have you not a word to say for yourself? What foundation is there for these infamous stories? You have been doing something to set tongues afloat. I have felt that for some time, but the hour has come when I demand to know what. I will not be kept on surmises any longer."

"You seem to me to be well posted," he said very quietly. "I am sure you have been pouring out information ever since I entered the house. What other particulars are there that you desire to know?"

"I desire to know the truth and not to be insulted with sarcasms. What have you been doing in an underhanded way to start these reports concerning you? Have you consented to be the tool of those rummakers to the extent that you are looking after their retail trade? If I had supposed that my recent gifts, of which I have been so proud, came from such a source, I would have thrown them in their faces rather than ever worn or shown them."

Ralph Bramlett straightened himself up at last and gave over trying to cleanse his hands; there were ink stains on them still. But he turned and gave his wife his full attention and spoke in the low tone that means, with him, suppressed wrath.

"You shall have every possible particular, Mrs. Bramlett; had I known that you were suffering in that direction I would have relieved your anxiety before. The gossips have been unusually successful this time; they have verged very near the truth. A few points only need correction. Instead of being an agent for the firm which I represent, I have the honor to be a principal in this matter. I have rented the corner store that has roused your wrath, and the men in charge are my clerks. I have found the business much more lucrative than that of bookkeeping, and the luxuries in which I have freely indulged you for the last few months are excellent proofs of the same. Is that sufficiently full information, or would you like to know something more? If so, do not hesitate to question me. I shall have pleasure in giving you every possible advantage over others in the amount of knowledge which you possess."

He could not surely have understood how cruel was the information he was pouring out, else he would have chosen a less dangerous time and a less insulting manner for his communication.

In truth, he was himself so much under excitement that it is questionable if he realized the force of his words; but it is also true that he did not understand the extent to which his wife was prejudiced against the retail liquor traffic. It is to be feared that he did not give her credit for strong principles in any direction; and the social degradation of such a business, as it would affect her, was something that he had not as yet thought of. She had borne the salary paid by the distillery, not only with equanimity, but to his certain knowledge had indignantly repelled Marjorie Edmonds's hints of available openings where the salary was not so large. Perhaps he could not be expected to realize what a difference the management of a liquor saloon would make in her estimation.

He was not left long in doubt. Estelle, whose every vestige of self-control had departed from her long before his studiedly polite sentences were concluded, burst upon him with a fury that for the moment half frightened him. She poured the vials of her wrath and contempt upon him in language such as he could not have imagined from her lips. She called him by every name suggesting hypocrisy that her imagination could frame; and her anger, instead of expending itself in this outburst, seemed to rise as she talked. Her words were checked at last, only by a realization of the fact that her husband had turned from her and hurried out of the room; nor was she greatly astonished when, a few minutes later, she heard the front door close with a bang.

Lena came to the door soon afterward to say that dinner was waiting on the table, and Mr. Bramlett had gone out again without eating a mouthful. Some impulse had prompted Estelle to rush to the door and lock it the moment she found herself alone; therefore, she was safe from Lena's intrusion. She had just presence of mind enough and sufficient command over her voice to call out to Lena that Mr. Bramlett had been unexpectedly summoned downtown, and that they would wait dinner until his return, then she gave herself up utterly to her misery. The patient Lena carefully removed and set to keep warm the dishes prepared for dinner, and settled herself to await further orders. An hour passed, and the master of the house did not return. Mrs. Bramlett came downstairs in the course of time and explained to Lena that she was afraid Mr. Bramlett would be detained beyond any reasonable hour for dinner. It was not worthwhile to keep the hot dishes waiting much longer; probably he would take only a glass of milk and some biscuits when he returned. For herself, she did not care to eat dinner alone; she would wait for him. But if he did not come in another half hour, Lena might clear away the dinner and consider herself dismissed for the night. Then she came back to the parlor and began her aimless fidget about the table and mantel that has been already described. With every passing moment her anxiety and indignation grew apace—anxiety to know how it would all end, indignation against her husband for adding yet this strain to her horrible day.

"It was no wonder that he ran away!" she told herself with a bitterly curling lip. If he should want to hide himself so completely that he could never be found, it would not be in the least strange after having brought such insufferable disgrace upon them all and been all but the murderer of his own father. She had not spared him this thrust also, in her ungovernable excitement; perhaps she had even dwelt upon it, because she could see that he winced under the words as nothing that she had said before had made him. She was by no means through, she assured herself. If Ralph thought to treat her as though she were a naughty child and stay away until she had recovered from her first excitement in the expectation of being received afterward as though nothing had happened, he would find himself utterly mistaken. She had not the slightest idea of enduring such a humiliation as he had planned for her. He must get out of that disgraceful business tomorrow, so utterly that it could at once be said, and with truth, that he had nothing whatever to do with it; nothing less than that would satisfy her. If he did not—she did not finish her thought. At the moment she heard voices, familiar voices, chatting and laughing. They were on the piazza now; she heard a merry sentence of Mr. Maxwell's as they waited for the bell to be answered. Of all the horrible times for a call from Marjorie Edmonds, this seemed to the half-distracted wife the worst. She would not see them; she would send word that she was not at home; no, that would not do, the parlor was brightly lighted and could be distinctly seen from the piazza. Well, then, she was engaged, very especially engaged, and could see no one. But she must have been observed from the windows, standing in the middle of the room doing nothing. Besides, it was too late; Lena was already at the door; she must see them.

They came in gaily, with cheerful greetings. Evidently they had heard nothing. They ran in quite often, these two, by way of helping to carry out their compact. It was all important for watching eyes and gossiping tongues to know that they were on extremely friendly terms with the dwellers in this house. As often as possible they chose an hour when the master of the house would not be at home; but on this evening, Marjorie had an errand with Estelle. They had come late so as to be able to make their stay short, but friendly.

The errand accomplished, Marjorie lingered, she hardly knew why. What could have happened to Estelle? She had never seen her in quite such a mood. She talked and laughed nervously, giving slight, apparently frightened, starts at every sound outside; she seemed not to know, some of the time, what she was saying. Could she be on the eve of a serious illness? If she was quite alone, ought they to leave her?

Suddenly her anxiety was broken in upon in the most startling manner. There was a curious fumbling at the night latch, as though one not acquainted with it was trying to enter; then the master of the house shambled into the hall, into the parlor, his face red, his eyes bleared, his whole appearance as unlike Ralph Bramlett as could be conceived.

"Halloo, Madge! you here!" he shouted, "and he's with you, of course. Say, why don't you two get married? You might as well; you've been long enough about it. There's nothing like married happiness, I tell you! What you doing here anyhow, you old smooth-faced hypocrite? You're a hypocrite! Do you know that? If it hadn't been for you, Marj'rie and I would have been all right. I want you to get out of my house; do you hear?"

Up to this moment the three listeners had stood transfixed with horror, the two women with almost equally blanched faces and strained eyes. Marjorie was the first to speak.

"He is insane!" she whispered. "Estelle dear, do not go near him! Oh, Mr. Maxwell!"

"Do not be frightened," said Mr. Maxwell, recovering speech; "it is not insanity. Mrs. Bramlett, let me manage this. Come, sir, you are not in a condition to appear before ladies. Let me help you to your room."

There was a moment's struggle, a half-insane yell from the master of the house, a determined grip from the hand of his guest, and the other yielded and allowed himself to be led muttering away.

"Your master has been taken ill," Marjorie heard Mr. Maxwell explaining to the frightened Lena. "Show me the way to his room, and then get me a pitcher of ice water. No, we shall not need a physician at present, my good girl. I know just what to do for him. It is a sudden attack that will soon pass."

"He is intoxicated!" said his wife, her lips as white as snow. Marjorie gave a low wail, as though it was she who had been stricken, and dropped back among the cushions, powerless for a moment to move or speak. Had the playmate of her childhood come to this? To one of her belief and environment, death itself was as nothing compared with such sorrow as this. She sat up after a moment and looked pitifully at Estelle. She knew not a single word to say to her; it was no time for pity, for sympathy even. She could not wonder that the wife stood as she had when her husband had been taken from the room, with her eyes fixed as if fascinated with it, on that closed door. To intrude a word upon her would have been to Marjorie horrible. After what seemed to her hours, but was in reality only a few minutes, Mr. Maxwell came downstairs.

"I have got him to bed," he said to Estelle. "He is entirely quiet now; sleeping, indeed, and you need be under no apprehension in regard to him. At the same time, if you would like me to remain part of the night I will—"

She interrupted him, "I would not. I have not the least desire for your presence. I know quite well what I shall do. The remainder of the night will be just long enough for me to make what preparations I must, and with the first streak of dawn I will go to my father's house that I was a fool ever to leave. Thank heaven I have friends who can take care of me; I do not need you."

Marjorie started up and came to her side. "Oh, Estelle dear," she said tenderly, "don't speak such words! You do not know what you are saying."

Estelle turned upon her fiercely. "Do I not, indeed! You would counsel me, I suppose, to stay beside a drunken husband. You would do it perhaps? It is a pity you have not the chance! For myself, no power on earth would make me so disgrace myself; I have borne enough."

"Mrs. Bramlett," said Mr. Maxwell, answering the mute appeal in Marjorie's eyes, "we cannot wonder at your excitement and—and pain; but let me remind you that your husband is not a drunkard. He is probably not in the habit of using stimulants and has been overcome in an unexpected way; it may be by some accident."

"Oh yes," interrupted Marjorie eagerly; "he must be the victim of some plot; I have read of such things."

"I tell you," said Estelle, stamping her foot, "I want nothing from you—neither sympathy nor explanation. I want you to go, and let me alone. Do you think I do not know that if it had not been for you my husband would never have so disgraced himself, would never have made my life miserable? You have intended from the very first to ruin my home; I wish you joy of having accomplished it."

"Mrs. Bramlett!" interposed Mr. Maxwell in his sternest tones. "We are certainly willing to hope now that you do not know what you are saying. I will take Miss Edmonds away at once, because I do not choose to hear her further insulted. In your saner moments, you will doubtless wish to apologize for words that you of course know to be false."

19

"I Don't Like It"

MR. Leonard Maxwell sat, with an open letter before him, staring thoughtfully into space. He had been so sitting for perhaps three quarters of an hour. There seemed, as he from time to time referred to it, to be some connection between the letter and his thought; yet it was a very short letter to have roused such grave and apparently unsatisfactory study. Less than a dozen lines comprised the whole; it ran thus:

MY DEAR LEONARD—*At last the impossible has been accomplished, and I am to have a vacation. To be entirely honest, I've done what you said I would, overworked. We have had a good deal of sickness this spring, and I've been run to death. When I got where I could not sleep nights, even though I had a chance, I determined to call a halt. I've arranged with Weston and Barnes to divide my calls between them, and I'm planning for a whole month of play. The question is, do you want me to come and play with you? I know you are at work; perhaps I can play for you when I can't with you. If there is room*

*where you are staying, wire me, and I'll come on at
once.*

> As ever, FRANK.

When the three quarters had lengthened into an
hour, Mr. Maxwell sprang up, letter in hand, and
hurried downstairs as though an idea had just occurred to him.

Mrs. Edmonds was in her sitting room alone.

"May I come in?" he asked; "I have a very large
favor to ask. I hardly know how to commence it,
because I am aware that you do not keep a boarding-
house; but—do you suppose you could be induced to
take pity on another man if I will agree to share my
room with him?" He laughed at Mrs. Edmonds's look
of bewilderment. "You think my sudden attack of
benevolence needs explanation? Why, it is just this
way; there are only two of us, my brother Frank and
I. Frank is a hard-worked physician who hasn't taken
a vacation since he graduated and now is to have a
month of enforced rest. Mother is abroad, as you
know, so he cannot be with her; and he naturally
thought of me. Is it asking too much?"

Mrs. Edmonds, greatly surprised, considered the
pros and cons, expressed courteous interest in his
brother and polite regret that she had not more room
to spare in her house, then asked tentatively what
seemed to be an embarrassing question. "Am I to
understand that you very much desire to make this
arrangement, Mr. Maxwell?"

That gentleman hesitated, a flush rising on his
usually pale face and slowly spreading until it reached
his temples. He laughed in response to her questioning look.

"Mrs. Edmonds, do not make me too much

ashamed of myself," he said hurriedly; "I have been fighting a battle with selfishness for the last hour. My brother Frank is the best fellow in the world, and there is not a man living that I so much desire to see; yet—can you understand a little how hard it is for me to deliberately put away from myself a portion of this summer?"

She felt that he must know she understood, and smiled gravely as she said, "Yet it must be a pleasure to you to think of having an entire month with the brother from whom you have been so much separated."

"Of course it must," he said quickly, "and if you can arrange for it without too much inconvenience I shall be grateful; otherwise, I ought to plan to meet him at some other point."

The evident distress in his tone as he added that last thought touched the mother's heart.

"Oh! we shall be able to arrange for it," she said; "it is only you who will be inconvenienced, on account of the limited number of rooms."

He thanked her hurriedly and went away to send his telegram, while Mrs. Edmonds sought her daughter and began to plan for the addition to their family.

"I don't like it," Marjorie said with a shadow on her face. "We are so cozy now and have such good times together, we three; a fourth will be almost sure to spoil it all; it isn't within reason to expect the other brother to be so nice as this one. Mamma, I am even afraid we shall dislike him."

"That would certainly be sad," said Mrs. Edmonds, breaking into a laugh; "but since he is this one's brother and wants to visit him, we could do no less than receive him; could we, dear?"

"Oh! of course not, but it will be disagreeable; you

see if it isn't. He will not be in the least like Leonard; brothers never are."

With which most ambiguous sentence she turned away without catching her mother's slight, quickly suppressed sigh; her daughter's preference for the present Mr. Maxwell was too outspoken for her to build any castles upon.

In truth, Mrs. Edmonds's castles troubled her not a little during these days. Absolutely certain of Mr. Maxwell's desires—and he made it apparent to her that they grew stronger with each passing day—she could not see that her daughter thought of him as other than a very exceptionally choice brother. Sometimes her impatience with the obtuseness of a girl who was so quick to observe in all other lines brought her to the verge of speech; it was only Mr. Maxwell's reiterated assurance that he would not for the world have Marjorie's peace disturbed that held the mother to silence. Meantime, the policy of the two to be always seen together was being literally carried out. The mornings, on Mr. Maxwell's part, were given to uninterrupted work; but every afternoon found him at leisure to walk, or ride, or read, according as Marjorie's mood dictated. Quite often now she yielded to her mother's wish to be left undisturbed at home and took long walks or drives with Mr. Maxwell.

Occasionally—and as the days passed this grew to be of frequent occurrence—they would call for Hannah Bramlett to accompany them. These excursions were more often than otherwise errands of mercy to the factory portion of the town. The gaping world must have looked on with exceeding interest during those long, bright summer days, as Mr. Maxwell drove gaily by, or sauntered leisurely along, with Marjorie Edmonds and Hannah Bramlett for his companions.

It was Mr. Maxwell who had first suggested Hannah as a companion. At least when Marjorie was expressing her indignation concerning the gossip and her sorrow that a good, well-meaning girl like Hannah Bramlett should have been its victim, he asked to what extent it had victimized her; and when Marjorie explained that she seemed to have almost no intimate friends and that some foolish people apparently stood aloof from her on account of the stories, though no respectable person believed them, he had said, "There is a remedy for such a state of things. Why don't we cultivate her acquaintance? If we were to call in friendly fashion and invite her to drive with us, for instance, occasionally, wouldn't it be helpful?"

Marjorie had clasped her hands in an ecstasy of satisfaction.

"It is the very thing!" she exclaimed. "Why do you always think of things to be done, and why do they never come to me?"

It is doubtful if Mr. Maxwell meant to inaugurate such a state of affairs as immediately followed. He might even have kept silence had he known that he would be so literally and constantly interpreted. Marjorie planned a walk for that very afternoon, with Hannah Bramlett for an accompaniment, and two days afterward proposed that she drive with them to the Schuyler farm where they were going to call. It was certainly hard to have a third person so frequently interposed; but Mr. Maxwell could not, despite this, help enjoying Hannah's evident comfort in these excursions and her mother's no-less-evident satisfaction over them. For the Bramletts were in more trouble during these days, and whatever contributed to their sense of self-respect was so much balm to their wounded sensibilities.

It was now nearly a month since the painful episode in Ralph Bramlett's parlor. All the people who suffered that night had a chance to grow accustomed to the pain and to try to accommodate themselves to the inevitable. So far as Mr. Maxwell and Marjorie's share in the scene, they had kept it quite to themselves; Marjorie could not be sure whether or not any other person knew of the manner of Ralph's homecoming and its disgraceful cause. How much the girl Lena surmised, or how far she was to be trusted, were matters of which Marjorie could not be certain; she deemed it safer to remain in ignorance than to ask questions. With regard to the insulting words spoken to herself, she had received from Estelle Bramlett a cold little note offering a semi-apology for any "thoughtless words" that she might have spoken in her distraction. Mr. Bramlett, she explained, had been overcome by fatigue and had hastily swallowed a tonic by a physician's advice; it proved to contain alcohol, and his system being entirely unaccustomed to the drug had responded promptly, hence the disgraceful scene which, she was sorry to say, Marjorie and her friend had witnessed. She supposed it was not necessary to remind her of the importance of its not being made known.

It is doubtful if Marjorie was not even more hurt by this note of apology. She showed it to Mr. Maxwell, her lip quivering a little as she said:

"That last fling is hard to bear; she was half insane with fear and grief the other night, and it did not matter what she said; but this is premeditated."

Mr. Maxwell had returned the note with a grave face, and had answered, "Still, Marjorie, you can afford to feel only sorrow for her. She is mistaken if she supposes that a few swallows of prescribed medicine put her husband into the condition that he was that night. I have the very gravest fears for his future. His is a temperament with which alcohol makes short work."

Marjorie had paled before the suggestion that his words implied; she said passionately that she *could not* have this friend of her childhood sink into a drunkard's grave. Why did he have fears? Did he not believe in prayer? and had not he covenanted with her to pray for Ralph until he was converted?

"No," he said in grave earnestness; "forgive me, Marjorie, if I pain you, but I did not make any such promise. Grace is free; there is no forcing process in the plan of salvation. What Mr. Bramlett *wills* must be; if he *will not* be saved, be sure that God will respect even that."

"Then what is the promise worth, 'Whatsoever ye ask in my name, believing, ye shall receive'?"

"My friend it is worth everything. If, in answer to my prayer, I receive God's assurance that that for which I plead *shall be,* then indeed I can continue to 'ask, believing;' it is like the solid rock to my feet, and I know I can claim its fulfillment though I may have to wait a lifetime, nay, long after my life here is over. Have you such an assurance in regard to Ralph Bramlett?"

"Yes," she said steadily; "I know Ralph will yet receive what I most desire for him."

"Then thank God for the assurance and hold to it. He never fails."

Yet Marjorie, even at the moment, could not help wondering whether the feeling that she had was assurance or a determination on her part that what she desired should be. The thought made her say almost complainingly:

"Sometimes, Leonard, I cannot help wondering why the way of life was made so hard, in a sense. Hard for obstinate natures, I mean. Why must one's diseased will be held in such honor? Why not save men in spite of themselves?"

"When you give entrance to such thoughts, do you remember what salvation really is? Would heaven be heaven to me if I did not want to be there, hated the Power that reigns there, desired to be free from his presence?"

"Of course not. I meant, why did not God compel people to love him whether they would or not?"

"Can you *make* yourself love a person, Marjorie?"

"No," she said, blushing under his earnest gaze; "but God could make me."

"Could he? What would such love be worth? How much could it be depended on?"

"Oh!" she said, turning away half impatiently, "I know I am talking nonsense; but it does not seem to me sometimes as though I could have people managing their lives in the way they do. I cannot help thinking that if I had the power I would *make* them do differently."

"I understand you; God himself uses that power continually, I suppose. 'The remainder of wrath he restrains,' you remember; but when it comes to forcing love and confidence, I can imagine what utterly disappointing machines we should make. I would not care for the allegiance of the very dearest being on earth, if it were a forced allegiance. Sometimes I think that this world of punishment about which we talk so much and understand so little is simply the gathering together of beings who *will not* accept the destiny for which they were intended, in a place by themselves, away from those whose bliss would only make their self-ruin the more complete. In other words, that God does for them the best that he can, since they refuse his best."

Poor Marjorie was obliged to confess to herself that she had very little outward appearance on which to build her assurance for Ralph Bramlett's future. It is true that he might have been taken unawares on that fateful evening, and such an experience might not happen to him again; but he was undeniably, and indeed openly, engaged in the liquor traffic. From the evening that he had boldly proclaimed it to his wife, he had not made the slightest attempt at further concealment. Indeed, before the next day was over he went to his father, and in a long argument labored to convince him that the step he had taken was in the interest of good citizenship. He had protected the imperiled corner from unprincipled persons and established a law-abiding business about which not a whisper of reasonable complaint could be made. His sister Hannah repeated these and kindred statements to Marjorie, her lip curling over them the while. Once she interrupted herself to ask, "Did you suppose that Ralph could ever become such a fool?"

What his wife thought, Marjorie could not positively discover. Evidently she had reconsidered her determination made on that dreadful evening and had not claimed the shelter of her father's house. She was to all appearances living her life in her husband's house as before. But Marjorie knew from Glyde Douglass, who was not only deeply distressed, but frightened as to what might come next, that the apparent calm was only on the surface. The distressed sister owned with tears that Ralph and Estelle did not even speak to each other. They sat together at meals as before and observed all the outward proprieties; but

Estelle had told her that she had not spoken one word to her husband since the morning after she had discovered the disgraceful business with which he had identified himself, nor did she intend to, until he should rid himself entirely of all connection with it and ask her pardon for the offense. What conversation passed between them before this period of ominous silence was reached, Marjorie could surmise better than Glyde.

Meantime, the tongues of the gossips ran freely. Those who were able to say, "I told you so!" rejoiced over those who had not believed the reports. Moreover, if rumor was to be credited, already the boasted quietness of the corner store was being interrupted, and scenes more or less directly connected with it were being enacted, not quite in accordance with good citizenship.

Such was the condition of affairs at the time that Mr. Maxwell was expecting his brother.

20

ENTER DOCTOR MAXWELL

"WITH your permission," said Mr. Maxwell, "I will drive to the station; the five-twenty train is just due, and we can take my brother home with us."

They were just returning from a trip to what was known as Factoryville, meaning that part of the town in which the factories and tenement houses for the operatives were located. Mrs. Edmonds and her daughter occupied the backseat of the carriage; and the vacant seat beside Mr. Maxwell had been filled by Hannah Bramlett, whom they had just left at home. They had been on an errand of mercy, every available space of the carriage having been filled with comforts for the homes where there was illness.

Reining in his horses at the station, Mr. Maxwell secured them carefully, shaking his head with a smile in response to Marjorie's offer to hold them.

"I always have an extra attack of prudence when I am near a railway station," he said; "I prefer the chain and ring to your hands, in case of any excitement."

Mrs. Edmonds proposed while they waited that she step across to the office of the laundry and make some business arrangements; and as Mr. Maxwell entered the station to consult a timetable, Marjorie was left to herself. Her thoughts were not enlivening. She dreaded the advent of the stranger more than she cared to have anyone understand. In her judgment, their party was now quite perfect; Hannah Bramlett was having the good times that had heretofore been denied her; and on occasion, whenever it was good for her, the dear mother could be depended upon to join them. What space was there for another?

"He will be out of sympathy with our ways and plans," murmured this malcontent, "and will demand the constant attention of Leonard when we want him ourselves. I wish he had stayed well and at work."

Then suddenly there was an excitement. She could never afterward recall just how it was; everything happened so quickly and so unexpectedly. Just as she became aware that the five-twenty express had shrieked itself into the station and that Mr. Maxwell and a stranger were issuing from the front door, she knew also that her mother was crossing the street in front of an electric car, and that another was gliding swiftly along in the other direction. Space enough for one who understood what should be done to make a safe transit; but Mrs. Edmonds became suddenly bewildered: the moving car that she had not at first seen startled her; and instead of hastening forward she jumped back, fairly into the jaws of the treacherous monster on the other track. At least so it seemed to Marjorie; and that the danger for an instant was imminent was evidenced by the immediate crowd that surrounded them. There was a sudden exclamation from the stranger, a bound forward, and before Mr. Maxwell, who was busy with the horses, knew, save for Marjorie's scream, that anything had happened, his brother was literally carrying Mrs. Edmonds toward the carriage.

"Ha! that was quick work, and brave work too!" exclaimed a looker-on in strong excitement; "who is that man?"

"Don't know," said a policeman; "a stranger, and a plucky fellow. He saved the old lady's life, I guess."

"Allow me to sit with her," said the newcomer to Marjorie. "No, Leonard, take the young lady in front, and let me get in here; I know better how to care for her. Does she belong to your party do you say? That is fortunate; we shall get her home quicker. Do not be alarmed, madam," to Marjorie; "she is not injured and has only fainted. It is simply a nervous shock."

"I believe you two have not been introduced yet."

This was Mr. Maxwell's remark some two hours later, when the excitement had somewhat calmed. The newly arrived doctor, instead of being welcomed to their home as they had planned, had himself taken the initiative. He issued his orders right and left and saw to it that they were obeyed. He had just come down from Mrs. Edmonds's room with the announcement that she was now quietly sleeping and was on no account to be disturbed, when his brother made the above remark, looking from the doctor to Marjorie with a grave smile on his face. Only he himself had any idea how often, during the last few days, he had imagined the meeting of those two and wondered how they would impress each other. Certainly no such meeting as had taken place had been imagined! Marjorie held out her hand impulsively:

"We need no introduction," she said, "or rather we have had one that will make us friends forever—he saved my mother's life!"

Naturally an acquaintance so begun progressed rapidly. Within a week Marjorie and Doctor Maxwell were the best of friends. It was a friendship, however, that from the first was as unlike as possible to that which she had given his brother. She never asked the doctor's opinion on any personal subject nor deferred to him in any way, save where her mother's physical condition was concerned; apparently they differed upon every subject under the sun and sparred continually in the merriest ways.

On one point she had been mistaken; so far from having no interest in their daily plans and occupations, Doctor Maxwell entered with zest into them all. He even seemed to be better acquainted with Hannah Bramlett before the first week had passed than his brother had become. He questioned intelligently with regard to their protégés at Factoryville and suggested certain sanitary improvements of which they had not thought. He went with Glyde Douglass to see her little crippled boy, Robbie, and before he had been there fifteen minutes improvised a rest for his back that was so simple it seemed strange that no one had thought to try it, and withal so restful that it brought the grateful tears to Robbie's eyes.

In short, by the time his vacation was half gone, Mrs. Edmonds was entirely willing to vote with her daughter that Doctor Maxwell was a decided acquisition and to mourn over the thought that he had but two weeks more.

"However, you didn't need those, so far as I can see," Marjorie told him gaily. "I believe he is a fraud; don't you think so, Leonard? Pretending that he needed rest, when all he wanted was a chance to come down here and play with his brother a little while!"

"That was it exactly," the doctor said, entering into

her merry mood; "Leonard and I haven't had a regular dew-down, as they say in the East, for nearly a dozen years. I began to fancy myself an old man, but I feel like a boy again. I don't know how it will be when I get back to my work." His face grew suddenly grave as he added, "What do you think it would be, Miss Marjorie, to spend your days and a great part of your nights among the sick and the suffering, listening to their woeful tales of sleepless nights, and racking pains, and wearing coughs; how long do you suppose your nerves would endure it?"

"I should think it would be a blessed life," she said, with a gravity as sudden as his own, and as sweet as it was sullen, "to be able to relieve pain, and quiet racking coughs, and bring hope and cheer where the shadows of awful fears had gathered—it makes one think of the Christ on earth again. 'The Great Physician;' I always liked that name for him."

"Ah, but sometimes one cannot relieve the pain; and in spite of every effort the poor human imitator of his Master may make, the shadows gather and deepen; what then? Even then," he added quickly, before she could speak, "one can always point them to that Great Physician who waits to care for them; that is true. But," with a sudden change of tone, "there are so many who grumble, you see, and groan; and those who have the least to suffer are the loudest groaners; young ladies they are, always, you understand." Then the merry sparring would commence again and be carried on as vigorously as though they had not just had a spasm of common sense.

It was difficult for Marjorie to realize that this merry-eyed man was his brother's senior by two years. He looked and acted nearly always like the younger man. The spirit of boyish fun seemed ready to bubble over at the slightest provocation. Mr. Maxwell referred to this one evening, as his brother, having lingered on the piazza indulging in a merry war of words with them all, finally took himself off to post a letter. "Frank acts like a schoolboy released," he said, laughing; "I can almost make myself think that old Father Time has traveled backward and that Frank is home for his college vacation, instead of being an overworked physician. You should see him at his work, Mrs. Edmonds; he is grave enough then; too grave. The fact is, responsibility rested too early and too heavily on his shoulders. He almost stepped into my father's large practice and became a burdened man at the time when most young physicians are looking for their first patients. He needs someone to keep his home life bright and strong."

Marjorie had glimpses occasionally of the physician. One day in particular she realized that her companion was a man, not a boy. They were driving together, she and Leonard, and Hannah Bramlett and Doctor Maxwell. The four drove often together and had such cheery times as almost made Hannah's face, that had aged too early, look young and pretty. Indeed, but for the sense of disgrace that Ralph's conduct had brought to her, and the fact that her father was steadily losing strength, Hannah could have been almost happy during this time. She had by no means dropped her interest in Jack Taylor; but because these new friends of hers claimed so much of her time, there had been little food of late for the gossips, and, their attention being engaged elsewhere, they had temporarily dropped her. Doctor Maxwell, who understood perfectly why his brother and Marjorie desired to shield Hannah by their attentions, entered into the scheme with great heartiness. They had been driving that afternoon to a celebrated falls, and on their return trip were to call for a moment at Susie Miller's, that Hannah might learn why she had not been at school for the past three evenings. As they neared the house, to their surprise Glyde Douglass opened the door and came out hurriedly.

"Oh, Doctor Maxwell!" she said, relief in her voice as she caught sight of the doctor and ignored the others, "would you be willing to come in here a few minutes? A little child is very ill; the doctor has not been here since morning, and sent word that there is no need for him to come, that there is nothing he can do; and the poor mother is almost distracted."

Before these explanations were concluded, the doctor had sprung from the carriage and was hastening toward the house, leaving the ladies to follow him, while Mr. Maxwell gave attention to his horses. It was the same little desolate inner room in which Glyde had watched the life go out from the poor little Miller baby a few months before. Only the disheartening features were enhanced this time, if possible, by the fact that although the day was not especially warm outside, yet in this little room, with its one small window coming within eight feet of a blank wall, the air was simply oppressive. The victim was a little girl of five or six, burning with fever and groaning with every breath that came from her swollen and purple lips. The mother, bending over her in abject, speechless misery, had evidently lost all hope and was only waiting the inevitable end. More children huddled in corners; and Susie, whose eyes were red with weeping, had to push them aside before she could make room for the guests.

Doctor Maxwell gave one glance at the bed and another comprehensive one about the room. Then he stepped to the door and surveyed the room through which they had made their way. Desolation reigned there; in the cookstove a small fire was burning, apparently for the purpose of heating water for the sick child.

"This room is better," said the doctor; "bring the child out here."

Then the mother spoke:

"The doctor said I mustn't move her, not change her in any way, or she would die."

"I am a doctor, madam; take the child in your arms and bring her out here. Miss Bramlett, open both those windows wide and pour some water on that fire. Miss Marjorie, let me have your fan, and wet this handkerchief dripping wet, and bring it to me. Leonard, see if you can raise some ice anywhere. Then I wish you would drive back and get my medicine case; you will find it in the top till of my trunk. I think if we work fast, we may save a life."

It was wonderful how promptly they all fell into obedience under the power of this master's voice. In less time than it has taken to tell it, his rapidly given instructions were obeyed, and Mr. Maxwell had headed his horses toward home and was driving at full speed.

"See if the mother will let one of you hold the child," was the next peremptory direction.

"Here, let me," said Hannah Bramlett, pushing forward and receiving the burden from the almost fainting mother.

"See to her," was the doctor's order to Marjorie with a nod toward the mother.

"She ain't eat anything today," volunteered Susie, coming to try to help her mother to the open door; "she was so awful anxious about Mysie, and that dreadful doctor wouldn't come! He said doctors were to help the living and that Mysie couldn't live. Oh, dear! Mamma, do you hear what he says? He is a great doctor from the city, and he thinks maybe he can cure Mysie."

Nearly two hours afterward the doctor came out to the little stoop where his brother and Marjorie were waiting for further orders. "I shall stay here tonight," he said; "the child is very ill, but there is a ray of hope for her. She will need the most intelligent nursing, and I can give it."

"But, Frank, do you think you are equal to an all-night strain?"

"Certainly I am, when it is such evident duty; the little one has been neglected. I suppose it is a case of an overworked doctor discouraged by the surroundings."

Hannah had come to the door to hear his opinion just as Marjorie asked, "Is there nothing that any of us can do to help?"

"Miss Bramlett has been helping," he said, smiling on her; "she is a born nurse. If one of you could stay tonight, it might enable that worn-out mother to get a little rest; she is nearly ill with anxiety and watching, and the daughter is too frightened to be of much service."

"I wish I could stay," said Hannah mournfully; "but mother cannot spare me at night while father is so feeble." Before her sentence was concluded, Marjorie had eagerly interposed:

"Let me stay; there is nothing to hinder me. I do not know a great deal about caring for the sick, but I can do as I am told."

"A rare qualification," said Doctor Maxwell; "I know of no higher one. Why not, Leonard?" in response to Mr. Maxwell's disapproving shake of the head; "she is young and strong, and it is an opportunity for service."

After that, no shake of the head could have deterred Marjorie. She dispatched a note to her mother for needed articles, among them a comfortable little supper, and saw the others depart with satisfaction.

In all her after years that night stood out vividly as the first one in which she had accepted and fully sustained her share of care and responsibility. Through all the night Doctor Maxwell was alert, watchful, patient, peremptory. He gave her directions in the same businesslike tone that he would have used to a medical student; he did not spare her in the least when there was need for her help; he even allowed her to sit for a full hour on guard while the child and the overtaxed mother slept, and he took a nap seated in the wooden-backed chair—the best accommodations that the room afforded—with his head on the window seat. Yet he watched carefully that the newly installed nurse did not needlessly exert her strength and sent her away to rest with as much decision as he did everything else.

In the gray dawn of the early morning, she prepared for him a little breakfast that her mother's forethought had made possible, and as he drank his coffee he said with a rare smile:

"I think you and I, with God's gracious blessing, have conquered. I wonder for what sort of a life we have saved that child."

21

BROTHERS INDEED

"THE very next thing to be done," said Doctor Maxwell to the people who appeared next morning to get their orders, "is to get that child and her mother into cooler and more comfortable quarters. No child would reasonably be expected to rally with such surroundings; and the mother is utterly worn out with care and anxiety and the want of suitable food. Unless she is rested in some way, a six weeks' siege, and then probably a coffin, are just before her. Is there no provision save the poorhouse made in this town for the poor whom sickness disables? A hospital isn't exactly the place for the mother at present, though she will be a candidate if we wait long enough; but I am told that your little hospital is overcrowded now."

"What sort of provision ought there to be, Doctor?"

It was the practical Hannah who asked the question.

The doctor laughed. "Such provision has not been made, I believe, this side of heaven, save for our very own. There should be a *home,* Miss Bramlett, worthy of the name; and half-time and cut wages and *rum* have made this father unable to furnish one. What is that large building on the first hill beyond the factories?"

"It is an empty house," said Hannah Bramlett eagerly; "it belongs to an old family who used to live here; there is some trouble with the title, and they can't sell it, and no one wants to rent so large a place, though the rent is very low."

"How low?"

Hannah named a sum at which the doctor smiled incredulously. "You can't mean those figures, Miss Bramlett!"

Yes, she was quite sure of them. She had wished so much that one of the girls in her class could be moved there for a while. She had even tried to raise the necessary money, but the girl had died before she accomplished it.

"Who will be a committee to secure a suitable bed and an easy chair or two, and, in short, the necessary articles of furniture for the removal of this mother and child to that house tomorrow?"

This question almost took Hannah Bramlett's breath away.

"But the money!" she said eagerly; and the brothers Maxwell responded almost in the same breath, "The money will be forthcoming."

"Send the bills to my brother," added the doctor with the merry look in his eyes. "Suppose you drive to the agent's at once, Leonard, and see what terms you can make for a month, say—or two months; no contagious disease. If he succeeds, the cleaning and furnishing part we will delegate to the ladies. Miss Bramlett, I think I will make you chairman."

"That Miss Bramlett," said the doctor as he drove

home the next afternoon, having settled his family, as he called them, in a great clean room in the breezy house on the hill, "is tingling to her fingers' ends with suppressed energy; it ought to be utilized. You should have gone in, Leonard, to see the room she arranged, with such a trifle of money, too. I was astonished at the sum she returned to me. She showed splendid sense; not an unnecessary expenditure, and yet real comfort. Poor Mrs. Miller looked as though she thought it was heaven as she dropped into the big armchair. It is my belief that that woman hasn't been really rested since her married life began. I told that husband of hers that one glass of rum would keep him from crossing that doorsill, so if he wanted to call upon his wife and child he must let it alone. I think the poor wretch would do so if he thought he could. The world has made it too easy for him to ruin himself and his family. What do you think Miss Bramlett said as she surveyed the kitchen and closet where she had arranged all the little conveniences for cooking nourishing food? 'I'd like to live here!' she exclaimed, 'and make good wholesome things for people to eat; and keep that room in there always ready for somebody who needed heartening up.' She looked positively handsome as she said it. She ought to have some such chance too. Her life expresses power run to waste."

"How would you like such a life as that?" he had suddenly lowered his voice and bent toward Marjorie, who occupied the seat with him, Glyde Douglass being in front with Mr. Maxwell.

"I would like to help," she said earnestly. "I feel as though to help other lives was the only thing that made this life worth living, but I don't know in just what way I could do it best."

"I do," he said. "I know just what you could accomplish; I should like to plan your life for you."

There was a heightened color on Marjorie's cheeks, and she began eagerly to talk to Glyde about some additional comfort for the new house; evidently she did not feel ready to have her life planned for her.

The next day a long-delayed storm held pleasure seekers closely at home—the first day that had been of necessity passed at home since Doctor Maxwell came among them. He, it is true, braved the weather and went to look after "his family," telling, with great glee on his return, that he had called for Miss Bramlett and taken her with him. "She is not one of your fair-weather philanthropists," he added, with a merry look for Marjorie. "I found her simply delighted with an excuse for ministering again. I'll tell you how it is with Miss Bramlett; she missed her playtime altogether. I know as well as I want to that she was a woman grown when she ought to have been a child, and that big room up there that she has helped to make into a home is her plaything. I'm charmed with the whole affair. I'd like to keep her playing there for a lifetime."

The evening closed in upon them, still stormy. The curtains were drawn early, and the great reading lamp lighted. It was not an unpleasant experience, this quiet, cozy evening. They had a dozen plans for making it one of the most enjoyable that had come to them, but the doorbell's ringing spoiled it all.

"Who can be coming to call on such a night?" asked Marjorie with a touch of impatience; then, as a voluble voice from the hall reached them, she turned to her mother in dismay.

"Mamma, it is Mrs. Kenyon! *Must* we have her

come in here? She will stay the entire evening, and she is quite the worst gossip of all."

This last offered in explanation to the doctor.

"Have her in, by all means," he said gaily; "I delight in gossip. No character, on the whole, affords a more racy study than a woman who talks because she cannot help it, and when she has nothing to say invents something."

Just as Mrs. Edmonds had murmured, "I think we must receive her here, Daughter; she is accustomed to it, you know," the caller pushed open the door and announced herself volubly, as usual.

"Oh, Mrs. Edmonds! How do you do? And Miss Marjorie. Good evening, Mr. Maxwell. Happy to know Doctor Maxwell, I am sure. Dear me! how cozy you look here! as though there wasn't any trouble in the world. Dreadful storm, isn't it? Almost like March outside; but I felt as though I must brave it to hear what you thought of the news. Perfectly dreadful! isn't it? I declare I never was so shocked, though I may say I have been expecting it this good while; at least, expecting something of the kind. I said to Mr. Kenyon only last night, 'You mark my words,' I said, 'if there doesn't come a crash of some sort before long, then my name isn't Matilda Kenyon. Even the liquor business,' I said, 'can't stand everything.' Such extravagance, you know; new lace curtains only last week, and she almost a bride yet one may say. It is the wife that has ruined him; I shall always stick to that. You see, I've been in a position to know a good deal about her goings on. Weren't you awfully astonished, Mrs. Edmonds? And Miss Marjorie, I expected to find her quite cut up about it, so intimate as they have been! Though to be sure, he has other things to think about now, if report is to be believed."

"You are taking us entirely by surprise, Mrs. Kenyon—" it was really Mrs. Edmonds's first chance for a word—"we have not heard any very distressing news of late."

She tried not to look at her daughter's glowing cheeks and to speak in her usual gentle tone. But her words were like an electric shot to the newsmonger.

"You don't say you haven't heard of it! Why, where have you kept yourselves all day? I know it's been stormy, but I saw him go out," with an emphatic inclination of her head toward the doctor, "and I made sure he would bring you back the news. Somehow I expected you to hear of it the first thing; you've been so intimate. And you really don't know that he has been took up for forgery? Yes, indeed! a plain case; and he's in jail this minute. Mr. Kenyon says he doesn't believe anybody can be found to go bail for him; it wouldn't be safe, you see; such a fellow as he has proved to be would take a leg bail, as they say, in a hurry. Just think of it! Behind prison bars tonight, while we all sit here so comfortable. I'm sorry for his poor father especially, being he's so feeble; but I must say I haven't any great sympathy for his wife; she has brought it all on herself—"

Marjorie moved across the room and laid her hand on the talker's arm.

"Mrs. Kenyon, *won't* you tell us about whom you are talking?"

"My patience, child! how you frightened me! Haven't I told who it was? I thought I had; and anyway, I supposed you'd know without any telling. Why, it's Ralph Bramlett, of course. There is no other townsman of ours, I should hope, that could disgrace us so. Child, you look like a ghost!"

Visions of tales that she would tell to eager listeners

must have begun at once to float through Mrs. Kenyon's brain; for she became somewhat distraught, although Mr. Maxwell held her steadily to talk in order to shield Marjorie as much as possible from her further observation. He fancied he could hear her saying, "Now, you mark my words, that girl is just as fond of him as she ever was, for all he is a married man, and she has two or three others dancing after her. She turned as white as a sheet when I told her the news, and I thought she was going to faint." This was so much Mrs. Kenyon's style of talk that it required no very great stretch of imagination to set her at it. Marjorie had dropped back into the shadow of the cozy corner. Doctor Maxwell bent over her, speaking low, "It is undoubtedly exaggerated; such stories always are. He has perhaps fallen into some financial difficulties from which we can help to rescue him. It is too late tonight to see the proper persons; but the very first thing in the morning, Leonard and I will see what can be done."

"Thank you," she said, her lips still very white. "He was the playmate of my childhood, and I have known his wife ever since we both were babies. It is awful! Is there nothing that we can do in the meantime, Doctor Maxwell?"

"Yes," he said, "as Christian people I think there is. Are you willing that I should suggest it, here and now, before that woman retires?"

Only half understanding, yet trusting him fully, she said simply, "If you think so."

Doctor Maxwell at once turned to the others.

"Mrs. Edmonds," he said, "if I understand the situation, an old acquaintance of yours has fallen into deep trouble; not only that, but he is a member of the church of Christ, and in that sense our brother; can we do better for him tonight than ask God to lead into the best ways for helping him and his?"

In a very few minutes thereafter, one astonished woman's mouth was effectually closed, and she was on her knees listening to as earnest a prayer for Ralph Bramlett as ever fell from human lips. Whatever else those prayers may have accomplished, they silenced Mrs. Kenyon and sent her home early and thoughtful. Perhaps there was given to her a new idea—that there was something better to do for people in trouble, even though that trouble was caused by sin, than to sit tearing open the wounds that sin had made, merely to gape at them.

After the brothers had gone to their room that evening, Doctor Maxwell was strangely silent for him. He stood staring out of the window into the blackness for some minutes without speaking. Suddenly he turned with a question:

"Can it be possible that such a glorious creature as she threw away her heart's wealth on that fellow?"

"If you mean Ralph Bramlett," said Mr. Maxwell, "no; she threw it away years ago on an ideal and lost that when she lost her respect for him. They were not engaged, but—pledged; she would have been loyal, but he deserted her, and so opened her eyes. But she is true, true as steel; he was her childhood friend, and she must always suffer for his sins. She believes that he will yet turn to God, but her faith is having hard blows."

Doctor Maxwell drew a long breath like one relieved.

"Thank you," he said. "How well you understand her! Have you any encouragement for me? She is capable of the holiest love, but am I the one to awaken it? You know how it is with me, Brother? When I first came here, I thought you must certainly have found your ideal; I do not yet understand how you, and she for that matter, could have helped becoming all in all to each other; but I thank God that neither of you see it in that light. Tell me, Leonard, could I not in time make her willing to become your sister?"

"That is a sort of joy with which not even a brother must 'intermeddle,' is it not?" he said. "I can only say as I have said of every effort of your life thus far, God bless you."

On his face was the look, strongly marked, that made others think he must certainly be the older brother.

The doctor came forward quickly and grasped his hand. "That is true," he said impulsively; "never was better brother born than I possess. It would go hard with me, old fellow, to run against your wishes in any way. I held my breath for the first day or two, until I understood. It might seem strange to some persons that I should have known my own mind so suddenly; but that is my way, you know. I wrote to Mother the night before I came here, in response to some of her motherly anxieties, that I never had seen the woman whom for five consecutive seconds I had desired to make my wife; and I told her in good faith that since there was a popular prejudice against a man marrying his mother, I thought I should have to remain single— and twenty-four hours afterward I should have had to write her a different story! We are strange beings, aren't we?"

Five minutes afterward the two were consulting earnestly as to the best ways of managing the effort that they meant to make for Ralph Bramlett at the earliest possible hour. An outsider would not have known that either of them had been strongly moved.

22

◄─┅◆┅─►

A Harvest

OF ALL the people who were plunged into the depths of distress by Ralph Bramlett's fall, no one was more surprised and dismayed than the young man himself. That night, during which he sat bolt upright in his chair, with the consciousness upon him that his door was locked, and that for the first time in his life he could not turn the lock at will, was one that aged him visibly. He was not so much surprised that the deed had been done as that he had been discovered.

The deed had been simple enough, merely the signing of the firm name as he had done, under orders, hundreds of times. To do it without orders had seemed so easy and so reasonable. It was not stealing; why should one have such an ugly thought in connection with it? Above all, that other uglier word *forgery* should not be applied to it! Of course he meant to replace the money; he had used only small sums for convenience, and meant at the earliest opportunity to make all right. Was he to blame that the opportunity had never come? Was he to blame because the liquor business had not been so lucrative as he had supposed?

In truth, the business had been misrepresented to him. Had he not been allowed to count on the support of certain men who, instead of appreciating their privileges, had been angry because a saloon had been opened in their neighborhood, and had given all their custom elsewhere? Moreover, there had been an appalling number of bad debts, and a few ugly accidents, that took money; then there had been those miserable debts with which he started, and others that he had been foolish enough to contract on the strength of his prospects. It had all been a wretched business from beginning to end. His days and nights for weeks past had been haunted with the troubles that were thickening about him; yet in his gloomiest hours he had not for a moment thought of locks and keys and a convict's dress.

He shuddered at the last idea and buried his face deeper in his hands, as if to shut out the picture. It had all come upon him so suddenly! That hypocrite of a junior partner, with his benevolent desires to start the younger man in a lucrative business! pretending that he did not care anything about the thousand dollars advanced—and he kept so close an eye on the expenditures as to trammel matters from the first, and wanted the surplus paid back to him before the new year had fairly opened. Then what business had he to come mousing among the books and examining papers in the bookkeeper's private desk? He was a contemptible hypocrite and nothing else! And the young man, who was at that moment under arrest as a forger of the firm name, a forger not once, nor twice, but at least half a dozen times, felt a certain sense of relief in applying the name "hypocrite" to one of the members of the firm! At the time it did not even occur to him that the same word was already in hundreds of mouths applied to himself.

But there came a harder night to Ralph Bramlett than that. It was after the heavy bail, which Mrs. Kenyon had been sure he could not secure, had been promptly guaranteed by the brothers Maxwell, and he was allowed to walk the streets again.

Following hard upon these first moments of relief came a summons to the home of his childhood. His father, from whom it had been found impossible to keep the dread news, had fallen under it as though it had been a blow.

Ralph remembered for years afterward, with a vividness that made every breath a pain, the horror of those hours during which he knelt, an abject, shrinking thing, beside his father's dying bed. Shrinking from the curious eyes of physician and nurse; turning even from the pitying gaze of his sister Hannah, to whom he had not spoken for months, not since he had angrily accused her of disgracing the family; shrinking most of all perhaps from the stricken face of his mother, yet waiting hungrily for some word from his father.

They had been afraid that he had come too late for that. The painful restlessness of the day, during which every effort was being made to hasten the tardy hands of justice and release the prisoner, had been followed by a night of stupor from which the attending physician believed the patient would not rally. Yet Doctor Maxwell, who had been called in counsel, moved around to the wretched young man's side just after the doctor had expressed this belief and murmured low, "Do not leave the bedside for a moment; I am confident that he will rally and ask for you, as they tell me he did at intervals during the entire day."

They waited, in that most miserable of all waitings, while a life slowly ebbed away, feeling that there was nothing to be done. For nearly an hour no one spoke. Mrs. Bramlett sat close to her husband, holding his work-worn and wrinkled hand in hers. From time to time she caressed it tenderly, as she might have done a little child's. Then bending low she would murmur fond, meaningless words in the dulled ears. Mrs. Bramlett had been in feeble health for years, and the husband had been the one to watch her comings and goings and save her steps where he could. She had thought that she would be the one to lie someday, breathing her life away, attended lovingly by the husband of her youth; but it had come to pass, as it so often does, that the stronger one had failed suddenly and become the invalid. She knew, poor mother, that the man who lay dying beside her had made his only son his idol, and when the idol disappointed him, the old man's strength gave way.

During all this waiting time, the mother did not so much as glance toward that kneeling figure at the foot of the bed; but it was because the mother heart was strong within her, and she knew instinctively that he could not bear to meet her eyes. As for Hannah, she kept her post immovably just at the bed's head, within sight of her father's face, yet within the shadow of the headboard. Her time had not come for tears; she had not shed one since she heard of Ralph's disgrace. She had hovered about her father, watchful of each murmured word or sign of need, ministered to him ceaselessly, and sought not so much as a word or glance of recognition in return. All during that wretched day, while the doctor came and went and shook his head more gravely at each coming, and the neighbors whispered in the kitchen, and one or two privileged ones tip-toed about the house doing needful things, Jack Taylor had appeared from time to time with messages for "Miss Hannah." "Mr. Maxwell had sent him to say that there had been unexpected delay in finding just the right man, but they were still hopeful." Or "Mr. Maxwell sent word that all was in shape now, and they hoped for a speedy hearing." Or later, "Mr. Maxwell feared it could not be accomplished before evening." And then, later still, breathless with the haste he had made, stumbling past the curious neighbors who would have asked questions, eager, silent, he made his way to Hannah, and whispered that "Doctor Maxwell and Mr. Bramlett were coming; would be there in ten minutes." And then, before she had had time to think what she should say to her brother, or whether she would ask her mother to go out and meet him, he had slipped past her and knelt at the foot of the bed, and covered his ghastly face with the bedclothes; and then they had waited.

Suddenly there was a movement on the part of the dying man. He flung his disengaged arm out one side and passed his hand along the bedclothes as if in search of someone.

"Where is he?" he asked distinctly; "where is my boy? Why doesn't he come?"

It was Hannah who bent over him, her voice clear and steady, "He has come, Father; he is here."

At the same moment Ralph arose and, aided by Doctor Maxwell, staggered forward, dropping on his knees again close to his father's side; his mother pushed back her chair to make room for him, and Hannah guided the groping hand to his head.

It rested there tenderly, as it had in the boy's childhood; and the father's voice was quite distinct as he said:

"I cannot see you, my boy; my sight is gone; but I know it is you. My hand would recognize your head among a thousand—my little boy's. Oh, Ralph! I remember all about it now; I haven't been the father to you that I ought, or it could never have happened. I take blame to myself; I will tell God so. But oh, my boy! my boy! speak to him yourself, and ask him to forgive you. Don't you know how merciful he is? 'Like as a father pitieth his children'—that gives me such comfort; for I have only pity for you in my heart. Begin again, my boy, begin again; it isn't too late. God will forgive you and bless you. I *must* see you again, Ralph; my earthly sight is gone; but your father mustn't miss seeing you in heaven. Promise me, Ralph, that you will be there."

The silence that fell while that answer was waited for was terrible.

"Speak to him!" It was Hannah's voice that broke in upon it, stern, commanding, yet with an undertone of such beseeching agony that it seemed as though a stone must have responded. The wretched young man raised his face for a single moment from his trembling hands, a face so utterly charged with woe that his worst enemy must have pitied him, and said two words:

"O God!"

"Yes," said the dying man, with solemn emphasis; "that is it, Ralph; never mind me; speak to God. O God, hear my boy! he cries to thee; for the sake of thy Son who died for him, hear my boy. Pray, Ralph, *pray!*"

He pray! Never before had the awful mockery of his prayers stuck on this man's soul. He could not have uttered a sentence had his life been at stake. But he clutched at the hand of the man who stood beside him and groaned out one word: *"Pray!"* And Doctor Maxwell, dropping on his knees beside the wretched son, said "Into thy hands, our Father, we commend his spirit, asking thee for Jesus Christ's sake to hear his last prayer."

And then a great wailing cry arose from the poor daughter; for she knew that her father's voice would be heard no more, and there came to her such a homesick longing to have only one word from him for her very self as she had not known her heart could feel.

Somebody thought of her and led her tenderly away; and somebody else put a pitiful arm about that poor old widow and supported her while she tottered out. As for the son, Doctor Maxwell kept a firm hand upon his arm and did not release him until the doors of his old room closed after him. Then he said, with a long-drawn sigh, "I will stand guard, but I think that such misery as his must be better borne alone."

And, in truth, he almost needed guarding; for it seemed to him at times that he must lose his reason. Such an abyss of hopeless despair yawned before him as only sin can make. He had loved his father more even than he had himself realized. A selfish love it had been, without doubt. All the emotions of his life thus far had been painfully mixed with self; but always there had been in the mind of the young man a lingering desire to do something great for his father and mother, to make their lives easier. The burdens incident to straitened means had pressed heavily upon him because of them. There had been times when he had hated the farm, old family homestead though it was, because it seemed to him the synonym for poverty and worry. In his boyish days his dreams of being a great lawyer had been always intermingled with dreams of the state of luxury in which he would establish his parents. In later years, his decision to take the position of bookkeeper in a distillery, though hurriedly made and with motives uppermost that made him blush to remember, had yet this undertone of comfort, that the large salary would enable him to help his father. It is true he had done nothing of the kind. Instead, he had almost immediately plunged into debt. He had always assured himself that this was his wife's fault; yet with that singular sense of double consciousness that had gone about with him despite his attempts at stifling it, he had known all the while that the lavish expenditure connected with his marriage and his establishing a home had been borne and fostered by his desire to show people that he was a prosperous man, despite the fact that Marjorie Edmonds had preferred someone else.

When months before he had awakened to the discovery that he was steadily running behind in his accounts, that his style of living was set on a scale that it would not be possible for him to continue unless his income was materially increased, and the rose-colored future pictured by the junior partner in the distillery had been pointed out to him, it was made especially attractive by the thought of what it would enable him to do for his father and mother. His father would no doubt feel bitterly prejudiced against the business; that was to be expected in so old a man; but his prejudices would grow less bitter from the day that the mortgage on the old farm was paid, and the land, every foot of which was dear to his father's heart, secured beyond question to the family name forever. Then, the debt once disposed of, he dreamed of the improvements he would make, still for the family benefit. Pipes should be laid from the grand old spring, and the water brought not only to the house but to his mother's room. The new stable, on which his father's heart was set so long ago, should be built, with the longed-for modern improvements for the comfort of horses. And his mother should have a summer kitchen with wire-gauze windows, and ventilating flues, and the most modern of ranges, and a kitchen cabinet, and every other device that could be found for making the daily routine of labor easy. Mother had had to do without such things all her life, and she should have them at last.

These were only dreams; alas for the realities! Not a penny had he been able to pay toward cancelling that mortgage; not a cent of the money advanced to him after the time when he pretended to be support-ing himself had been returned. Instead of making the lives of father and mother easier, he had deepened their anxieties in a hundred ways. He had come to them with complaints of his sister, and criticisms concerning her, which, however much deserved, had accomplished nothing save to make their lives harder. Very plain words had been spoken to him by his wife. She had not hesitated to tell him that his last business venture, which he assured himself had really been made for their sakes, was killing his father; that if he died, as he would before very long, his son would be as surely his murderer as though he had taken a knife and stabbed him. The words had pierced the son's heart when they were spoken and had sent him out, as he bitterly told himself, to his ruin. If it had not been for his wife's words! Up to the very moment of the exposure that had shut him for a single, horrible night within prison walls, Ralph Bramlett had steadily shielded himself and accused others.

23

"It Might Have Been"

WILL there ever be a longer night than the one which that poor self-ruined man spent alone in the room peopled with memories of his childhood? He could not help looking about him occasionally and recalling memories. It was a long time since he had been in that room. Over there was the bed into which his mother had so often tucked him on cold winter nights; and when the blankets were just to his mind, she had bent and kissed him and said cheerily, "Pleasant dreams." How long ago that was! He must be at least a hundred years old now! Yonder was the table where he had sat when he wrote the essays of which they had been so proud. He remembered the one that took the prize. He could see, as if it were but yesterday, his father bending over it with him, asking his opinion about a certain word, offering a bit of shrewd advice about a sentence, which advice his son never took— he had been sufficient to himself and wiser than his father even in those early days. He could hear his own voice again:

"Every word of it is mine, Father—" spoken with

swelling pride. And then, with an accession of superiority, "some of the fellows in school copy awfully." Then his father's voice, "That is right, my boy; whatever else my son becomes in the world, I hope he will always be strictly honest in word and deed."

At that very table he had practiced his lately acquired art of shading letters, making what his father considered beautiful writing; they had been proud of his penmanship. He drew out the old drawer that creaked a good deal and came out crooked, and, halfway, refused to go farther; it had been an old table even so long ago as when this man, who felt so old, was a boy. Within were the very papers he had left when he went out from home. They were a family not given to change, and both mother and daughter had had a fancy for preserving this room of Ralph's just as it was. He turned over the papers—scraps of all sorts of youthful effort. He found a paper that stabbed him; it was simply names, written all over in different styles of writing—his father's name, his uncle's, his teacher's, the minister's. He could hear his own voice distinctly now:

"Look, Father, see how I can imitate Mr. Burr's handwriting. I don't believe you could tell that from his." And the father had shaken his head and said, "A dangerous talent, my boy; I should not care to cultivate it; I have known of its getting more than one man into mischief." That had been long ago, when he was the merest boy. Had the words been prophetic? They brought back suddenly to Ralph Bramlett his awful present. He shut the drawer with a groan and turned away. Yet where should he turn? The room was peopled with images. Let his eyes fall where they would, they brought him instantly stories of his youthful, comparatively innocent, past. And between that past and this awful night lay a great gulf.

Given to dreaming from his childhood, there had scarcely been a phase of possible experience that this young man had not at some time lived mentally. When he was a lad of fifteen, there had been a death in the neighborhood that had left a young man fatherless, with a mother and two little brothers dependent upon him. The scenes connected with that time had impressed the boy vividly. In imagination he had put himself forward into manhood and arranged a similar experience. His father's sickbed, that presently became a deathbed, and himself the stay and comfort of all concerned. It had been he to whom his father had looked for strong and tender helpfulness; he alone had been able to change his position, administer medicine or food. It had been his form that his father's failing eyes followed; his name had been the last word spoken by the paling lips, spoken in gratitude and trustfulness, commending his mother and sister to his care. Afterward he had been his mother's refuge. He had supported her with his arm during the last trying moments; he had carried her fainting from the room; he had hung over her in self-forgetful tenderness all through the hours that followed, ministering to her every want. He had upheld his sister with kind, brave words and had been told by her and by his mother again and again that they could not live but for him. He had thought of everything, been ready with directions to the outsiders who waited for his orders, been wise and thoughtful above any young man ever known before, and his praise had been on all lips. Such was the dream. Here was the reality, and how awful the contrast!

Some facts had repeated his dream; only across the

hall his father lay at that moment dead. His mother had been carried half-fainting from the room; but he, the son and brother who was to have been all in all to her at that hour, had not dared to so much as raise his eyes to her face. Nobody consulted him, nobody thought of him. Ah! not that last. He knew that everybody thought of him—with contempt, with indignation, with shame. For a man like Ralph Bramlett to be able to conceive of the world as thinking of him with scorn and aversion was almost enough to dethrone his reason. As the hours wore away, and his haunting memories became more and more keen and piercing, he sprang up almost in terror. He began to walk the floor with rapid strides. How was it all to end? How could he get out of this room, this house, away from everybody who had ever seen or heard of him before? Was there not some refuge? He could not face those people and read their opinion of him as he glanced. He would rather have been left in prison, locked in from these awful retributions. It was a cruel kindness that had opened those prison doors and let him come forth. No, no! He did not mean that! He could not have borne it not to have heard his father's voice again. And his name had indeed been the last upon those dying lips. But oh, could he ever, even when death mercifully released him from this horror of living, forget the reason? Even the wife of fifty years had been apparently forgotten for the son's sake. But the reason! Oh, the *awful reason!* It would drive him wild! Yet he had been forgiven. "Like as a father pitieth—" He could seem to hear the familiar voice once again repeating the words. And that last word—that very last. What had it been? "Pray, Ralph, *pray!*"

"O God!" he said again in agony, "I cannot! I don't

know how to pray. I have never prayed in my life. I have been a hypocrite always and only. When I joined the church I was a hypocrite; when I married my wife I was a hypocrite; when I went into what I called business I was a hypocrite. I have deceived everybody, most of all myself. I have ruined my life! I am a felon, a convict, or soon will be. I am a murderer! I have killed my father; I shall kill my mother. If I could only kill myself! Yet I dare not do this. Could I risk the chance even of meeting my own father again?"

It was an awful experience. Yet one who had a real heart-knowledge of human experience, and of the Refuge established for the sin-haunted, might have had a more hopeful feeling for that young man's future than ever before. At last he had been entirely frank with himself. For a single moment he had laid aside all subterfuges, all confessions of the sins of others, stripped himself of excuses, and stood with his naked soul before him, taking in not only its "might have been," but its awful poverty. If only such gaze can last long enough, an honest soul must be driven from itself in search of refuge; and it is then, if ever, that the claims of the Lord Jesus Christ may be urged.

Meantime, outside, there were anxious conferences.

"I don't know what to do," said Marjorie Edmonds in great distress. "It seems cruel to leave him to himself for so long; he may be almost insane with grief. This is no common sorrow; he ought to have some refreshment, at least. Think what a night the last one must have been to him, and the day that followed it! Now it is almost morning again. Somebody ought to go to him."

They were standing together for a moment, Doctor Maxwell and herself, near one of the eastern windows, consulting as to the various questions that had come up for decision. Doctor Maxwell, comparative stranger though he was, by reason of his profession had been very closely allied to the tragedy that was being enacted. Hannah Bramlett, having seen evidences of his skill in the restoration of the little child at Factoryville, had insisted on his seeing her father. She had been equally determined to have Marjorie with her, begging her so earnestly to stay when she called the evening before that it seemed cruel to deny her. So Marjorie had, of necessity, assumed a degree of management; the neighbors generally seeming to recognize in her an intimate friend. Mr. Maxwell had but a short time before being driven home with Mrs. Edmonds, Marjorie agreeing to wait until she should see Hannah again. As she spoke, they both noted that the gray light of another morning was struggling into the sky.

"Who is there that can go to him?" Doctor Maxwell asked. "I thought that at first it would be better to leave him quite alone; but we may be overdoing that part of it, as you say. By the way, where is his wife? I do not remember to have seen a glimpse of her. Is not she the one to help him now?"

Marjorie shook her head mournfully.

"She has not been here at all. She went to her father's as soon as she heard the news—that other news, I mean—and refused to come out here, or to see her husband again. I saw Glyde for a few minutes last evening. She and Mr. Burwell were here. Mr. Burwell came last night, and Glyde told me that he exerted all his influence to induce Mrs. Bramlett to come with them and be here when her husband arrived, and failed."

Doctor Maxwell's face darkened. "Is that your idea of the meaning of marriage vows, Miss Marjorie?"

"No, but there is something to be said for poor Estelle. She has suffered a great deal, I think; sometimes I fancy she is hardly in her right mind. There has been an estrangement between them for some time—indeed, I believe they have not even spoken together for weeks. Oh, I do not uphold her, of course; but—don't you think it is very hard to determine what one would do under such terrible circumstances as hers?"

"Perhaps so. Do you think it hard to determine what one should do?"

"Oh no, indeed! I feel very sure that she ought to come; but I am afraid she is in such a condition mentally just now, that that word *ought* has no power over her."

"Did it ever have? I beg your pardon if I seem to be unduly criticizing your friends; but I have wondered if most of the trials of the unhappy husband, and possibly of the wife also, had not grown out of their inability to grasp the force of that word *ought,* and make it a power in their lives. He seems to me peculiarly a man who has, perhaps from his early boyhood, allowed himself to do that which for the time being he chanced to feel like doing, without weighing results, until he has educated himself into an overmastering desire to carry out his passing will, let the results be what they may."

"It is precisely his character; at least, I suppose it is," she added humbly. "My mother has had that feeling concerning him ever since his boyhood. I used not to think so; and there was a time, when we were girl and boy together, that I think I might have helped him and did not; it is that thought which makes it so hard for me to—"she did not complete her sentence.

Doctor Maxwell looked down at her with a grave smile. "Are you, too, haunted by that torturing 'it might have been'?" he asked. "I think half the misery of wrecked lives must be comprehended in that phrase. I cannot believe that you can have made very grave mistakes, so young as you are; and yet I can well understand that to a sensitive conscience a memory of what one might have accomplished for another, and did not, has power to sting. I know all about it by bitter experience. I stood side by side one evening with a young man, a boy, my friend and classmate, and felt impelled—I doubt not now by the power of the Holy Spirit—to say to him, 'Come with me into the room yonder, where people are being shown the way to Christ;' and I did not say it. I told myself that it would be of no use, that he was not in the mood for serious things; that he would possibly turn the whole matter into ridicule; that I might much better wait until some quiet time when we were alone together. And I never saw him again, Miss Marjorie; he never reached his home. An accident overtook him on the way and proved fatal. Do not you think I should be well able to understand the 'might have been' of life?"

Marjorie had never seen him so moved. Yet, after a moment, he turned promptly, as his fashion was, from thoughts of self to the needs of the hour. "What about the sister? Could not she be depended on in this emergency?"

"Hannah? Oh no! not to go to Ralph; at least, I think it would do no good. He is angry with her, has refused this long time even to speak to her. Indeed, Doctor Maxwell, you must think we have strange friends! I never realized the smallness of all these exhibitions so much as I do now. What a strange, terrible deathbed scene it was! But I do not think poor Hannah is to blame—I mean, that she does not feel bitterly toward Ralph; she keeps away from him only because she fears to do more harm than good. It is difficult to know what to do."

At that moment the door near which they stood opened, and Mrs. Bramlett came slowly out. She had been a brisk little woman all her life, notwithstanding her feeble health; but she tottered now and put her hand out in a pitiful way, in search of the wall for support. Her face had a drawn, haggard look; and altogether the weight of many added years seemed to have fallen upon her in a few hours.

Marjorie moved swiftly toward her, speaking tenderly.

"Dear Mrs. Bramlett, we hoped you were getting a little sleep. Will you come into the front room and let me bring you up a cup of tea and something to eat?"

Mrs. Bramlett shook her head. "No, dear," she said; "I don't feel the need of it. Do you know where my boy is? I want to go to him."

"He is over there in his old room. Dear Mrs. Bramlett, are you strong enough to see him now? Won't you take just a little nourishment first? The teakettle is boiling, and I could make you a bit of toast in a very few minutes."

"I couldn't eat now, child; the first mouthful would choke me. I ought not to have left Ralph so long; it was selfish in me, poor boy."

As she spoke, she tottered toward Ralph's door, tapped gently, received no answer, tapped again, then, turning the knob, entered and closed the door behind her.

"These mothers!" said Doctor Maxwell, brushing a mist from before his eyes. "We might have known that she would come to the rescue; there is nothing that they cannot endure when their children are at stake. How one's sympathies are drawn two ways at once under such circumstances as these! I find myself feeling so glad that she is moved to go to him and that his door was not locked against her; yet at the same time I feel how despicable it is that the strong arm on which she ought to be able to lean in this time of her greatest human need has so utterly failed her. One does not know whether most to despise or pity that young man. If he has any heart at all, how it must goad him now to realize that in this hour of his opportunity he is a broken staff!"

24

THE UNEXPECTED

IN MANY ways the days that followed were hard ones, even to those not immediately connected with the Bramlett family.

Poor Ralph gave very little trouble to those who could forget the rare glimpses they had of his face. He kept to his room closely, not even coming to the family table, which, thanks to Mrs. Edmonds's thoughtfulness, was kept supplied with comforts, and served with care. Glyde Douglass came as though she, instead of her sister, were a daughter of the house; and her friend Mr. Burwell might have passed for a son-in-law, so untiring was he in his efforts to serve the stricken household. It was he who carried choice portions from the table to Ralph's door; never entering, however, for Mr. Burwell had been distinctly shown more than once that his very presence was distasteful to that young man. It was always the old mother who received the tray at his hands and made an effort to force the appetite that had almost entirely failed.

As for Estelle, she steadily resisted all attempts to

bring her to a show of propriety. The people whose influence she apparently feared, she disposed of by declining altogether to see them. As she kept her room and was guarded and cared for by her elder sister, this was not a difficult thing to accomplish.

Among those to whom she had utterly refused admittance was her sister Glyde; so that Marjorie, who had depended on Glyde for information, could not be sure as to the poor woman's state of mind, save as it was shown by her determination not to do what was desired of her. Even her mother, who in general sided with Estelle, was of the opinion that she should attend the funeral. As for Marjorie, she was intensely anxious that this should be done; so much shame, it seemed to her, Ralph might be shielded from. Since he must appear before the public to be gazed at, surely his wife might bear the ordeal with him and thus close the eager mouths of the gossips in this direction. Moreover, his mother's heart was set upon it; so they all labored in various ways to bring it to pass, and failed.

"I do not know a person who has influence over Estelle," said Marjorie mournfully, "except Ralph himself; since he has failed, it seems useless for anyone to try."

"Has he made the effort?" Doctor Maxwell asked.

"Oh yes! Didn't you know? Glyde says he sent a note to her last night, asking if she would do that one thing for his mother's sake; and the sister who stays with her said she read it and turned her face to the wall, only shaking her head when asked if an answer was to be returned."

"Then she is utterly hardened," said Doctor Maxwell, with the stern look on his face which made one realize that he was a man, instead of what he sometimes appeared, a merry-hearted boy.

"No," said Marjorie; "she is only a naughty child who cannot get the consent of herself to give up the *role* she had resolved upon; so many people seem to me never to have grown up. Poor Ralph is one of them. See how he treats Mr. Burwell! yet he came from New York at this time on purpose to try to be of assistance to Ralph himself."

"Who is Mr. Burwell?"

"Don't you know? He is engaged to Glyde Douglass; but that doesn't tell you who he is, does it? He belongs to the firm of Peel & McMasters of New York. He was admitted to the bar only a few weeks ago and retains his position in their office; not exactly a partner, I suppose, but still associated with them in such a way that it is said his business success is secured."

"If that is so," said Doctor Maxwell eagerly, "young Bramlett would do well to retain his influence. Such names as Peel & McMasters to back one are not secured easily."

"I suppose not; but it seems as though poor Ralph was always bent on working against his own interests. He has a prejudice against Mr. Burwell, an entirely unreasonable one, I think. Years ago he had an opportunity to enter the office of Peel & McMasters himself, as a student. He had been eagerly waiting for some time in the hope of securing the next vacancy; but owing to an absence from home he missed the telegram summoning him, and, by some misunderstanding, Mr. Burwell secured the vacant place. I could not learn that there was anything in the least underhanded about it, but Ralph persisted in thinking that there was. He has brooded over it all this while; and now, although Mr. Burwell is his sister-in-law's promised husband, refuses to have anything to say to him."

"The more I hear about that personage," said

Doctor Maxwell, "the more surprised I am that he has not ruined himself even earlier in life. He is in all respects so completely the spoiled boy."

"Is it ruin?" Marjorie asked in a low voice, her face paling at the thought.

"No; not ruin, but salvation I hope, and to a degree believe. It seems to me that that last prayer of his father's will surely be answered. But as the average man looks at these things, I am afraid it is ruin. That is, I fear that there is no escape from the punishment that the law demands. I need hardly tell you that Leonard and I will do our utmost for him; and this young man Burwell is a powerful ally if he has the position you think he holds; but there is a powerful enemy to meet. The firm of Snyder, Snyder, & Co., never noted for excessive kindness of heart, seems to be especially vindictive in this case; more particularly that junior partner, who, I am told, Mr. Bramlett looked upon almost as a personal friend.

"There is another side to the matter, Miss Marjorie,—"this last added after a pause of some seconds— "I am to do, as I told you, my utmost to save him from the penalty of the law; but I confess that I do it under protest and out of regard for his friends, rather than for himself. On general principles, I am inclined to think that the best thing that can happen to a transgressor is to suffer the penalty. I am not sure but this is especially the case in the present instance. To make wrongdoing easy to a man like Mr. Bramlett is, if I understand his character, to help him to self-ruin. Yet I am being overruled by my interest in his friends and shall do my utmost, without any prospect of success."

The dreaded day was lived through, and the worn-out body of Ralph's father was consigned to its last rest. The expected crowd gathered, many of them sympathetic, some of them curious to the last degree. There was not a great deal on which to feed their curiosity. None of the family were to be seen, save in their transit from the upper hall to the carriage; then the curious had opportunity to observe that the widow leaned heavily on the arm of her daughter, and that her son walked behind her in solitude, though the three entered the same carriage.

"Shouldn't you have thought that she might have had the decency to come to the funeral!" the voluble voice of Mrs. Kenyon was observing just as Doctor Maxwell returned from assisting the last departures into their carriages. Mr. Maxwell, with Mrs. Edmonds and Marjorie, had followed in the procession to the cemetery, after the fashion of the locality; but Doctor Maxwell had tarried behind to be of use as occasion offered. He gave his first attention to Mrs. Kenyon.

"It just shows what a miserable hussy she is! I am sure father Bramlett never did her any harm, whatever may be said of the son; even if he had, she might come and see him laid away in the ground. Anybody that will carry spite to such a length as that I've no patience with. I just as good as know there was some horrible trouble between her and him that drove him to the forging business; her actions now show it."

"If you are speaking of Mrs. Ralph Bramlett, she is not out today because, as a physician summoned to give his opinion, I positively forbade her leaving her room." It was Doctor Maxwell's clear-cut voice just behind her that made the gossip start and turn hastily.

"I want to know!" she said humbly. "Is the poor thing sick? It is the very first I have heard of it. Well, well! troubles never come singly, they say; how true it is. I'm sure she is excusable if she is sick. I will take pains to let folks know it. She isn't dangerous, I hope?"

"She is suffering a good deal," said the doctor ambiguously, as he hastened away from further questioning.

But the evening before, he had taken Glyde Douglass home; and while waiting for a package that he was to take to Marjorie, had been hastily summoned to Mrs. Bramlett. She had been ill all day but had utterly refused to see a physician; now she had fainted and frightened her mother and sister into action. It was a relief to those especially concerned, to be assured the next day by Doctor Maxwell that Mrs. Ralph Bramlett was much too ill to think of leaving her room.

"It is eminently more respectable to be able to speak of her as ill," said Mrs. Edmonds with a grave smile, "than to be obliged to admit, at least by silence, that she is sulking at such a time as this."

Mindful of those words, Doctor Maxwell had taken pains, by informing Mrs. Kenyon, to give the fact of illness as wide a circulation as possible.

All things considered, it seemed to the Edmonds household as though months must have intervened since they gathered in the family sitting room. Now they had come to the last evening of Doctor Maxwell's stay with them. Already he had extended his leave of absence two weeks beyond the original period and knew that he must not under any pretext tarry longer. Yet apparently he was as loath to leave his resting place as the others were to see him depart.

"I really don't know what we are going to do without your brother," Mrs. Edmonds had said that afternoon. "He came to us so short a time ago a stranger and now it seems like parting from one of my own children, to say good-bye to him."

But she spoke cheerily, dear innocent lady. She liked and admired Doctor Maxwell; next to his brother she felt that she liked him better than any of her friends, and of course it would be hard to part with him; but after all, she told herself, it was not as if Leonard were going. She could see reasons why, for a time, it would actually be better to have the brother away. Next summer, perhaps, he could come to them for the entire season, and because of circumstances feel even more at home with them than he did at present; but just now—and so the dear little mother dreamed her dream and smiled, and planned to make that last evening as social as possible. It is simply incredible how blind even very astute people can be at times, when their minds and hearts are filled with preconceived ideas.

Her social evening did not develop as she had planned.

"It is almost too pleasant for the house," she had said at the tea table; "yet I think we shall all want to stay at home tonight, and in the house; we have been through so much of late. Besides, we want to make the most of the doctor's last evening and be where we can all look at him at once."

A burst of laughter had followed this suggestion, and Doctor Maxwell had made much of it in the merriest way during the remainder of the meal. But no sooner was the late tea disposed of than Mrs. Edmonds's household disappeared—melted away, one might say, before her eyes, or at least during an absence of a very few minutes. She went to the kitchen to give some directions to her maid, and on her return no one was to be seen. Within the pretty parlor everything was in order for a family gathering. Mrs. Edmonds, rejoicing that the evening was cool enough to admit of lights, made the room bright, wheeled the easy chairs into positions suggesting rest and comfort, and waited for her family. Ten minutes, fifteen, a half hour. It was very strange what had become of them. Marjorie was not in the habit of disappearing without a word to her mother. An occasional movement overhead suggested that one of the gentlemen was in his room; perhaps both were there, but in that case where was Marjorie? Another half hour passed; and this mother, who had been so tenderly cared for heretofore, began to have a curious sense of desertion and general ill-treatment. Then there came slow, measured steps down the stairs, and Mr. Maxwell entered quietly.

"Alone?" he asked, but in the tone that people use when they feel that something must be said, rather than that they care for an answer.

"Why, yes, I seem to be. Have you any idea where Marjorie is? She said nothing to me about going out."

"I think they went for a walk, Mrs. Edmonds; she and Frank."

"That is very strange! I mean, it is very unusual. Marjorie is so accustomed to mentioning all her goings to me that I have fallen into the habit of expecting it as a matter of course. Besides, I thought we were all to have a sort of 'at home' evening together?"

Mr. Maxwell seemed to have no reply ready for this interrogative remark. He went over to the piano and struck a few notes apparently at random; then, still standing, played through the melody of a hymn that was a favorite with him. Mrs. Edmonds, who was also very familiar with it, said over mentally the words, as the melody proceeded.

"If through unruffled seas
Toward heaven we calmly sail,
With grateful hearts, O God, to thee
We'll own the favoring gale."

The strains continued, being repeated and repeated, as though the player were also giving the words with his inner consciousness. Mrs. Edmonds could not think of the next verse; she strained her memory as people will after the unimportant; but the only other words she could recall were:

> *"Teach us in every state*
> *To make thy will our own;*
> *And when the joys of sense depart,*
> *To live by—"*

The melody came to a sudden pause, and the musician came over to where she sat.

"Do you know what is going on out there in the moonlight, my friend?"

She lifted startled eyes to his face. "How should I? What do you mean?"

"I hope you like my brother Frank very much; I assure you he is in every way worthy of respect and love."

It was impossible not to understand his meaning. Look and tone added what was lacking in the words. The mother gave a little involuntary start, a murmured word of exclamation, then sat quite still for several minutes. Mr. Maxwell began a slow walk up and down the quiet room.

Presently she broke the stillness. "It may seem a strange question for a mother to ask, but do you know what the outcome will be? I mean, do you think that Marjorie—"

She stopped, unable to ask another whether her daughter's heart had been given away.

"I have no knowledge on the subject, Mrs. Edmonds, other than that which my inner consciousness gives me; but my belief is that it will presently be my duty to congratulate you."

Then, with a sudden start, she realized the effort that it must cost him to say these words to her.

"Oh, Leonard!" she said, a mother's tenderness in her voice; "what can I say to you?"

He paused before her with a grave smile on his face. "Mrs. Edmonds, do you know the words of the tune I was playing?

'Teach us in every state
To make thy will our own.'

Can these things be mere accident? Must we not trust our Father through whatever path he leads us?"

Footsteps were heard on the lawn, and a murmur of voices.

"Good night," added Mr. Maxwell abruptly; and taking his hat from its station in the hall, he passed through the side door as Marjorie and her companion entered the front one.

Doctor Maxwell went directly upstairs; but Marjorie came to her mother and put loving arms about her.

"Oh, Mother!" she said, "I am afraid we have spoiled your quiet, social evening; but Frank had something to tell me. Can you guess, Mamma, what it is?"

25

JUNE AGAIN

"MAMMA," said Marjorie, pausing at her mother's door, "there has been a change in program. Frank will drive you to Park Place and wait for you, if you don't object. I want to go with Leonard to make that promised call at Hill House. It is just the morning for a walk as long as that, and I want to have a quiet talk with Leonard."

"Very well," said Mrs. Edmonds in a satisfied tone of voice, "arrange it to suit yourselves; I certainly shall not object to Frank's company, if he doesn't to mine. There will have to be considerable waiting for me I am afraid, this morning; and Frank is more patient than you are, Daughter."

"I know it," Marjorie said with a happy little laugh. "Frank is more everything than I am, Mamma. You can't make me jealous of him if you try." She ran gaily down the stairs as she spoke, and joined Mr. Maxwell in the hall.

Mrs. Edmonds had had ample time to grow accustomed to, and satisfied with, Doctor Frank Maxwell. For more than a year he had been her son-in-law. It was quite two years since that evening that they had planned to spend socially together, and had in reality spent much apart. On the following morning they had separated, Doctor Maxwell returning to his work, and the others trying hard to take up life where they had left it on the day of his arrival; every one of them realizing that the old life could never be taken up again—six weeks had made such radical changes as would tell for all time. Only happy changes to Marjorie. Her face was radiant during those days with her newfound joy in life; and thanks to the watchful guardianship of mother and friend, she was not allowed to know, either then or afterward, that she had shadowed a life.

Within a week of his brother's departure, Mr. Maxwell also took leave of his summer home. He had not expected to go so soon, at least Marjorie had no idea that he was to go until October; but a letter from his mother, announcing her arrival in this country several weeks earlier than she had at first intended, had changed his supposed plans; so Mrs. Edmonds and her daughter were left to themselves. Marjorie grumbled about it a little.

"It is ever so lonesome, Mamma, without Leonard, isn't it? One expected to have to get on without Frank, but I thought we were sure of Leonard until October. I wonder if his mother thinks any more of him than we do? Dear me! I wonder what the mother is like? I believe I feel half afraid of her. My own little mother has spoiled me for any other, and she is the only one in the world of that sort."

The sentence was frequently interrupted by gay little kisses, which Marjorie placed on her mother's eyes, her nose, her chin, on any improbable place. She had gone back in those few days to the light-heartedness of her early girlhood. Mrs. Edmonds, watching her, and noting how entirely the shadows had lifted from her fair face, could not but be happy in her daughter's happiness, and hide away her own sore disappointment. Sometimes she feared it was not entirely hidden. For instance, at that moment Marjorie, with her mother's face between her two hands, drew back and scanned it closely, as she said, "I believe you are the only one who is not entirely satisfied and happy. You had such an absurd little daydream to be carried out, and we all disappointed you so. Poor Mother! to have failed in your only attempt at matchmaking! You wanted Leonard and me to be lovers, and we would persist in being only the best of friends. Mammy, I warn you, if you give the least little speck more of your heart to Leonard than you do to Frank, I shall be jealous of him." Then, with a sudden change of tone, "Mother dear, doesn't it seem almost too bad that Leonard does not find some strong, sweet woman who is in every way worthy of his heart, and give it to her? There must be such a woman in the world. Or has she, possibly, gone to heaven? Perhaps it is the memory of some sweet early friend that has given his face such a different look from other faces. Only, if it were so, I almost think he would have told me, so intimate as we have been. I was tempted to ask Frank confidentially about him; but the brothers have been so separated of late years that I think perhaps we know Leonard better than does his own family. Isn't it blessed, Mamma, to have such a brother—and to have found the brother first! That is unusual, isn't it?"

Mrs. Edmonds kissed the bright face close to hers and suppressed her sigh, and said, "I would not ask Frank about him, Daughter, if I were you. Since he has not chosen to give you his confidence, would it not be better to respect his reserve?"

"Of course, mother; you are right, as usual. But I cannot help wishing there were some angel good enough for Leonard. It seems hard that he should have to be content with only a very faulty sister."

"Why are not your sympathies drawn out toward Frank, my dear, since you see your faults so plainly?" Mrs. Edmonds could not help indulging herself in this little study to discover, if she might, why the one brother had been so entirely successful where the other had signally failed.

"Oh, Frank!" Marjorie said with a rich blush, and the happiest of little laughs; "he is not perfect, like his brother; I assure you, Mamma, I shall be much better for him than any angel that was ever created."

And the mother could not doubt it.

Very swiftly had the fall and winter sped. Broken at the holidays by a hurried visit from Doctor Maxwell, who brought his brother's regrets, that gentleman having deemed it advisable to spend Christmas and New Year's Day with his mother in a distant part of the state.

In the following June, within two days after Doctor Maxwell was freed from college life, there was a quiet wedding in Mrs. Edmonds's front parlor, no guests not immediately connected with the two families being present save Glyde Douglass Burwell and her husband, and Hannah Bramlett.

Nothing more unlike the dreams and fancies of Marjorie's early girlhood could have been imagined than this very simple, very private wedding.

"I used to think," she said to her mother, as they stood together in the bridal chamber a few minutes before the hour for the ceremony, "I used to think,

Mamma, that if ever I married, I would have a magnificent church wedding, with flowers and ribbons, and carriages, and point lace, and bridesmaids, and maid of honor, and all the fineries and follies that such an occasion could possibly offer an excuse for. I planned regardless of expense, precisely as though you were a rich woman, you understand; I think girls often do, and grow into the idea that such accompaniments are necessities. Positively, I have come to believe that even such trivial matters as these have a great deal to do with the mistake marriages, of which there seem to be so many. Girls, young and thoughtless, become fascinated by the display that surrounds the marriage ceremony, the mere outside show I mean, and accept the husbands as necessary adjuncts to that hour of splendor, with almost no serious thought about their future. Mother," with a sudden little tremble in her voice, "I came so near, so very near, at one time, to making one of those awful mistakes! Can you think how it makes me feel to remember where he is today?"

And Mrs. Edmonds knew that her daughter had gone back to her early girlhood, to the time when she had expected to be Ralph Bramlett's bride. Even the mother shivered at the thought; for Ralph Bramlett that day wore a convict's dress. Every effort that had been faithfully and persistently put forth in his behalf had failed, and three months before Marjorie's marriage day he had received his sentence. What if he had been her darling's husband!

"Daughter," she said, a sudden trembling seizing her as she clung to the beautiful white-robed girl, "it frightens me to think of what might have been." Then, after a few moments, during which she was caressed and soothed as though she had been the daughter, she said:

"Dear child, forgive the question I am going to ask; it seems to me that I must. You have so often told me since that early time that you believed that you were not like other girls, that you should never marry; will you tell me—are you sure, quite, quite sure, that you were mistaken in yourself and that your highest and holiest needs are met in this marriage?"

"Mother!" the girl bent over her and wound the silken robes about her in a tender embrace that was almost maternal. "My little mother! do you think I can have you worrying your heart with such questions? I was very much in earnest in what I said, very sincere; and I should have kept my word, I am confident, if I had not met Frank Maxwell. But that, you see, overturned all my intentions. I am very, very sure that no other man on earth could have done it." And then that all-conquering man had knocked at the door, and they had gone down to the parlor, and in five minutes more the mother's one darling had become Mrs. Frank Maxwell.

One bit of gossip that floated afterward to the ears of the bride had sent her into heartiest laughter.

"I want to know if she is really married!" Mrs. Kenyon was reported to have said. "Well, now, which one was it? I never could be sure myself, and I don't see how she could be. The professor certainly had the most chance, and she seemed to divide herself equally between them when they were here together; and I didn't know but at the last minute she would change her mind and take him."

The doctor had carried his bride away with him that evening; and Mr. Maxwell had lingered, taking possession of his old room and giving the lonely mother much of his time and care, until, in September, she was ready to join her daughter in her new home. The following June had brought him to the old home again with Mrs. Edmonds, and now for two happy weeks Doctor and Mrs. Frank Maxwell had been there also. It was Doctor Maxwell's first vacation of any extent since that six weeks' one in which he had accomplished so much; and he was enjoying it with all the abandon that had characterized his earlier days. Many were the rides and walks and visits the four had already enjoyed together.

"Quite like old times," Doctor Frank was fond of saying; though at least one of the party felt distinctly the sharp contrast between the present and the past.

On the particular morning with which this chapter opens, Marjorie Maxwell had elected, for reasons best known to herself, to divide the company and keep her brother-in-law to herself.

There was certainly a strong flavor of the past in this leisurely walk together through the familiar streets. They could scarcely help talking of old times, or at least of old friends, as they passed houses and corners that recalled them vividly. Especially was this the case when they passed the house where Ralph Bramlett's brief and stormy married life had been spent, and noted that windows and doors were thrown open to the morning, and the voices of happy children at play floated to them from the little side yard.

"You see him occasionally still?" inquired Mr. Maxwell, as they both looked earnestly at the house where they had been so often guests; he had no need to use names.

"Occasionally, yes; Frank tries to see him regularly every two weeks; and Glyde, I think, never misses a visiting day, though she is crowded with work and care. Hasn't she been a faithful sister-in-law?"

"And is Frank as well pleased with the change in him as ever? There has been so much to talk about since we met that I haven't asked particularly concerning him."

"Oh, Frank is more than pleased. He says that people who have not seen him since that time would not recognize him; there is such a radical change in looks as well as manner. And I, who see him less often, probably notice it even more; besides, his record there shows for itself. Mr. Adams told Frank that everyone in the house respected him. Isn't it strange that he should have had to go through such an ordeal before finding the right road, or at least before being willing to walk in it?"

"Yet the change came before the legal punishment began."

"I know—did Frank tell you about it? That second night beside his father's coffin. I hope the father knew it right away! Frank says it is very touching to hear him tell it. Has he told you the particulars?"

"Ralph wrote to me," said Mr. Maxwell, speaking with evident effort after a moment's hesitation. "It seems he had an old grudge or prejudice against me—I am sure I did not know it—and felt that he wanted to apologize. There was no need, but he wrote an earnest, manly letter; such a one, I confess, as I had not thought he could write; and among other things he told me the story of that night. In his extremity, he said, the Lord Jesus Christ came and held out his hand. How many witnesses he has to a like experience with like results! Does it not seem strange sometimes that there should be any doubters? There is no better attested fact in all history than that personal contact with Jesus Christ transforms lives.

"Does Mrs. Burwell ever hear from her sister in the West?"

"Not at all. Doesn't it seem too sad? She has alienated herself from them all. Now that her mother is gone, there is apparently no link between them. The eldest sister is with Glyde, you know; but she never hears, either. The uncle with whom Estelle is, writes occasionally to Glyde; but he was never given to letter-writing, Glyde says, and if they do not hear from him once in six months, they are not surprised. He mentions Estelle only in the most casual and fragmentary way. I am afraid that such mention tells too much; for the uncle is very fond of Glyde—why, he is the Uncle Anthony about whom she used to talk so much—and if there were anything cheering to say, he would be sure to say it. However, he is evidently very good to Estelle; if she had not had such a refuge, I do not know what would have become of her—father and mother both gone. Nothing any sadder than those two wrecked lives has come to my knowledge. There are times when it seems as though I could not have it so. Now that Ralph is a changed man, I feel as though something ought to be done to bring them together. Only think of it! He has never seen his little boy; and, if this continues, is not likely to."

"Yet; if she is not a changed woman, could their coming together work out anything but misery? That she is utterly silent toward her husband augurs very ill for her. I have old-fashioned notions about marriage vows, Marjorie."

Thus they talked of old acquaintances and new experiences, and moralized after a fashion that belonged to them, moving slowly the while toward

"Hill House," as the building on the hill above the factories had come to be known. The Maxwell brothers had continued its rental since that month when Mrs. Miller and her sick child had been removed there. Many others had since enjoyed a week or a month, or, on occasion, three months' respite from their hard lives by a sojourn there. Among the initiated in Factoryville they called the place not Hill House but "Heaven," speaking the word reverently. A few other rooms had been furnished in simple and sanitary fashion, and it was well understood that Hannah Bramlett and her mother had the general supervision of the entire house. No great expenditures in any direction had been necessary; there was nowhere any lavish display of funds, and yet the necessary money for doing what manifestly ought to be done seemed always to be forthcoming. Altogether Hill House was a very unique and interesting mystery to many curious people.

Mrs. Marjorie, though undoubtedly enjoying her talk, had all the while, to those who knew her well, the manner of one who has something more important in reserve that she means to reach when the set time shall arrive. At last she reached it by the question:

"How is Hannah prospering?"

26

─────

HALF THE STORY

"HANNAH," said Mr. Maxwell, "is a comfort in many ways, and a success. She is in her element in managing Hill House. I think you would be surprised to see how wisely she administers affairs there. Her talents ought to be utilized in a much larger way. At present, however, she owes her first duty, of course, to her mother. But the dear little old lady grows feeble; Hannah will wait alone for Ralph's homecoming, I fear."

"It was so good of you to plan to let her stay at the old farm," said Marjorie gratefully. "I heard the story of the mortgage all over again from Hannah's eager lips; she could not tell me enough about it."

"Hannah is very generous to her friends."

"Do the gossips let her alone nowadays?" was the next question, asked a little timidly. The reply was prompt and free.

"Ah, that reminds me; I have great news for you. I hope you remember Bill Seber, and the trouble he used to give Miss Hannah by paying too much attention to her pretty pupil, Susie Miller? She was so tried about it that she enlisted Jack Taylor in Susie's behalf. Jack, you know, always enters into things with a vim; and he prosecuted his duties as protector of Susie with such vigor and success that the girl forgot Bill Seber entirely and gave her allegiance to Jack. Result, a charming little wedding that is in prospect. I fancy it is to be held at Hill House; and if I am not greatly mistaken, you and Doctor Frank will be honored with invitations. Great excitement prevails in regard to the minutest details. You will be glad to know, as an instance of what may perhaps be called poetic justice, that Bill Seber seems to be chief man. Does that story answer your question? Even the gossips have discovered that Jack Taylor is otherwise engaged; and as for Miss Hannah, I believe she has learned the lesson that diffusive helpfulness is the best and truest kind. She has not selected any substitute for Jack, but has any number of special protégés now and is certainly one of the most helpful workers they have at the mission or the evening school. Don't you remember Frank used to say when he first met her that she was an illustration of energy run to waste?" And then Mrs. Marjorie resolved to make her opportunity without waiting for a more favorable time.

"Leonard," she began, a touch of timidity in her voice, "I am just the same as your 'truly' sister am I not, and may speak to you quite as plainly as a real sister might?"

"Assuredly I cannot conceive of any words from you that I should consider too plain. I think you must know how I appreciate my place on your list of relatives."

She laughed lightly. "Do not take me too seriously, Leonard, or I shall be afraid to proceed. I'm going to criticize you if you do not frighten me out of it; and it is a line of criticism to which I am certain you are not used. Do you remember speaking very plain words to me once about poor Ralph, and the mistakes I made in trying to help him? Has it never occurred to you that possibly you might be making a mistake in the same direction?"

That it had not was evidenced at once by his look of utter bewilderment.

"This is worse than a conundrum," he said cheerily, "and I was never known to guess one of those creations. Speak plainly, my dear sister; I assure you I am quite prepared for the worst!"

It was impossible not to laugh, and several more minutes were wasted in fun; then Marjorie grew suddenly grave.

"Seriously, Leonard, there is something that I very much want to say to you, and to say it with delicacy and dignity; but the subject matter is so foreign to you that I do not know how to set about it. Let me put it in plain language, I do not like circumlocution. I am afraid that because of your kindness and thoughtfulness and perfect courtesy toward one woman, you are awakening not expectations, perhaps, but feelings that you would not like to arouse, and making wounds that will be hard to heal. Remember, I am sure before you tell me so, that you have not had such an idea. Perhaps you will even find it hard to believe that I am right; but I know I am."

Her listener's face expressed only amazement.

"I was never at a more utter loss to understand one's meaning," he said, speaking gravely enough, but yet with that cheerful air which said, "You are evidently laboring under some sort of mistake that I can set right in two minutes, if you will be so kind as to enlighten me with regard to it."

Marjorie hesitated and almost wished that she had not begun. It was so at war with all her ideas of friendship, this laying bare the sacred secrets of others.

"Has it never occurred to you," she said slowly, choosing her words with great care, "that Hannah, being a woman, and having a warm, true heart, might be giving it unawares in a direction that could cause her only pain?"

And then she felt a sudden irritation against this brother who had heretofore seemed all but perfect. His face expressed only sincere perplexity. Why need he be so absurdly obtuse? Because he was superior, apparently, to the weakness of an absorbing human affection, need he therefore forget that he was surrounded by people who were very human indeed?

"My dear Marjorie," he said gently, "I must be very stupid; no such thought has for a moment occurred to me. I cannot think, indeed, I am sure, that you do not refer to Jack Taylor. I assure you, she is simply delighted with this approaching marriage; her whole heart is in it."

"Jack Taylor, indeed!" Marjorie could not help an outburst of laughter, though feeling much inclined to cry instead with something akin to vexation.

"Oh, Leonard! Of all absurd creatures, a man under certain circumstances can be the most so. I am talking, or trying to talk, about *you*. Don't you know that you have been very especially kind to Hannah of late, and that she has not had many friends, and that she has a great, true, appreciative heart? Can you not step down from your heights of superiority long enough to conceive of the mischief you might do?"

He was silent for so long that she began to fear she had offended him and glanced timidly at his face. It expressed only distress.

"I hope and believe that you are mistaken," he said at last. "It would give me deeper pain than I could express in words to cause Miss Hannah, or for that matter any other lady, a moment's suffering, or to be the means of any misunderstanding. I cannot think it possible that a woman who has shown herself to be so sensible could—however, I need not pursue the subject further; it were discourtesy to her to do so. I need hardly tell you, Marjorie, that I appreciate your motive and have to thank you, as usual. It may be that in my preoccupation I have been sufficiently careless to set those gossiping tongues, of which you used to stand in such fear, at work again; if so, I am truly mortified. Part of my creed has been that no gentleman should so conduct himself with a lady as to make her the subject of unpleasant remark."

He began immediately to talk of other matters and held Marjorie so closely after that to interests connected with Hill House that neither then, nor on their return trip, was there opportunity to add another word. She felt a trifle sore over it. The interview had not been what she had planned. She had believed that this man, who had shown her a brother's kindness always, would be frank and communicative with her, instead of closing her mouth almost as he might have done Mrs. Kenyon's. She said something of the kind to her husband at the first moment of privacy; and he had soothed her with the reminder that Leonard was not like any other man living and must not be judged by the same rules.

"He lives in the clouds," said that wise brother, "and always did; just the warmest human love that he knows anything about he gives to mother and you, and it simply bewilders him to suppose that anyone could imagine him as having more to give. But he will do the wise thing by your friend Hannah in some way; see if he doesn't."

Feeling that at least she had done her best, and vaguely fearing lest in some way it should prove to be, nevertheless, her worst, Marjorie tried to dismiss the matter from her thoughts with ill success. Mr. Maxwell she saw little of during the afternoon. He remained in his room, "at work on his everlasting book," her husband reported; and the evening gathering was therefore looked forward to with something like solitude on Marjorie's part. But directly after tea, Mr. Maxwell went out without explanation to anybody; when he returned it was late, and Marjorie and her husband had been long in their own room. After that, life went on much as usual. Not even Marjorie could detect the slightest shade of difference in her brother-in-law's manner toward her; and it was not until years afterward that she learned how he spent that evening.

As a matter of fact, the textbook that he was preparing received very little of Mr. Maxwell's attention that summer afternoon; instead, he gave himself to thought and prayer as to his present duty, in view of the revelation that Marjorie had made to him. The more carefully he considered it, the more sure he was that she was right and that he had been culpably blind and careless. By evening his way seemed clear; and he took himself, as early as propriety would admit, out to the Bramlett farm and sat down in the large old-fashioned parlor near Hannah, whose grave face had brightened visibly at the sound of his voice.

There were matters of interest to talk about, as there always were, connected with Hill House; especially so in view of the approaching marriage ceremony to take place there. After duly considering various questions of expedience that had arisen since their last talk, Mr. Maxwell deliberately made the conversation personal by saying:

"This planning marriage festivities and housekeeping details is queer work perhaps for a confirmed bachelor like myself, is it not? But I assure you I enjoy it. I do not think that even you can take a stronger interest in this young couple than I do. I fancy that some of the pleasure of my life will be found in watching others set sail on the stream that I shall never by experience know anything about. I like to give a little pull now and then with the oars, as by your kindness I am permitted to do in this case."

The hand visibly trembled that was turning over the papers on which the names of guests to be invited to Hill House had been written; and Hannah's voice was constrained as she tried to say lightly:

"I should think you were young to talk about being a confirmed bachelor. You'll be setting sail yourself someday."

He shook his head and spoke with exceeding gravity:

"No, Miss Hannah; possibly I am peculiar; I do not profess to know other men very well, but I believe I know myself. It is possible, no doubt, for a man to meet two women who, at different stages of his matured life, he might desire to marry. For me there was only one. Her I have lost, and I am as sure as though the grave had already closed over me that no woman will ever share my name and work."

"Did she die?" It was after some minutes of ominous silence that Hannah trusted her voice to ask, speaking very low, that simple question.

"No; she lived and married, and is a happy and honored wife, and never knew, and will never know, what she was to me. You, my friend, are the only person to whom I have ever deliberately told the story. You know, of course, that I have a reason for thus laying bare my heart; let me tell you briefly what it is. I have plans connected with this scheme of ours that will involve a much greater money outlay than we have had thus far. You have managed admirably with what there was; but of course you know that Hill House has been trammeled in many ways for want of an assured financial basis. My salary as a teacher is more than sufficient for my personal wishes, and entirely separate from that there is a small fortune that I inherited with unlimited rights. My mother and brother are both so situated as to money that there is not a reasonable fear of their ever needing any of mine. Such being the case, I have determined to make Hill House a permanent place where we can at leisure experiment on some of our ideas. I say 'we' in connection with it all, because I fully realize that, while some of us have furnished the money, it is really your patient and persistent thought and care that have made it the success that it is. I know your heart must be fully committed to the enterprise. I have intruded my personal affairs upon you because I foresaw that you would have criticisms to answer with regard to what some people will consider a lavish one of means; and I feared that your own thoughtful heart might be troubled about a possible future. So I determined to make very plain to you that no future ties of mine would ever call in question my right to thus dispose of my stewardship.

"Am I not right, Miss Hannah, in committing you unreservedly to this enterprise and believing that you will give it all the time and strength that you can spare from higher duties?"

He did not make a very long tarry after that, believing that neither Hannah nor he was in the mood for commonplaces. Neither was he ready for his room and bed. Instead, he walked away beyond the Bramlett farm, out into the quiet country. The night was warm and still and the moonlight brilliant. It all brought vividly back to Mr. Maxwell's mind a walk that he had taken with Marjorie years before. She had been frightened at finding herself alone on the lonely street, and his coming had relieved her fears. She had clung to his arm all in a tremble for a minute, and he had felt then and there the mysterious thrill of soul that comes sometimes to link another soul to one's own. He put the thought quietly from him. Marjorie was his sister, God bless her; all the past had been lived through and put away. He thought of Hannah, and walked back past the Bramlett farm. A light still burned in the room that he chanced to have discovered was Hannah's own. Poor Hannah! He had done the best that he knew to cover over a mistake that Marjorie believed he had made; there was a dull pain at his heart as the belief thrust itself upon him that Marjorie was right. How could he have been so careless and cruel? There was but one thing left for him to do for Hannah; he walked slowly back along the country road, praying.

Hannah Bramlett sat in her little low-backed rocker, bolt upright, hands clasped in her lap, no tears on her face nor in her eyes. This was not the time for tears. She had her own heart's secret to struggle with and bury. How glad she was that it was all her own. It seemed to her that she must have died had anybody known. She had not realized what had happened to her until Mr. Maxwell's own words had revealed herself to herself. How good he had been! and unselfish and true, just as he always was. To think of anyone preferring anybody—to him! Hannah tried to be true to her friends, even in her thoughts.

Well for her that she was not, and knew that she was not, at the mercy of a hopeless love so that her life must be ruined and the lives of others marred in consequence. She must rise above this thing as a matter of course; she must remember first of all that she had given her heart to the Lord Jesus Christ and was his, body and soul, for time and for eternity.

Even before she went to her knees she had settled it. She would live her life, the busy, helpful life that Mr. Maxwell's generosity made possible, and prove to herself as well as to others that "grace was sufficient."

When Mr. Maxwell found that the small light in the eastern window of the Bramlett farmhouse had disappeared, he went home.

"I was so astonished the other night over what you planned to do that I did not answer you very clearly, I think. I'll help at Hill House in any way that you think I can and be glad of the chance. I will give my life to it." This was what Hannah Bramlett said to Mr. Maxwell the next time she met him. After a moment, during which she had flushed and paled and cleared her voice, as though she had more to say when she could trust herself to say it, she had interrupted the kindly commonplaces with which Mr. Maxwell was answering her, to add:

"And, Mr. Maxwell, I thank you for telling me what you did the other night; it was kind of you; I won't ever forget it."

This was the only reference that either of the two persons concerned ever made to that important evening in their lives.

27

OPPORTUNITY

MRS. Frank Maxwell was in her nursery, where small Marjorie was being prepared to abdicate her throne for a few hours, and give herself to sleep. This was holiday time for both father and mother. No trivial thing was allowed to interfere with that half hour alone with their little girl. Doctor Maxwell had just departed in response to a call from his office—not without a few grumbling words to the effect that a doctor never had time to even kiss his baby—when the mother, too, was summoned.

A lady was waiting in the parlor who would not give her name but said that she must see Mrs. Maxwell immediately.

That lady arose with a sigh; this looked suspiciously like one of the numerous calls that came to her in the name of a need that had been reached through devious windings along the paths of sin. Mrs. Maxwell had found that the Christian wife of a Christian physician in large practice in a large city not only had need for the grace of patience but also must become, in the most important sense of that phrase, a careful student of human nature.

She lingered to give a few more good-night kisses to little Marjorie, with a thought of prayer in her heart, not only for the baby, but for what might await her downstairs; then she went. The parlor was dimly lighted; and her caller stood in shadow—a tall woman dressed in black, with a veil that partly obscured her face.

"Will you not be seated?" said the hostess, advancing. "What can I do for you?"

The lady turned and threw back her veil, stepping forward toward the light as she did so. Instantly Marjorie exclaimed, "Estelle Bramlett!"

"You know me, then? I did not feel sure that you would. The years have made such changes. Yes, I am Estelle Bramlett. I have not been half an hour in your city and have come to you at the very first. You can do—everything for me, perhaps. Marjorie, I want to see my husband. I feel that I *must* see him. I do not know whether I ought or not; but I think I have borne this life just as long as I can. Will you help me?"

She had changed very greatly; it was not strange that she should have been in doubt as to whether her old acquaintance would know her. The abundant hair, of so dark a brown that it would almost have been called black, was now so abundantly streaked with white that, in connection with the deathly pallor of her face and the dark rings under her eyes, it made her look almost like an old woman. Yet Marjorie, though she struggled to speak quietly, had only aversion for the woman that she felt had been heartless and cruel.

"I do not know of any reason why you should not have seen your husband at any time during these long years," she said; "your sister has constantly done so, and other and newer friends than she have been faithful."

"I know it; oh, I know it all! Marjorie, do not look at me so coldly. You who are a happy wife and mother, have a little pity on me. Do you think I have not suffered? Don't you know why I have kept away from him all these years, kept myself from writing to him, or hearing from him, save now and then through others? May I sit down near you, Marjorie, and tell you the whole story?"

Of course she must be heard. Mrs. Maxwell carried her to her own room, gave peremptory orders that she was engaged and could see no one, then closed and locked the door and sat down opposite the hollow-eyed woman, who had dropped into the nearest chair.

It was a long, sad story. During the days immediately following the knowledge of her husband's disgrace and ruin, Estelle admitted that she had been hard and cruel. She believed she was insane. She did not know what spirit possessed her. She tried at times, and could not *make* herself do other than as she did. For a while she believed that she hated her husband, hated her sister, hated even her poor mother, who bore with her and tried in pitiful ways to help her. If it were not insanity, what could it be called? For certainly she had always loved her mother. More than that, she hated, it seemed to her, everyone who bore the name Christian, everything that had to do with Christianity. In her wildness she dated the beginning of Ralph's downfall to that time when he joined the church and professed to be interested in such matters and did so many things that she did not understand and that were not like him. When he was convicted and sentenced to state prison, she had felt for a time that she must take her life to get rid of the horror of it all. Then suddenly she had remembered her Uncle Anthony, whose favorite she once had been. She knew that he lived alone, with only a housekeeper to care for him; and she knew that he had repudiated all interest in religious things long before. If he would but take her in and shield her from the hateful world, from everybody who had ever known or seen her—above all, from church members and ministers and all the dreadful people who had awakened at the eleventh hour to try to "do her good,—"she believed that she might possibly keep, for a time at least, from that last awful crime of suicide. So she went away in the night, unknown even to her mother, and made her way to Uncle Anthony's western home. He had received her and cared for her like a father; but she had not been in his home for twenty-four hours before she made a discovery that filled her insane soul with a kind of terror. Uncle Anthony had become a man of prayer, a churchgoer, a church member, identified with all the interests from which she had run away!

She told her story well and briefly. How, by degrees, Uncle Anthony gained an influence over her, calmed her strange fears, and made her see that that from which she had shrunk as from an enemy contained the only hope or help for her in this world; until there came a time when she would have gone home, only then it was too late—mother and father were gone, and she had no home. Up to that point she had talked on steadily, with a kind of suppressed intensity, controlling with firm will any expression of emotion; but when she spoke of her father and mother and the broken home, there came a burst of tears, and she buried her face in her hands. Only for a moment; then she brushed the tears away and continued her story.

By degrees, what she had supposed to be the faith

of her childhood, or, rather, such faith as her childhood had never known, came to her; such a sense of the power, not only, but of the goodness of God, and such a realization of the fact that he called upon her to be his child and trust him fully, as she had not known was possible, filled her soul. From that hour she began to order her life, to the best of her ability, as she believed God would have her.

At this point Marjorie interrupted her for the first time, "But, Estelle, under those circumstances, how was it possible for you to maintain such utter silence toward all your old friends, toward your husband especially, when you must have known something of what it would add to his misery?"

A sudden change came over her guest's face; the hands clasped on her black dress trembled visibly, and her entire attitude was that of one trying to hold some intense feeling in check.

"You do not know what you are talking about," she said at last, not passionately, but with an air of hopeless conviction. "I knew only too well that for my husband to hear from me, or even to hear of me, with the feeling that I was holding him in any way, would but add another drop to his cup of misery—a very large drop. I came to know, long before I took that last step, which I meant should separate me from my home and all my old associations, that my husband had made a fatal mistake; that he did not love me and never had; and that for me to go away from him, so far that he need never hear from me again, nor have to do with me in any way, would be the best effort I could make toward fulfilling the spirit of my marriage vows."

A soft light broke over Mrs. Maxwell's face. This confession, made in abject sorrowfulness, was a revelation to her; it explained much that had been terrible in the conduct of this friend of her girlhood. She even began to understand the processes of reasoning by which this half-insane woman had reached her strange conclusions. She asked another question, her tone much more sympathetic than it had been.

"Have your ideas or feelings changed in any degree of late, Estelle?"

The look of abject misery on Mrs. Bramlett's face lifted, and she turned eager eyes on her hostess.

"Yes, they have; that is, my ideas of what is right have changed very greatly. I have come to feel that in isolating myself from my past, or trying to do so, I was wrong, as I have been in almost every act of my life. I have come to realize that when I made that resolve, I took counsel of wounded feeling, instead of looking to my Father in heaven for direction. I have come to understand better what marriage vows mean and to feel that, bitter as the mistake may have been, and hard as the result may be, there is nothing for me, nothing for him, but to abide by those vows. You see, Marjorie, he is the father of my child and has duties toward him which he cannot lay aside at will; and for the sake of him, as well as for the sake of truth and honor, we must *together* do the utmost that we can with what life we have left. Is not that so? Am I not right this time? I have not arrived at such a conclusion hastily; indeed, there is a sense in which I may say that I did not reach it at all. The feeling came to me. I have thought over it and prayed over it, until at last it seems to me a conviction; but I have as yet taken no step to disturb Ralph. I came directly to you. It seemed to me that you would be sure to know what was right, better than any other person to whom I could appeal."

"What do you want to do, Estelle, aside from this conviction of what is right? I mean, if you could have your choice, and feel that either course would have God's approval, which would be yours?"

For the first time the pallor on the worn face before her disappeared, and a deep crimson took its place.

"You are afraid I am taking counsel of feeling, instead of duty!" she exclaimed. "I have been afraid of it myself—so afraid that it has made me hesitate long, yet it seems to me now that I am going in the direction pointed out; but I will be very frank with you and leave you to decide. I want, above all things else in this world, to make what atonement I can to my husband for his wrecked life. He ought not to have married me, Marjorie, knowing that he did not love me—I cannot close my eyes to the facts; but after that, almost everything that has happened since has been, I think, my own fault. I was so exacting, so hard, so cruel! Oh, you have no conception of the life I led him! It is no wonder that it ended as it did; I goaded him to it. I think there is no other word that would describe the condition of things. And I have a consuming desire to tell him that and to get him, on my knees, to forgive me and let me try again. I have forgiven him utterly; but what I had to forgive, the real sin against me, was when he asked me away back there to be his wife. So far as my own marriage vows were concerned, I have nothing to confess; I meant them fully. That I have failed ignominiously in keeping them, I do confess in shame and bitterness of soul; but when I took them upon me, my whole heart went with them. I loved him, Marjorie, and I love him now. I love him so much that if it is the right thing to do, I am willing to keep away from him forever and live my life alone; yes, I am even willing—"but then there came a look of inexpressible agony into the dark, sad eyes—"to give up my little boy—*his* little boy—to his care and love, if God directs me to do so. But, oh, I do not see it so now! I cannot but feel that together we might cover over some of the mistakes and bring up our child for God; and I cannot but feel that he means we shall try to keep the solemn vows which we called him to witness were made until death parted us. Oh, Marjorie! can you help me? How does it seem to you? Am I right, or wrong?"

She must have noticed the change in Marjorie's face; for Marjorie's eyes shone with a tender light, and her voice was tenderness itself.

"My dear friend," she said, "my sympathies and hopes are with you. I believe you are being led by the Spirit of God, and that you are to be given such an opportunity as perhaps does not come to many for redeeming the past. Have you heard anything about Ralph of late?"

"Nothing," said Mrs. Bramlett eagerly. "I would not allow myself to question Glyde. I thought it was not being true to my resolve to let him be entirely freed of me. I thought it was due to him, after the way in which I had treated him, that I should not even mention his name. I lived up to my resolve literally; I might have been trying to do so still, if I had not been taught by my boy. When he began to ask questions, to say, 'Where is my papa? Has my papa gone to heaven like Robbie Stuart's?' then I felt that there was another life to be considered. There was an innocent boy who ought not to be deprived of his father's love and care because of his mother's sins; and I resolved to come and ask Ralph if we could not begin again. But in order to be utterly sure that I was doing what was right and not simply what I wanted to do, I resolved, as I told you, to come first to you. We did not even go to Glyde's; we stopped at a hotel, Uncle Anthony and my little Ralph and I. Uncle Anthony has been good to me through it all. He took me home to his heart at once and bore with all my miseries and follies almost as an angel might. I believe he thinks I am doing right at last, although he has said not one word to influence me in any direction. He said he was afraid to interfere, that he had interfered in lives before and done mischief, and he wanted God to lead me. But he himself proposed to come East with me; and when I told him I wanted to see you at once, he ordered a carriage as soon as my little boy was asleep and promised to watch beside him until I returned, and let me come away quite alone, as I wanted to. Why did you ask me if I had heard from Ralph lately?" she broke off abruptly to inquire, her face paling over a sudden fear, "Oh, Marjorie! he is not ill?"

"No," said Marjorie with quiet promptness; "he is quite well; my husband saw him only yesterday. I will help you, Estelle; be sure of that. I am glad that I can. My husband goes so frequently to see Ralph and understands so fully what is necessary, that he will be able to make all arrangements for you to meet him. Can you come—wait, let me think—I shall talk with Doctor Maxwell tonight, of course, as soon as he comes in, and—can you wait one day more, Estelle, until five o'clock tomorrow? I am afraid it cannot be managed before that hour."

"I will do whatever you tell me," said this curious shadow of Estelle Douglass, who was so like and yet so utterly unlike her former self that there were moments when Marjorie almost asked herself if she were not dreaming.

She went herself to the door to see her guest to her carriage, then awaited with feverish impatience her husband's return.

28

ANOTHER CRISIS

A WONDERFUL bit of news she could have given her caller, had she been sure as to the wisdom of doing so. From the wife's point of view, Ralph Bramlett had still another full year of servitude before he could go out into the world again; and he must go always thereafter, she believed, with the prison stain upon him. But, as a matter of fact, in less than twenty-four hours from that time, Marjorie expected to receive Ralph Bramlett as her guest, with the assurance that those terrible iron doors had opened to him for the last time. Very earnest efforts had been made during these years, both by Mr. Burwell and the Maxwells, to secure the young man's pardon; and each time they had been unsuccessful. The governor, owing to certain recent experiences, was more than usually difficult to move; and though almost everything possible was in the prisoner's favor, most of his friends had finally despaired. It was almost against the judgment of his brother that Mr. Leonard Maxwell made another effort, so that all were prepared to be not only joyful, but astonished, over his success. It had been arranged that Doctor Maxwell should go the next day at the appointed hour, in his carriage, to bring Ralph Bramlett, *citizen,* home with him as his guest.

Glyde and her husband were to come for the day; and Hannah Bramlett had been telegraphed for and was expected to arrive by the late train that evening.

"Be sure to bring the baby," Marjorie had admonished Glyde, "and I will keep little Marjorie awake for the occasion; we must have everything as cheerful and unembarrassing as possible, and the children will help toward that end."

Estelle's unexpected advent had disarranged the program. Mrs. Maxwell's quick brain saw a certain tableau that could be arranged, the viewing of which, she believed, would do more to welcome Ralph Bramlett back to the world than most of them realized. She knew certain facts that the others did not. More than one earnest talk had she held with the friend of her youth during the intervening years. They had not talked very much about the past; it had not seemed to her wise; instead, she had striven to help the repentant man to think of the duties and responsibilities of his future. But one day he had begun to speak to her quite as though they had been talking about Estelle:

"I do not want you to blame my poor wife overmuch, Mrs. Maxwell," he had said; "I made her life anything but a happy one, even from the first. It is probably the very best that she can do for her future happiness to free herself entirely from me, as she has. She has a legal right to do this, you remember, and I certainly should be the last to blame her for taking advantage of it; yet if I had my chance again, I think I could make her life at least a peaceful one. Sometimes in my dreams I go through some of the scenes that might have been; I have my boy in my arms, and can feel his kisses on my face, and hear him call me 'papa.' Can you imagine what it is to me to waken from such dreams to the reality?"

Marjorie had gone away from that talk with her heart swelling with indignation against Estelle, feeling that she had done a monstrous thing in thus utterly repudiating her marriage vows. Now her heart throbbed with sympathy as she thought of the surprise in store for both. Surely the desire of her life in being instrumental in bringing those two together again, under changed relations, seemed about to be realized.

"Hurry!" she said to Doctor Maxwell two hours later, as she waited at the head of the stairs for him to ascend. "How very late you are! Yes, Hannah has come, and gone to bed hours ago. Do hurry, Frank! Never mind the mail; I have something wonderful to tell you—something that will not wait. Who do you think has been with me this evening?"

"The President of the United States and all his Cabinet, at the very least, to judge from your excitement," he said, smiling, as he bent to greet her.

"It is a much more important event than that. Frank, Estelle was with me for an hour or more."

"Mrs. Bramlett!" he said, with lifted eyebrows. "I did not know that it would give you very special delight to have a visit from her."

"You are not to talk in that horrid way, nor put on your superior look. I have a wonderful story to tell you. Estelle is so changed that you would hardly think she could be the same person."

"I am glad to hear it; the greatest good that Mrs. Bramlett's old acquaintances could wish for her, would be that she would become utterly unlike herself."

"Hush!" said Marjorie with pretty imperiousness. "Save your sarcasms; wait until you hear what I have to tell."

The talk that followed lasted away into the night—into the early morning, rather; and before all the details of the coming day were arranged to their satisfaction, the doctor was called to a patient. However, he left his wife quite satisfied with the interest he had shown and the enthusiasm with which he had entered into her altered plans.

It is probably useless to try to picture, even to ourselves, the tumult of feeling that surged through the soul of Ralph Bramlett as he sat alone in Doctor Maxwell's library on that afternoon which marked another solemn crisis in his life. One may be deeply sympathetic with certain experiences, and yet be unable to imagine their depth and power on the heart of another. Such ordinarily trivial things help at times to swell the tide of feeling. Take the mere matter of dress, for instance; consider what it was for this man to find himself attired in citizen's dress once more, the hated garb of prison life put away from him! How strange and new, and yet how old and familiar, must have been the sensation as he sank into the depths of that richly upholstered chair and felt, rather than realized, that his feet gave back no sound as he made his way to it. Once more he was in a home! Once more he was surrounded, enveloped as it were, in an atmosphere of refinement and quiet. It was such a spot as he had planned once to call his own—it might have been his own!

The years that had wrought such changes upon others had by no means passed him by. His pale face was paler and thinner than it used to be; and his hair, that had been intensely black, was now so plentifully streaked with gray as to give one an impression of many more years belonging to him than he needed to claim. This idea was intensified by the heavy lines on his face, made generally by years. Of course it was not strange that under such experiences as his, he should have aged rapidly; but there was another change, subtle, indefinable in words, yet unmistakable. He had been in a strange school, certainly, to acquire the look; yet, for the first time in his life, a student of human nature would probably have said of him, "That is a man to be trusted." Such is the tribute which men of the world often unconsciously make to the power of the Holy Spirit; for with Ralph Bramlett it was simply the old story—his was the face of one who had sinned and suffered, and yet had come off conqueror "through him that loved him." "O the depth of the riches both of the wisdom and the knowledge of God!"

Nevertheless, it was of necessity a sad face, and there was abundant reason for the shadows. Only a few weeks before this, Ralph Bramlett had shed perhaps the bitterest tears that would ever fall from his eyes, over a few penciled words written by his mother's worn-out hand—a hand that was at rest now. Very simple the message had been; there was not the slightest reference to the heartsick longing that she had had to see his face and hear his voice on earth once more. She had reached the place where she could sink her own desires and fully understand his.

Oh, the longing that there had been in his heart to hear his mother's voice say, "I forgive you!"

"Dear boy," she had written, "how could you ask your mother if she had truly forgiven you? There is a verse in the Bible for you: 'As one whom his mother comforteth, so will I comfort you.' God could not have told me anything better about himself than that. Dear Ralph, I long so to comfort you! I am going, in a few more hours, to see your father. Think what blessed news I have to tell him! Oh, I make no doubt that he knows it already, but still he will like to hear me say, 'Ralph is coming, too; he will be here in a little while;' then together we will watch for you."

There had been not the shadow of a doubt expressed as to what his future would be. The little mother who had feared and trembled and worn an anxious face all her days, at that hour spoke exultantly of the strong, brave life her boy would henceforth live—even a happy life. She assured him that that was what his mother and father desired for him—a happy life. She even rose to the heights of human self-abnegation and spoke a tender word for the wife who, she believed in her heart, had led him astray and then utterly repudiated him. She, the mother, had forgiven her, and hoped that he could forgive her and pity and pray for her. The poor young man, still young, though looking middle-aged, thought of this letter as he waited in the library for what was to come next. A blessed letter, a comforting one. He believed that in the years to come he could read it over and get comfort from it, as she had meant he should. But just then he felt only a longing for a touch of the vanished hand. She had breathed out her life without him; and he might have been at her bedside and held her hand, and gone with her tenderly to the very verge of death's river. He had thought to do so if, in the natural order of events, he should outlive her. Oh, that awful "it might have been"! Was he never to get away from its horror? He sat here waiting for what was to come next; and, whatever it was, he dreaded it. How, for instance, was he to meet his sister Hannah, fresh from her solitary following of their mother to the grave? He shrank from the thought of Hannah; he shrank from everything—from life itself. Oh, if a merciful God had only heard his cry and permitted him to get away out of the flesh to that other world, where his mother was, where God was! For just then, at that frightened moment when the flesh shrank away and said, "I cannot, O God! I *cannot* meet the reward of my own doings," there came to his soul, like the undertone of a wondrous oratorio, the memory of some words he had learned in his childhood, and thought not of them: "I, even I, am he that blotteth out thy transgressions for mine own sake; and I will not remember thy sins." For the first time he noted that potent phrase, "for mine own sake." Why should He want to? Strange and almost terrible as the thought was, it must be that God loved him, *loved him!* There was no one left on earth who did; but in the strength of such a love as that which God in Christ offered him, could he not live, after all?

Then the door opened softly; and slippered, noiseless feet came in hesitatingly, and advanced with slow, shy steps. Midway into the room they paused, and their owner gazed earnestly at the man sitting with bowed head and covered eyes. Evidently he had heard no sound. The steps advanced again, a small hand rested with velvet touch upon his arm, and a soft voice said, "Papa! Are you my papa?"

Ralph Bramlett started as though an angel's tones had arrested him, and looked at the expectant little face before him.

"Are you my papa?" said the soft voice again, whose strains stirred some tender yet undefined memory in the listener's heart. This could not be Marjorie's child! He leaned forward and gathered the vision to his arms, while he answered the earnest question:

"Oh no, my darling! What put such a strange thought into your mind? What is your name?"

"Why, yes, you are! My name is Ralph Douglass Bramlett; and she said my papa would be here."

"Who did?" The man was trembling so that he could hardly hold the little form in his arms. The child looked at him with great wondering eyes, as he replied:

"Mamma did; she told me that my papa was in here, and that I might come in and climb into your arms and say, 'Papa, I love you.' You are my papa, aren't you? I knew you would come, because I asked Jesus to let you. He is the one to ask when you want things very much; and I wanted you to come. I missed you. Harry Williams has a papa, and he kisses him. Don't you want to kiss me?"

A less courageous child might have been frightened over the convulsive clasp in which he felt himself drawn to that hungry father's breast, and the rain of passionate kisses that covered his face. But he laughed gleefully, kissing back with energy and saying, between the breaths, "I guess you love me as much as Harry's papa loves him. Mamma said you would. Papa, have you come home to stay and take care of Mamma and me, like Harry's papa does?"

Poor Ralph! What waking dreams he had had about that boy of his who was away off somewhere in the West, and who would never be taught to call him father! He had tried to school his heart to bear that, as a part of the cross that he had made for himself. This sudden surprise almost bewildered him; for a moment it seemed as though God must have heard some of his despairing cries, and this was heaven.

"Here's Mamma!" exclaimed the child, giving a sudden spring forward. "Oh, Mamma! I found him, and he loves me! He has kissed and *kissed* me, more than twenty-'leven times."

"Ralph," said a voice at his elbow, in tones that trembled with feeling, "won't you forgive me and let me come, too, and try again?"

"Keep away, all of you, for a while," said Doctor Maxwell in the hall outside, speaking in what Marjorie called his "voice of authority"; "there is time enough for the rest of us. Let the man have his wife and boy entirely to himself for a while."

29

•⊷⊶•

"FOR ME—HEAVEN"

JUNE again; and, as so often before, the Edmonds family and their friends were gathered at the old home. Each summer since Marjorie's new home had been established, they had managed to come together to this old resting place, away from the weight of work and care that lay upon each. Marjorie Maxwell in her new home had found work for others that taxed her energy and strength to their utmost. Sheltered as her life had been, she had not known before, the awful need for work as it is revealed to the city physician who toils with a constant acceptance of Christ as his Master. Mrs. Edmonds, too, had thrown her whole heart into the new service that this changed life opened before her, so that their few weeks of rest had come to be looked upon as a necessity. Great was the joy of the young people of various connections, who had fallen into the habit of coming to the country with them, when Doctor Maxwell was able to announce the date of his vacation.

At this particular time the house was fuller than usual, as some who had not been in the habit of gathering with them were among their guests. The Bramlett homestead was closed, and Hannah was staying at Hill House until other arrangements could be made. Thither went also Mr. and Mrs. Burwell as her guests; but Ralph Bramlett and his wife and boy were staying with Mrs. Edmonds.

The house was thrown open as usual to all the influences of the summer day, and the merry voices of children could be heard on the lawn; but within, unusual quiet reigned. Although it was nearing the hour when, according to custom, various members of the family would be gathering in the pretty back parlor that Doctor Maxwell's young cousins called "the home room," it was still quite deserted. The chamber doors were all closed, and only a low murmur of voices could be heard within. In short, the whole house was pervaded by that indefinable atmosphere which marks a special day—a day set apart by some great joy or sorrow, from the commonalities of everyday life. The story, as is so frequently the case, could be compressed into a single sentence; and it is so often the same sentence! They had but just returned, the occupants of this house and their friends, from a newly made grave. They had left sleeping therein one of their number. Perhaps Ralph Bramlett was the only one who could be said to have been prepared for the news; to the rest of them it had come as a shock from which even now they seemed unable to rally enough to fully realize that it had come.

Immediately following the reunion of Ralph Bramlett's wrecked family, before he had had time to consider what was best to be done next and while they were still Doctor Maxwell's guests, there had come a summons from Professor Maxwell. Since he was unable to leave, at present, would Mr. Bramlett run down to him for a day or two? He had some very special matters of business to talk over with him.

Doctor Maxwell heard this bit of news with hearty satisfaction.

"I knew Leonard would have some scheme," he said to Marjorie, "and it is sure to be the best that could be devised; I have been holding on to hear from him. The wife and boy would better stay with us, would they not, until Bramlett returns?"

It was finally arranged in that way, and they watched Ralph depart with a sense of great comfort. Leonard would know just what to say to him; and it was actually better to have him away for a few days, to give them time to get used to the new order of things.

"I grumbled over the idea that Leonard could not get away from college to be with us when Ralph should come," Marjorie said to her mother; "but see how nicely it has all been overruled. It is much better to have Ralph go to him; and Leonard is sure to know what ought to be done next."

There had been some fear lest Ralph Bramlett would not be willing to obey the summons; but he was found to be not only willing but eager to do whatever Leonard Maxwell might suggest.

On his arrival at the college town, he found, to his surprise, that Professor Maxwell had not been out of his room for several days.

"Laid aside for a little while," that gentleman said, smiling, in answer to Ralph's earnest inquiries; "nothing new, only a more marked visitation from an old friend of mine. Never mind me; let us talk now about more important matters while there is time. I am glad you came to me so promptly, my friend."

There had followed a great deal of talk, some of it of a character to almost overpower Ralph Bramlett.

During these last hard years of his life he thought he had come to know this man of God very intimately; but there were revelations made in connection with those talks that sent him to his knees in almost pitiable self-humiliation and gratitude. In the light of the unselfish greatness of that other life, perhaps he saw his own smallness as never before.

Between times he had many anxious thoughts about Mr. Maxwell's state. He made light of his illness as something that was so slight as not to be worthy of note; yet Ralph Bramlett believed that he recognized increasing weakness and besought him to send for Doctor Maxwell.

There came a morning when, the moment he entered Professor Maxwell's room, he recognized that there had been a change.

"Yes," said the professor, smiling quietly in response to Ralph's look of consternation, "you are right; I have had a night of suffering, but I am much better now, quite free from pain, indeed. I believe now that the time has come for me to tell you something. I thought I should rally from this attack as I have from others, and that there would be no occasion for causing my friends anxiety. I believe I was mistaken. My promotion is coming earlier than I had any reason to expect or hope. Why should you be so distressed? Surely, my friend, you can rejoice with me! I thought I was perfectly willing to stay here and serve; but I will confess that the thought of soon serving in His visible presence has set all my pulses to throbbing with a new, strange joy. It is different with me from what it is with most men. I have strong family ties, but no duties or responsibilities. And my mother, for whom I meant to live, is waiting for me to come to her on the other side. Why should I not be glad?"

There had been much talk after that. Ralph, at his own request, was installed beside the sick man, with permission to stay until the end. Mr. Maxwell agreed at last to having his brother and Marjorie sent for, but had believed that there was no occasion for startling them with a telegram; a letter would reach them in twenty-four hours, and there was really no immediate haste. Indeed, the doctor had said that he might linger for several weeks. But it came to pass that within twenty-four hours of the time that Ralph had written at Mr. Maxwell's dictation a letter that taxed all the writer's power of self-control, he had followed it with a swifter messenger, and an hour afterward had sent another with the astounding news that Mr. Maxwell had gone to the other country!

In accordance with his distinctly expressed desire, they had brought his body to the town where so many of his rest hours had been spent, and where his brother had a family lot. Their mother had died abroad the year before and been buried there, beside her father and mother and the friends of her youth.

⋙ ⋘

The first violence of the shock was over; and as they lingered in their several rooms that June afternoon, they talked together tenderly of their friend who was gone, and of the effect that his going would have upon the living.

"Poor Mamma!" said Marjorie. "I think, Frank, it is almost harder for her than for us; because, you know, we have each other. You cannot think how deeply attached Mamma has been to Leonard, from the very first of their acquaintance. I have always fancied that she saw in him some mysterious soul-likeness to the little boy who went to heaven before I was born. At least, the tie between them has been peculiar and strong.

"What a strange influence he had over people! I could but think of it today, when I saw the crowds from the factory and from the mission, and noticed that there were tears on almost every face; and yet this was not his home, only the place where he spent his resting time! Such 'rests' as he took must make very bright crowns, must they not?"

In Estelle Bramlett's room, Ralph sat by an open window which overlooked the lawn where his boy played; and Estelle, with her head on his shoulder and her hand firmly clasped in his, talked ramblingly and tenderly of that part of the past on which it would do to touch:

"Do you know, Ralph, I used to fear and almost hate Mr. Maxwell? 'He is altogether too good for this world,' I used to say contemptuously to Glyde, when she would try to tell me something he had said. I told her that I did not believe in such perfect men, that they were nearly always hypocrites! But Oh, Ralph! I came to know him in a way that I have not been able as yet to tell you about. I have some letters to show you, written during that dreadful time! I cannot tell you what they were to me; they seemed almost like the voice of God."

"I can imagine!" he said tremulously. "I had letters too, and talks. And *deeds*," he added with a peculiar emphasis after a moment's silence; "something that I have not yet told you, Estelle. We will go over it by and by, after the boy is asleep; we must go down to him soon. When you know all, you will understand, even more than you now do, what we owe to him. We must see to it, my wife, that our lives are, after this, what he planned they should be; else I can almost conceive of his being disappointed, even in heaven."

"I am sorry for so many people!" Estelle began again, breaking the tender silence. "Did you notice the crowds from the factory? Poor Jack Taylor! The tears just rolled down his face; and that Bill Seber was almost as much affected. Then there is poor Hannah. Oh, Ralph! do you suppose Hill House will have to be given up, or did he make some provision for it? I almost feel as though it would break Hannah's heart if her work there could not go on."

"I do not certainly know," said her husband, "but I do not believe Mr. Maxwell forgot Hill House; I think he thought of everything and everybody."

Poor Hannah! At that moment she was shut and bolted into the utmost privacy of the neat little room that she occupied at Hill House and was on her knees, trying to get strength to look her future in the face and take in the probabilities of the life that stretched before her. The old home gone, Hill House gone; for Mr. Maxwell had died suddenly and probably did not even remember that the lease would expire in another month. Ralph had his wife and boy; everybody had ties and plans and hopes, save herself. This one friend of hers, with whom God had let her work for a few precious years, gone, like the rest! What should she do to earn her living? What would the poor girls do, whose faithful friend and helper she had been during these years? Prosaic thoughts? Yes, some of them. Hannah had reached the years when she knew she must meet and face the common realities of life. She did not touch, even with her thoughts, that other, deeper wound. She had given that part of her life entirely to God.

Meantime, locked also into the privacy of her own

room, sat Mrs. Edmonds, an open letter in her hand, the tears quietly following each other down her face. Ralph Bramlett had handed the letter to her as soon as he arrived. It was sealed and bore, beside her name, this direction: "To be read in some quiet hour, after my body has been laid to rest."

Thus it read:

> *My very dear Friend:*
>
> A precious bit of knowledge has come to me within the last few hours; it is that I am quite soon to be permitted to go home—to the home toward which I have been so long turning my thoughts. I had planned for a vacation with you all, as usual; but instead, I am to need no vacation, and am to enter upon my work for eternity. Isn't that a wonderful thought?
>
> I think I need hardly attempt to tell you how glad I am. I have been at peace in my work here and interested in it all; but—well, how can I be expected to tell you what it feels like to think of being there!
>
> Meantime, there are some matters to set in order before I go. At least, I think I have them arranged and would like to tell you about them in detail, that you may be able to advise intelligently, without waiting for the regular processes of law. It is known to you, I believe, that I have been entrusted with an important stewardship; and it is perhaps a peculiar fact that I have not a relative in the world who seems likely to need a penny of it for himself. There are not many of our family left on this side, you know. Well, I have told Ralph Bramlett that I think he ought to carry out the desires and hopes of his early

years and become a law student; and I told him that I had arranged matters so that he could care for his family and do so. I hope, my friend, you will think I have done right? I have left him twenty thousand dollars; not, as I once heard a censorious person say in a similar case, as a "premium on dishonesty," but because I believe him to be the Lord's freed man. And when the Lord puts a man's past behind his back, what are we? "Who shall lay anything to the charge of God's elect?" I have one deep regret; had I tried to help him earlier, much that is past might not have been. Yet God in his mercy has overruled all our mistakes.

About Hill House; my heart is very much in that enterprise. I believe that our friend Hannah has a work before her there, whereat the angels rejoice now, and over which we may have joy together through the ages. Therefore, after a few gifts have been made to kind friends and a few tokens offered as memorials to some who have been more than friends to me, I have left the remainder of my property, amounting, I believe, to something more than seventy-five thousand dollars, in trust to Hannah Bramlett, to be used according to the plans of which she and I have often talked. There are trustees, of course, and advisers. I have taken the liberty of naming you as one, and my brother Frank and his wife, and others whom you can trust. I think it has all been arranged in correct business form. It is by no means a hasty step; for although my summons has come earlier than I had expected, it is proper that you should know that I have for a year or two been aware that my life was strung on a very uncertain thread. I have been able to do with my means just what I desired to do.

To you, my dear friend, I may say one thing more, a word that will not be spoken elsewhere. My joy in doing this is, I hope and believe, first, because it is the Master's thought; what he would have me do in his name. But secondly stands the conviction that I am doing what my sister-in-law Marjorie would do if she could, and what she will be grateful to me for doing. It is too late for me to hide, if I would, that she has been the human mainspring of my life. My one love! How strange it all seemed to us years ago—to you and me—that our plans should miscarry as they did! And yet, cannot you see today the overruling Hand? For her, not early widowhood, but a strong, true heart to lean upon through the long happy years, I trust; and for me—*heaven*.

One more favor I ask of you, my dear friend; I do not suppose it is in the least necessary, yet I will mention it.

Let my carefully guarded secret be buried with me. Do not, for any possible reason, shadow Marjorie's life by the knowledge of what she has been to me. I know her so well that I am sure it would cast a shadow for a time. She would immediately begin to accuse herself, to mourn over some things that she might or might not have done; and I love her so well that I would have no shadow touch her life, save those of the Master's sending.

There is much more that I would like to say, but my strength is failing. I can only wait to add an earnest good-bye for your own dear self.

When you read this I shall have been for some-days—as we count time—at home!

I remember with pleasure, while I write, that the years are falling fast upon you, and that it may soon be my privilege to welcome you. Until then, dear trusted friend, Good-bye.

LEONARD MAXWELL.

⟫+ +⟪

"Are we to see the letter, Mamma?" Marjorie asked a few days afterward, when they had been talking over that and other matters connected with their loss.

"No, dear," said Mrs. Edmonds, brushing away a quiet tear; "there is a bit of privacy connected with it, for my eyes alone. You know I had to be his mother after she went away."

"Poor Leonard," said Marjorie with a gentle little sigh; "I always knew there was a lost chord in his life. I hope he has found it now."